M CLEMENT
Clement, Blaize.
Raining cat sitters and dogs
: a Dixie Hemingway mystery
/ Blaize Clement.

# Raining Cat Sitters and Dogs

ALSO BY BLAIZE CLEMENT

*Curiosity Killed the Cat Sitter*

*Duplicity Dogged the Dachshund*

*Even Cat Sitters Get the Blues*

*Cat Sitter on a Hot Tin Roof*

FOUNTAINDALE PUBLIC LIBRARY DISTRICT
300 West Briarcliff Road
Bolingbrook, IL 60440-2894
(630) 759-2102

# Raining Cat Sitters and Dogs

*A Dixie Hemingway Mystery*

BLAIZE CLEMENT

MINOTAUR BOOKS
A Thomas Dunne Book
New York

This is a work of fiction. All of the characters, organizations, and events portrayed in this novel are either products of the author's imagination or are used fictitiously.

A THOMAS DUNNE BOOK FOR MINOTAUR BOOKS.
An imprint of St. Martin's Publishing Group.

RAINING CAT SITTERS AND DOGS. Copyright © 2009 by Blaize Clement. All rights reserved. Printed in the United States of America.
For information, address St. Martin's Press, 175 Fifth Avenue, New York, N.Y. 10010.

www.thomasdunnebooks.com
www.minotaurbooks.com

Grateful acknowledgment is given for permission to reprint the following:

"Nothing Twice" from *View with a Grain of Sand,* copyright © 1993 by Wisława Szymborska, English translation by Stanislaw Baranczak and Clare Cavanagh © 1995 by Houghton Mifflin Harcourt Publishing Company, reprinted by permission of the publisher.

Library of Congress Cataloging-in-Publication Data

Clement, Blaize.
Raining cat sitters and dogs : a Dixie Hemingway mystery / Blaize Clement.—1st ed.
p. cm.
"A Thomas Dunne Book."
ISBN 978-0-312-36956-9
1. Hemingway, Dixie (Fictitious character)—Fiction. 2. Women detectives—Florida—Fiction. 3. Pet sitting—Fiction. 4. Sarasota (Fla.)—Fiction. I. Title.
PS3603.L463R35 2010
813'.6—dc22

2009039814

First Edition: January 2010

10 9 8 7 6 5 4 3 2 1

Acknowledgments

I am indebted to the "Kitchen Table Writing Group"—Linda Bailey, Greg Jorgensen, Madeline Mora-Summonte, and Jane Phelan—for their support and encouragement. Watch for those names. You'll soon be seeing them in your local bookstores.

A huge thank-you to Suzanne Beecher of DearReader.com, who has generously introduced Dixie to her thousands of book club members. Suzanne's generosity in helping writers is matched only by her lavish distribution of chocolate chip cookies. I'm honored to have her friendship.

Many thanks to homicide detective Chris Iorio of the Sarasota County Sheriff's Department, who always patiently answers my law enforcement questions. Thank you.

A big thank-you too to the Siesta Key Chamber of Commerce for their support, to all the deputies who keep Siesta Key its calm, laid-back self, and to Siesta Key residents for not minding that I add fictional neighborhoods and businesses to the real ones. I appreciate that.

Many thanks also to Marcia Markland and Diana Szu at Thomas Dunne Books, along with all the terrific production, promotion, and marketing people. Their efficiency and hard work make it possible for writers and readers to connect.

I'm also deeply grateful to readers who share their pet stories and tell me how much Dixie means to them. Thank you from my heart!

And to my expanding family, you continue to fill me with joy and pride.

Even if there's no one dumber,
if you're the planet's biggest dunce,
you can't repeat this course in summer:
this course is only offered once.

—Wisława Szymborska, from
"Nothing Twice" (1957)

# Raining Cat Sitters and Dogs

# 1

Every now and then you meet somebody you like on sight, even when everything about them says they're bad news. Jaz was like that. The first time I saw the girl, she was sobbing hysterically and rushing across Dr. Layton's parking lot with a towel-wrapped bundle in her arms. A large man trailed behind her with reluctance making heavy weights on his feet.

She looked about twelve or thirteen, with beginner breasts making plum-sized bulges under a stretchy tube top, and the thin, coltish awkwardness of adolescence. She had cocoa-colored skin and a long mop of tangled black curls. Her cutoffs were frayed and had the mulled look that clothes get when they've been slept in.

The man was around fifty, with pale jowls beginning to sag, and graying hair that looked more mowed than barbered. He wore a navy blue suit and a paler blue tie, both too unwrinkled to be anything except polyester. With his pulled-back shoulders and drip-dry shirt taut across his chest, he looked like a junior high school principal who had learned too late that he hated kids.

I'm Dixie Hemingway, no relation to you-know-who. I'm a pet sitter on Siesta Key, an eight-mile barrier island off Sarasota, Florida. I used to be a deputy with the Sarasota County Sheriff's Department, but something happened almost four years ago that caused me to go howling mad-dog crazy for a little while, so I left with the department's blessing. I'm still a little bit tilted, I guess, but not more than the average person. Like they say, a person who's totally sane is just somebody you don't know very well.

Now that I'm more or less normal, I have a pet-sitting business that I enjoy, and I end every day feeling like I matter to the world. I mostly take care of cats, with a few dogs and an occasional rabbit or hamster or bird. No snakes. I refer snakes to other sitters. Not that I'm snake-phobic. Not much, anyway. It just gives me the shivers to drop little living critters into open snake mouths.

I had come to the vet's that morning to pick up Big Bubba, a Congo African Grey parrot who had seemed under the weather when I'd called on him the day before. When a bird sneezes and looks lethargic on his perch, I don't take any chances. As it turned out, Big Bubba had merely been having a bad day. Dr. Layton had called the night before to tell me I could pick him up that morning, so I was there to take him home.

The crying girl and the man went in ahead of me. When I got to the reception desk, one of Dr. Layton's assistants was taking the bundle from the girl, and the receptionist was making sympathetic sounds and patting the girl on the shoulder. She was crying so hard that her words came out slurred and broken.

The only thing I could clearly understand was, "He hit him!"

The receptionist and assistant looked up sharply at the man, who heaved a great sigh.

"It's a wild rabbit," he said. "It ran in front of my car. It was an accident."

The girl turned and screamed at him. "But it *matters*! It may just be a rabbit, but it *matters*!"

Now that I could see her face, she was older in the eyes than I'd expected, and they a surprisingly pale aquamarine. With her tawny skin and wild black curls, the improbable eyes testified to ancestors from all over the world, a coming together of genes that can either be a societal blessing or curse. From the set to her jaw that was both defiant and desperate, I guessed in her case it had not been a blessing.

Everything about her said, *I'm young, I'm pissed, and I'm miserable.*

The man said, "Okay, okay, okay," and looked around with jittery uneasiness.

Dr. Layton bustled out from the backstage labyrinth of examining rooms and boarding areas. A comfortably plump African-American woman roughly my age, which is thirty-three, Dr. Layton has the ability to soothe and command at the same time. With a quick glance at the injured rabbit lying suspiciously limp in its towel covering, she turned briskly to the man.

"It ran in front of your car?"

"It was an accident. I wasn't going more than ten miles an hour. It wasn't like I was speeding."

The girl seemed close to a complete meltdown. She buried her face in her hands, her whole body quivering with the intensity of her sobbing. The receptionist and the vet's assistant looked like they might cry at any minute, just in sympathy, and people and animals in the waiting area stretched their necks to look at her.

Dr. Layton said, "What's your name, dear?"

She said, "Jaz." At the same time, the man said, "Rosemary."

The girl shot him a hostile glare, and Dr. Layton studied him.

She said, "Are you this girl's father?"

Too firmly, he said, "Stepfather."

Dr. Layton put a calm hand on the girl's shoulder. "Jaz, go sit down while I check the bunny. I'll let you know if I can do anything for it."

To me, she said, "Dixie, do you mind waiting a few minutes? I want to have a word with you."

I nodded mutely and followed the man and girl to the waiting area. His hammy hand was wrapped around her upper arm in a tight vise, while she continued to heave with sobs. When she felt the edge of the chair against her legs, she shrank into it and drew her knees up to her face, sobbing as if she had lost her closest friend.

I took a seat across from her. Around the room, a handful of people and their pets were looking at her with sympathetic eyes. Two seats away from her, Hetty Soames was there with a new puppy. She gave me a quick smile and discreet wave, the way people do when they see somebody they know at a funeral, and then turned her attention back to the crying girl.

If Hetty weren't so busy raising future service dogs, she could be an Eileen Fisher model. An ageless take-charge woman, she has sleek silver hair and looks elegant in loose linen pants and tunics that would look like pajamas on any other woman. The new pup with her was the latest in a series of pups she raises for Southeastern Guide Dogs. Raising future service dogs isn't like raising other puppies. They need the same love and attention, but they have to be socialized differently. Those little guys will one day need to focus solely on doing their job and not get sidetracked by things other dogs might explore out of curiosity. Raising them takes thousands of hours of patient work, not to mention a heart big enough to pour out lots of love on a puppy and then hand it over to somebody else. Hetty has been doing it for years, and the only way you can tell she's sad when a young dog leaves is that the spark in her eyes dims for a few weeks, only to come back when a new pup comes to live with her.

The girl's distress obviously bothered Hetty. It bothered her new pup too. A three-month-old golden Lab-shepherd mix, his little ears were up and he was watching the girl with concentrated attention. We all were.

Jaz was like the mutt you see at a shelter, the one that reason tells you is not a good choice to take home, but the one that tugs at your heart. Huddled as she was in the chair, we could see that the golden sparkles had mostly worn away from her green rubber flip-flops. Her toenails were painted black, and several of her toes wore gold or silver rings. Her ankles were amateurishly tattooed with flower bracelets, but a well-done black tattoo in the shape of a dagger ran several inches up the outside of her right ankle.

If I'd got a tattoo when I was her age, my grandmother would have sanded it off with a Brillo pad.

The man kept making uneasy shushing sounds, as if the girl's despair embarrassed him. Teenage angst affects people the same way that a pet peeing on the furniture does—it brings out basic traits of either patience or meanness.

Hetty's pup must have decided that since no human was going to do anything constructive, it was up to him. He darted away from Hetty's feet, reared on his hind legs, and pawed at one of the girl's toes. She took her hands away from her face, looked down at him, and laughed. Her laughter was a rusty, croaking sound, as if it had been jerked from her throat.

Hetty leaned forward in an anxious moment of hesitation, but the girl bent down and scooped the pup into her arms. With no hesitation whatsoever, he proceeded to lick the tears from her cheeks and to wriggle as close to her as he could get. She giggled, and everybody watching gave a collective out-breath of relief at hearing that normal adolescent sound. Jaz wasn't so far gone that she couldn't laugh, then, not so damaged that she couldn't respond to love. I think we had all been unconsciously afraid she might have been.

Hetty said, "Looks like you've found a new friend. His name is Ben."

As if to make sure Jaz understood, Ben gave the tip of her nose a wet kiss, which made her giggle again.

Dr. Layton came from the treatment rooms and walked to stand in front of the girl. "I'm sorry, Jaz. There was nothing we could do for the rabbit. I think he died instantly. I don't believe he suffered."

That's what they always tell you. That's what they told me when Todd and Christy were killed. I never knew whether I could believe them, and I could tell the girl wasn't sure she could believe Dr. Layton, either.

She pulled Ben closer, took a deep shuddering breath, and nodded. "Okay."

The man came abruptly to his feet, digging in his hip pocket for a wallet. "How much do I owe you?"

Dr. Layton said, "There's no charge."

As she turned to walk away, a loud male voice yelled from the vet's inner sanctum.

"Get that man!"

The man swiveled toward the sound with his right hand diving under his suit jacket toward his left armpit.

Instinctively, all my former law enforcement training made me leap to my feet with my arm stiffened and my palm out like a traffic cop. "Hey, whoa! No need for that!"

In the voice of one who hopes to defuse a tense situation, Dr. Layton said, "That was a bird. An African Grey."

As if on cue, Dr. Layton's assistant came out with Big Bubba inside one of my travel cages. Big Bubba hated little cages, which is probably why he swiveled his head toward me and hollered again, "Get that man!"

With an embarrassed twitch of his hand to the girl, the man said, "Come on, Rosemary."

Jaz and Ben exchanged a long sad look, which may

have been the final impetus that caused Hetty to do something that made my mouth drop.

Getting to her feet and taking Ben from Jaz, she said, "I need somebody to help me with this puppy. Just a few hours a week. It doesn't pay much, but it's easy work and I think you'd like it."

That was probably the biggest lie Hetty Soames had ever told. Not the part about the work being easy, but the part about needing help taking care of Ben. She had simply taken a shine to the girl, knew she was in some sort of situation that wasn't good, and wanted to give her a helping hand.

Jaz and the man spoke over each other again. He said, "She can't do that."

She said, "Yeah, I can do that."

I tried not to grin. Anybody who knows Hetty knows she usually gets what she sets her mind on. I figured she would have the girl at her house within the hour, maybe sooner. Dr. Layton seemed to think so too. With a happier look on her face than she'd had before, she motioned me to the reception counter where Big Bubba waited in the travel cage.

At the counter, I looked over my shoulder at Jaz and her stepfather. He had jammed both hands in his trouser pockets and was gazing at the ceiling with the look of a man at the end of his rope. Jaz had moved to squat beside Ben and pet him while she talked to Hetty.

Dr. Layton said, "There was a touch of eosinophilia in Big Bubba's tracheal wash, but I suspect he's reacting to the red tide like everybody else. Keep him indoors until it's over. If it gets worse, I can give him some antihistamines, but I'd rather treat it by removing the allergen."

I wasn't surprised. A bloom of microscopic algae, red tide's technical name is *Karenia brevis,* but by any name it's nasty stuff that causes respiratory irritations and watery eyes for people and pets. We get the bloom almost every September when Gulf breezes begin coming from the west, but this year it had started a month early. I promised Dr. Layton I would keep Big Bubba indoors for the duration of the bloom and carried him out the door.

I don't imagine Hetty or Jaz or the man noticed me leave. They were all too caught up in their own intentions.

Afterward, I would look back on that brief encounter in Dr. Layton's waiting room and wonder if there was any way I could have prevented all the coming danger. At the time, all I knew was that a girl who called herself Jaz but was really named Rosemary was desperately unhappy, that her stepfather's nerves were shot, and that he wore an underarm holster.

# 2

I left Dr. Layton's office with Big Bubba's travel cage draped with a sheet and strapped in the backseat of my Bronco. The sun was knee-high on the horizon, giving the early August air a gauzy quiver that made all the lush foliage and flowers look even more beautiful than usual, like a scrim laid over the world to hide tiny imperfections.

Siesta Key is a semitropical island, so our landscape is a riot of greenery and color. It doesn't make a lot of horticultural sense, but plants grow like crazy in our sandy soil. Gardeners on the key do more cutting back than fertilizing, and they're always behind in keeping up with the rampant growth. Bougainvillea climbs all over the place, orchids nestle in the crotches of oak trees, hibiscus flings red and yellow flowers in every yard, ixora gets trimmed into red-blossomed hedges, and every flowering tree in the world seems to find its way here. We're definitely a technicolor island.

The few extra minutes I'd spent at the vet's had eaten

into my time, but I drove more slowly than I usually do so as not to throw Big Bubba off balance. The sheet covering his cage kept him from freaking out at the passing trees, but he was so upset at being away from home that every now and then he squawked "Hey!" just to let me know he wasn't happy.

Siesta Key lies between the Gulf of Mexico and Sarasota Bay, and stretches north to south. I'm told it's about the same size as Manhattan, which may explain why so many New Yorkers have second homes on the key. I don't know how many people live in Manhattan, but Siesta Key has around seven thousand year-round residents, with that number swelling to about twenty-two thousand during "season," when it's cold in Manhattan and other unfortunate places.

Two drawbridges connect us to Sarasota, and every hour or so a tall-masted boat sails through while cars wait. For the most part, we're a peaceable community. So peaceable that only one sworn Sarasota County deputy is assigned to handle our crimes—*sworn* meaning carrying a gun. Otherwise, for things like lost bikes or squabbles over who's responsible for the damage done by a fallen tree limb, unsworn officers of the sheriff's Community Policing unit keep us on the straight and narrow.

Midnight Pass Road runs the length of the island, with condos and tourist hotels sharing space with private walled estates, and narrow lanes twisting off to residential areas. We have fifty miles of waterways inside the key, so most of our streets are as meandering as the canals they follow. Our sunsets are the most spectacular in the world, our trees are full of songbirds, our shorelines are busy with stick-legged waterbirds, and our waters are inhabited not just by fish but also by playful dolphins and gentle manatees. I've never lived anywhere else, and I never will. I can't imagine why anyone would.

On the key, you live either on the Gulf side or the bay side of Midnight Pass Road. Big Bubba lived at the south end, on the bay side, in a quiet, secluded residential area too old to have a formal name. A swath of nature preserve separated the private homes from a plush resort hotel on the bay.

Big Bubba's human was Reba Chandler. She had recently retired from teaching psychology at New College and was on a boat gliding down some river in the south of France. I had known Reba and Big Bubba since I was in high school, when Reba had trusted me to take care of Big Bubba while she was away on vacations. Back then, it had been a teenager's way to make easy money. Now it was my profession. Funny how life loops back on itself like that.

Like most of the houses in Reba's old-Florida enclave, hers was at the end of a shelled driveway with a thick wall of palms and sea grape screening it from the street. Reba called it her "birdhouse" because it had been built when people planned ahead for flooding, so it stood on tall stilty legs. Most people who have houses of that era have enclosed the lower part, but Reba had left hers as it was originally, with ferns growing under the house and a flight of stairs to a narrow railed porch. Built of cypress, the house had weathered silvery gray. Hurricane shutters that had begun life a deep turquoise had become pale aqua over the years, giving the house the look of a charming woman who had become more lovely as she aged.

When I pulled up to the house, my Bronco's tires made loud scrunching noises on the shell, a sound that Big Bubba must have recognized.

From his covered cage, he hollered, "Hello, there! Hello, there! Did you miss me?"

I parked in the driveway and opened the back door to get his cage. "We're home, Big Bubba."

He made aaawking sounds and yelled "Did you miss me?" I grinned because that was what Reba had always said to him when she came home from school.

I carried him up the steps and unlocked the front door. Ordinarily, Big Bubba lives in a large cage on the screened lanai, but to protect him from the red tide invasion, I took him to his smaller cage in the glassed-in sunroom. African Greys are temperamental birds. When they're upset they can take a good-sized chunk out of your finger, so I placed the travel cage so Big Bubba could hop from one cage to the other by himself. Back in familiar territory, he marched back and forth on a wooden perch, bobbing his head and giving me the one-eyed bird glare while I put out fresh seed and water for him.

Congo African Greys are the most talkative and intelligent of all parrots, and they're strikingly beautiful. With gleaming gray feathers, they sport white rings around their eyes that look like spectacles, and they have jaunty red feathers partially hidden under their tail feathers. Like all intelligent creatures, they bore easily. If they spend too much time without something to entertain them, they're liable to become self-destructive and pull out their tail feathers. People who take on African Greys as companions have to be smart and inventive or they'll end up with naked birds.

Big Bubba said, "Did you miss me?"

I said, "I counted every minute we were apart."

He laughed, bobbing his head to the rhythm of his own *he-he-he* sound.

I said, "It's not funny. You're a real heartbreaker."

Reba stored Big Bubba's seeds in glass jars lined up on a wide wooden table next to his cage. While I exchanged witty repartee with a parrot, I poured fresh seed from the jars into his cups. Then I cleaned the sides of the jars holding the seeds. I also cleaned the table the jars sat on. I like to keep things tidy.

I tossed the paper towels I'd used for cleaning in the wastebasket. I said, "I'm going now, Big Bubba. I'll see you this afternoon."

He said, "Sack him! Sack him! Get that man!"

Big Bubba was a great talker, but not so hot as a conversationalist.

His TV set was on the table with the jars of seed, and I bent to turn on his favorite cop show. Big Bubba was crazy about shows where police chase killers through the streets and knock over fruit stands. I didn't know if it was the fast cars or the flying fruit that excited him, but he couldn't get enough of them.

Before I turned the set on, I heard a sound behind me and jerked upright. Three young men stood shoulder to shoulder in a narrow shaft of sunlight streaming through the windows.

I may have made a small shriek, I'm not sure. I'm strong and I know how to defend myself, but there were three of them and only one of me.

They looked to be around senior high school age, and they were almost comical in their studied scariness. Eyelids at half-mast, lips twisted in identical pouty sneers, hair so messy it might have hidden spiders. They would have looked even scarier if their baggy jeans hadn't been belted so low that their underwear ballooned around their hips.

One of them, the tallest, oldest, and meanest-looking, said, "We're looking for Jaz."

Somehow I wasn't surprised at the coincidence of hearing the name of the girl from the vet's office. People with strong personalities seem to turn up all over the place, either in person or in reference, and Jaz certainly had a strong personality. I also wasn't surprised that she knew these young men. She had the combination of innocent tenderness and hard-shelled toughness that would make her fall for street-gang swagger.

I swallowed a large lump that had formed in my throat, and tried to think of something within reach that I could use as a weapon.

I said, "I don't know anybody named Jaz."

Three pairs of grudge-filled eyes stared at me. For a moment, nobody said anything, and I almost thought they might leave.

Then the big one that I had decided was their leader said, "Don't fuck with us, lady."

I took a half step backward, and in a high voice that I hoped sounded like a clueless dimwit, I said, "Is Jaz somebody you know from school?"

One of the boys tittered, and the big one scowled at him. "We ask the questions, you answer. Understand? Now get Jaz out here."

The middle boy, whose jeans hung so low the crotch dangled between his knees, said, "We won't hurt her, ma'am."

The big one said, "Shut up, Paulie."

I traced an X across my chest with my finger. "I swear to God, I have never met anybody named Jaz. These houses all look alike, you probably just got the wrong address."

The director in my brain said, *That's good. Don't act like this is a break-in, act like it's a normal drop-in by friends. If they rush you, grab a jar of birdseed and bash it on one of their heads.*

Big Bubba took that moment to decide he was being ignored. "Helloooo," he hollered, "did you miss me?"

The most sullen of the three stretched his arm forward with a switchblade knife making a silver extension of his hand.

The boy called Paulie said, "C'mon, don't do that."

I took another half step backward. With my heart pounding like a jackhammer, I flashed all my teeth and tried to sound perky.

"He's an African Grey. He sounds like he knows what he's saying, but he's just imitating sounds he's heard."

The boy with the knife said, "You got that bird in Africa?"

I said, "He's *from* Africa, but I didn't go there and get him."

As if he'd had a sudden epiphany, Paulie, the middle boy, shuffled to the table where Big Bubba's food was arranged. He had to hold his pants up with one hand to keep them from falling. He picked up a glass jar of sunflower seeds and studied it. Probably one of the few things he'd ever studied.

He said, "This is for birds, ain't it? I always knew this stuff was for birds. Man, my sister eats this stuff!"

The one with the knife said, "I seen a show one time where people from Africa were squeezed in the bottom of a ship, all chained together. Man, that was bad."

The tall one looked as if he'd like to bang their heads together. He said, "That bird wasn't on no slave ship, stupid."

Paulie set the jar of seed back on the table. The jar now had gummy-looking smudges on it, which made me want to snatch the paper towels from the trash and make the kid clean it.

I took another half step backward and wished I had pepper spray with me.

Big Bubba hollered, "Get that man! Get that man!"

I said, "He watches a lot of football games."

"Hello," yelled Big Bubba. "Hello! Hello! Did you miss me? Touchdown!"

The boy with the knife clicked it closed and jutted his jaws forward. "I'd like to have me a bird like that."

The big one said, "Dickhead! How you gone travel with a bird that talks? You need any more attention than you already got?"

I guess that's why he was the leader, he was the one who thought ahead. He gave me a long look, most likely wondering how long it would take me to dial the police if they left me conscious.

To the dickhead, I said, "You might like a parakeet. They talk too. But if you get one, be sure it's a male because female parakeets don't talk. Not like in the human world, huh?"

Three sets of vacant eyes swung toward me. I smiled. Broadly. Inviting them to share my humor. Only Paulie smiled back. I'd forgotten that criminals are too stupid to have a sense of humor.

In a woman's high treble, Big Bubba crooned, "I'll be loving yoooo . . . alwaaaaays." He sounded like he meant it.

Maybe it was because I was doing an Academy Award job of acting like a dithery blonde. Or maybe it was because Big Bubba was making them nervous. Or maybe they were just apprentice thugs who could still lose their cool.

Whatever the reason, the tall one said, "We're outta here."

Within seconds, all three had melted out the door and disappeared.

I waited, straining to hear my Bronco's motor turning over from a hood's hot-wire, but the only sound was my own heartbeat.

Dry mouthed, I took out my phone and dialed 911.

Deputy Jesse Morgan was at Big Bubba's house in less than five minutes, crisp and manly in his dark green uniform, his belt bristling with all the items that law enforcement officers keep handy. Morgan is a sworn deputy, and the fact that he answered the call meant the sheriff's office took the incident seriously.

Morgan and I knew each other from some other unpleasant incidents. When I opened the door he didn't speak my name, just tilted his firm chin a fraction in greeting. Maybe he thought saying my name would bring him bad luck.

"You called about a break-in?"

From his cage in the sunroom, Big Bubba shouted, "Hold it! Hold it! Hold it!"

I said, "That's a parrot."

Morgan held his pen poised above his notebook and waited.

I said, "It was three boys, Caucasian, late teens, all in baggy pants with their underwear showing. They just walked in on me."

"Just now?"

"Five or ten minutes ago. I called as soon as they left. One of them had an automatic knife."

"They threaten you?"

"Not exactly. He just flicked the knife open to let me know he had it."

Saying the word *flicked* made me tense a little bit, sort of preparing myself to tell the part I dreaded.

"They said they were looking for a girl named Jaz. They seemed to think she lived here."

He looked up from his notepad. "You spell that J-A-Z-Z, like the music?"

"I guess so. I don't really know."

"You know this girl?"

"No, but I saw her this morning at Dr. Layton's office. I was there getting Big Bubba—he's the parrot—and this girl was there with a man. She seemed like a good kid. They had a rabbit the man had run over, but Dr. Layton couldn't save him."

"The rabbit."

"Yeah. The man claimed he was Jaz's stepfather. Only he called her Rosemary."

He raised an eyebrow and studied me for a moment. "Sounds like you didn't believe him."

I wasn't going there. "How would I know? I never saw them before."

"Except at the vet's."

"Except there."

His face didn't give away a hint of whatever he was thinking.

He said, "You're taking care of this parrot?"

"Yeah, for Reba Chandler. I come here twice a day. I had to leave him at the vet's overnight, but he's okay. He's been having a little reaction to the red tide."

"Who hasn't? You have any idea why they came here looking for Jax?"

"*Jaz*. It's *Jaz*. I guess they just got the houses mixed up. She seemed like a nice kid."

I knew I was repeating myself, but for some reason I didn't want Morgan to think badly of Jaz just because some thugs were asking about her.

He said, "Jaz doesn't know Miss Chandler?"

I gave him the look you give people who've asked a really dumb question, and then I realized it wasn't such a dumb question after all. The fact that *I* didn't know Jaz didn't mean Reba Chandler didn't know her. Maybe she did. If Jaz lived in the neighborhood, it would be like Reba to befriend her. Except I didn't believe she lived in the neighborhood.

I said, "Maybe I haven't made it clear those guys were scary."

"Anything more specific that might identify them?"

"One of them was named Paulie."

I clapped my hand to my forehead like somebody remembering they could have had a V8. "Oh, I forgot! The one named Paulie picked up a jar of birdseed. It would have prints on it."

Morgan stopped writing and followed me to the sunroom. He and Big Bubba gave each other the once-over while I scurried to the kitchen to get one of Reba's canvas grocery bags. Back in the sunroom, Morgan covered the jar's metal lid with a paper towel and carefully transferred the jar to the bag. Paulie's latent prints would be lifted from the jar and run through IAFIS for a match. If the kid had ever been arrested by city, county, state, or federal law enforcement officers, his prints would be in the Interstate Identification Index of IAFIS.

I said, "Another thing, one of them said something about traveling."

"What'd he say?"

"He said, 'Dickhead, how you gone travel with a bird that talks?' See, one of the guys said he'd like to have a bird like Big Bubba, and this one, I think he was the leader, said, 'How you gone travel with a bird that talks?' "

Morgan picked up the canvas bag by its handles. "You know how to get in touch with Miss Chandler?"

I shook my head. "She's in the south of France on a boat that stops at four-star restaurants."

Reba had left me the number of the cruise line that I could call in an emergency, but I wasn't about to disturb her vacation just because some teenage hoods had come in her house while I was there.

Morgan looked as if he knew I could call Reba if I had to, but he didn't press it. As he went out the front door, he said, "We'll keep a closer watch on the area."

I nodded, knowing full well that all the trees and shrubbery on the street did a good job of hiding a lot of innocent behavior. It would hide criminal behavior too.

I gave Big Bubba some sliced banana in case he'd got upset listening to me and Deputy Morgan. Then I turned on his TV and went back down the steps to the Bronco. As I drove down the lane, I saw a pale form through the fronds of an areca palm. I stopped and looked, and for a heartbeat I thought I saw Jaz's face watching me. If it was her, she was instantly swallowed up by green trees and hanging vines.

I thought for a minute, then drove a few lanes over to Hetty Soames's house. If Jaz was mixed up with those young toughs who'd come into Reba's house, Hetty needed to know about it before she got involved with the girl.

# 3

Like Reba's house, Hetty's was hidden behind trees and foliage, but it wasn't wooden or built tall on stilts. Instead, it was pale pink stucco and sat low under oaks and pines. I followed a side path to the lanai, where Hetty and Ben were playing fetch-the-ball. Racing back and forth with puppy glee, Ben thought he was just having fun, but Hetty was gently training him to return to the same spot each time he brought the ball to her. In a few weeks, he would know to touch her leg with the ball and wait for her to take it.

Hetty's cat, Winston, sat in a cane chair calmly grooming his white socks. A gray mixed shorthair with a white ruff and Cleopatra eyes, Winston surveyed the world and all its inhabitants with the patient tolerance of the Dalai Lama. Winston could have worn a saffron toga and still keep his dignity.

Pups raised to be service dogs are introduced to just about every situation under the sun. In addition to the regular places that all dogs go, service dogs in training go to church, to movies, and to restaurants. They learn to live serenely with other pets and children. They learn to keep their cool no matter what happens, so that when they are eventually teamed with a person who needs them to be their eyes or ears, they're unflappable. Ben hadn't learned that yet. When he saw me, he forgot all about the ball game and charged over to check me out.

Hetty followed him and knelt beside him to keep him from jumping on me.

She said, "I'll bet I know why you're here. You're concerned about Jaz, aren't you?"

I said, "I've just been at Reba Chandler's house, and some young toughs came in looking for her."

With one hand on Ben's neck, Hetty looked sharply at me. "Did they hurt you?"

"No, but they were scary. I called nine-one-one and a deputy came and got the information. He said they would keep extra watch on this area, but I wanted you to know about it."

Leading Ben, Hetty went back to her chair. "You think those boys are friends of hers?"

I nudged Winston to one side of his chair and sat down beside him. I scratched the spot between his shoulders, the acnestis that animals can't scratch by themselves, and he looked up at me and smiled.

I said, "They asked for her by name, so she must know them. And another thing: When I was leaving Reba's house, I think I saw Jaz hiding in the shrubbery."

Hetty nodded, her eyes clouded with worry. "She lives nearby."

"You got her address?"

"No, but she said she was close enough to walk here. She's coming tomorrow morning."

Winston stretched his head back so I could scratch his neck. He did it with great poise. I wish I were more like Winston.

Hetty said, "Jaz seems like such a sensitive girl. Why would she be friends with boys like that?"

"Sensitive girls can be dumb as anybody else."

"I wouldn't call it dumb. She's just young."

I couldn't argue with that. Even under the best of circumstances, adolescence is a god-awful age—too young to have learned from experience but old enough to act on impulsive decisions. No kid is truly immune to taking a wrong turn, and only the lucky ones who go wrong get a helping hand. From the look of her, I didn't think Jaz had had an easy life, and I doubted she'd had many helping hands.

I moved my scratching fingers to the top of Winston's head.

I said, "Do you really believe she and her stepfather live in this neighborhood?"

"Not really."

Neither did I. Except for old-timers like Reba and Hetty who had bought before prices skyrocketed, most of the residents in that exclusive tangle of lanes and canals were modestly rich. Hetty and I both knew that rich girls don't have Jaz's pissed-off fear, and rich men don't wear shiny polyester suits like Jaz's stepfather.

Hetty said, "Tourists?"

"Maybe."

When you live in a resort area, you get used to a river of

strangers flowing through. But if Jaz was a tourist, why had those young men come to Reba's house looking for her?

Winston decided he'd allowed me to scratch him long enough and bounded to the floor. For a moment, he and Ben touched noses in a kind of neutral acknowledgment of each other's presence. Then Winston leaped into Hetty's lap and Ben trotted away to see if the ball still needed to be picked up. Heads of warring nations could learn a lot about how to achieve lasting peace by watching dogs and cats who live in the same house.

I said, "I'll stop by tomorrow after I leave Reba's house."

Hetty's lips tightened, and I knew she was annoyed that I thought she needed help. Independent as she is, though, Hetty's also a realist, and she didn't argue.

With my stomach sending urgent reminders that it was time for breakfast, I drove through the ramble of lanes from Hetty's house. I peered into the foliage for a sign of Jaz, but I didn't see her.

The Village Diner is in the part of Siesta Key that the locals call "the village," meaning the bulgy part of the key toward the north end. The Chamber of Commerce and the post office are located there. Restaurants and real estate offices share space with trendy boutiques, and shops sell touristy T-shirts and giant seashells that people will be embarrassed they bought when they get back home. You have to drive carefully in the village because sunburned tourists in skimpy swimsuits and straw hats are apt to step into the street without looking. They're on their way to Siesta Beach, and either the negative ions of the seaside make them temporarily goofy or they're blinded by the sun. Being compassionate people, we wouldn't run them down even if they were locals, but we probably wouldn't be quite so patient if it weren't for the fact that our entire economy depends on them.

At the Village Diner, Tanisha, the cook, always starts my breakfast the minute she sees me come in the door. Judy, the waitress, has my first mug of coffee poured and waiting for me by the time I get to my usual booth. That's how much of a regular I am.

Judy is tall and lanky, with pecan-colored eyes and a sprinkle of freckles over a pointed nose. She and I have never met anyplace except the diner, but I know everything there is to know about all the no-good men who've disappointed her, and she knows about Todd and Christy and how crazy I went when I lost them.

At my booth, I dropped my backpack on the seat and took a few deep glugs of the coffee that was waiting. Tanisha stuck her wide black face through the pass-through from the kitchen and waved to me so vigorously her cheeks shook. Tanisha's another friend I only see at the diner.

A second before Judy materialized with my breakfast, Lieutenant Guidry of the Sarasota County Homicide Investigative Unit tapped me on the shoulder and slid into the seat opposite me. As usual, my heart did a little tap dance when I saw him. Guidry is fortyish, with eternally bronzed skin, steady gray eyes, short-cropped dark hair showing a little silver at the temples, a beaky nose, and a firm mouth. Laugh lines at the corners of his eyes and lips. Nice lips. Those lips have kissed mine a couple of times and I can attest that Guidry is one fine kisser. Oh, yes, he is.

Guidry and I had a kind of on-and-off sort-of relationship, meaning that every now and then some strong magnetic force sucked us together, and then we'd pull back as if it hadn't happened. I didn't know why Guidry stepped back, but for me it was just flat too scary. Falling in love with another cop carried the risk of losing him, and I wasn't sure I could take that risk again. I wasn't even sure I wanted to love anybody again. I'd lost too many people already. I didn't think I could bear losing anybody again.

On the other hand, my body didn't seem to pay much attention to what my head wanted.

I looked across the table at him and tried not to let it show that I felt like a sixteen-year-old in the presence of the captain of the football team.

Judy plopped my plate down and splashed more coffee in my cup.

She said, "What'll you have, sir?"

From the respectful way she spoke, nobody would have dreamed she called him the hunky detective behind his back.

"Just coffee, thanks."

He was silent while she scooted to get a mug for him. His mouth looked as if he'd been chewing on something for a long time and wished he could spit it out. Other than that, he looked his usual self—more like an Italian playboy than a homicide detective.

When I first met him, I'd thought he really was Italian, but he'd told me once that Italian was one of the few things he wasn't. I'd also learned that his easy elegance came from growing up wealthy in New Orleans. I knew his whole name too, but I'd had to prize it out of him. Everybody called him Guidry, but when I pushed he'd admitted that his mother called him Jean-Pierre. Which made him some kind of New Orleans French. That was all I knew, other than the fact that his father headed a big law firm in New Orleans and that his mother was a soft-hearted woman. Not that I'd pried, or that I was overly curious. I had merely asked very casually. And I would never try to get any more information because it was absolutely none of my business. None whatsoever.

After Judy brought him coffee, he said, "Tell me about the boys who accosted you this morning."

"They didn't exactly *accost* me. They came in Reba Chandler's house and scared me."

"The fingerprint people got a good print from the jar, but we haven't got a report back from IAFIS yet. Deputy Morgan said one of them had a knife?"

"Switchblade. I imagine they all had them, but he was the only one who got nervous and showed it."

Guidry pulled out his notebook and flipped some pages looking for notes, probably searching for what he'd got from Deputy Morgan.

He said, "This girl they were looking for, you didn't hear a last name at the vet's office?"

I shook my head. "Dr. Layton just took the dead rabbit from her. Jaz was crying, and the receptionist was calming her. They didn't have her fill out any forms with names and addresses."

"Dead rabbit?"

"The man had run over a rabbit. It was wrapped in a towel, but it was dead."

Guidry gave me the blank look he always gets when I mention animals.

I said, "Last time I looked, you were a homicide detective. I'm pretty sure you're not investigating the death of a rabbit, so why the interest in Jaz and those boys?"

I could see him debating whether to tell me, and if so, how much.

He said, "An elderly man was killed in his house last night. He lived alone and apparently woke up and surprised somebody in the act of burglary. There was a tussle, and he got stabbed. One of his neighbors reported seeing three young men loitering near the house earlier in the evening. Their description fits your guys."

I shrugged. "Lots of young guys look like them. Half the boys on the street have baggy drawers."

Guidry drummed his fingertips on the table. "Most of those guys showing their underwear are just high on the fumes of their own testosterone. That's normal stuff that kids do just to outrage adults. Robbing and killing is not normal, it's gang behavior."

I hated to think of gangs in our lovely part of the world. Most people think of gangs as swaggering street thugs shooting at one another, but today's gang member is just as likely to be the teenager next door, the one whose parents are too busy or too dumb to notice that their kid suddenly has a lot of spending money. Gang leaders recruit kids to rob or sell drugs, relatively small-time stuff, but a lot of those kids who aren't killed or put in prison go on to big-time drug smuggling, big-time fraud, sometimes big-time assassinations.

I thought about the kid with the knife at Big Bubba's

house. Yes, he had been stupid enough and weak enough to be recruited by a gang. So had the others. And they had asked for Jaz. I thought about the tattoo on Jaz's ankle and wondered if the dagger was a gang symbol.

I said, "Guidry, that man with Jaz wore an underarm holster."

He made a note in his little black book. "Anything else?"

"When I was leaving Big Bubba's house, I think I saw Jaz's face through the bushes. She and her stepfather didn't look like they could afford that neighborhood."

He said, "Big Bubba?"

"He's an African Grey. A parrot. Talks like nobody's business."

Guidry passed the back of his hand across his forehead as if he'd suddenly suffered a pain. Another thing he does when I talk about animals.

I said, "There's something else. Hetty Soames offered Jaz a job helping her with a new puppy. She expects the girl at her house tomorrow morning."

"I'll have somebody in the area."

I looked bleakly at him. He couldn't have somebody from the sheriff's department watch Hetty's house around the clock.

He said, "Morgan said you outtalked those guys that came in on you."

"I played dumb blonde. Not a big act."

His mouth played with a smile. "The sisters used to warn us about smooth-talking girls like you."

His eyes had a spark that looked like he meant it as a compliment, but I was still a bit put off. It was hard enough to wonder what his parents' opinion of me might be if I ever met them. Not that I ever would, but I might. I sure didn't want to have to worry about his sisters too.

I said, "Are they much older than you?"

He frowned. "Who?"

"Your sisters."

He laughed. "I meant the nuns at school. They were forever warning us boys about the danger of Protestant girls."

"What about Jewish girls?"

"They didn't think we'd ever meet any Jewish girls, and I doubt they'd ever even heard of Buddhist girls or Muslim girls. But they knew damn well there were loose Baptist girls hiding behind every bush ready to jump out and make us get them pregnant so they could trap us."

"Did that scare you?"

He grinned. "Scared the hell out of me."

He stood up and dropped bills on the table. "Dixie, if you see those guys again, don't interact with them. Stay away from them and call me. And if you see the girl or the man, try to find out where they're staying. I want to talk to them."

He touched my shoulder again, letting his fingertips linger a moment longer than necessary, and left me sitting there with my hormones racing as wildly as my imagination. Guidry always has that effect on me. The hormone part, that is. Well, the imagination part too.

Judy scooted to my side with her coffeepot in hand and an inquisitive look in her eyes. "You and your hunky detective been to bed yet?"

I glared at her. "He's not mine, and we most certainly have not."

"Hon, when a man looks at a woman the way he looks at you, he's hers. And I don't know what you're waiting for. If you don't use it, it'll rust."

I rolled my eyes and slipped out of the booth. "I'm going home."

She grinned. "Girl, when you finally give it up, you're liable to kill that poor man."

I made a face and hurried away. The mortifying thing was that I was pretty sure Judy was right.

# 4

My morning schedule is practically set in concrete. I get up at 4:00 A.M., splash water on my face, brush my teeth, pull my hair into a ponytail, drag on shorts and a sleeveless T, and jam my feet into clean Keds. By 4:15, I'm out the door, and by 4:20 I'm working my way north calling on all the dog clients. Then I retrace my route and see to all the other pets. I spend about thirty minutes with each pet—there are usually seven or eight, ten at the most—so with traveling time and occasional glitches to slow me down, it's usually about ten when I've fed and groomed and played with the last pet. Then I head to the Village Diner for breakfast. After I've convinced my stomach that it isn't starving to death, I head home for a shower and a nap.

My apartment is above the four-slot carport that I share with my brother and his partner. They live in the two-story frame house where my brother and I grew up with our grandparents. The house and garage apartment are at the end of a twisting lane on the Gulf side of the key, on a hiccup of sandy shore that alternately erodes and rebuilds with shifting currents. That continual shape-shifting makes our property considerably less valuable than most Siesta Key beachfront land and keeps our property taxes in the lower stratospheric reaches.

When my grandparents moved to the key back in the early '50s, they ordered their frame house from the Sears, Roebuck catalog. The carport was added later, and the apartment wasn't built until after my brother and I moved in with them. Our father had been killed saving somebody else's children in a fire, and our mother had run off with another man. I say "run off" because that's how my grandmother always described her daughter's desertion. I doubt that she really ran when she left. More likely, she skipped.

I was seven when my father died, and nine when my mother left. My grandfather built the garage apartment when I was about twelve. At the time, he meant it to be guest quarters for visitors from up north. He never dreamed I would end up calling it home.

When I came around the last curve in the drive, I saw Michael and Paco under the carport by Michael's car. Michael is my brother, two years older than me and my best friend in all the world. A firefighter like our father, Michael is built like a Viking god. He's strong and steady as one too, and so good-looking that women tend to grow faint when he crosses their line of vision. Too bad for them, because Michael's heart belongs to Paco, who is an undercover agent with the Special Investigative Bureau of the Sarasota County Sheriff's Department.

As slender and dark as Michael is broad and blond, Paco also gives women hopeless fantasies of turning a gay man straight. His family is Greek-American, but he can pass for just about any nationality, which is a strong asset in his line of work. He's also a master at disguise, and there have been times when our paths crossed while he was working undercover and I didn't recognize him. Since I've come close to blowing a few drug busts that way, he now gives me a secret hand signal if we meet when he's in disguise—usually his way of telling me to back the heck off. After thirteen years as my brother-in-love, Paco is almost as dear to me as Michael.

Michael works twenty-four/forty-eight at the firehouse, which means he's on duty twenty-four hours, then off forty-eight. Paco doesn't have any set schedule, and Michael and I never question him about where or when he's working. He wouldn't tell us if we did, and we're better off not knowing because we would worry a lot more than we already do.

Michael's twenty-four-hour duty had ended that morning at eight, and from the looks of the bags of groceries he and Paco were hauling out of his car, he had apparently left the firehouse and hit every supermarket in Sarasota. Michael is the family cook. He's also the firehouse cook. If it were possible, Michael would be the world's cook. I don't think it's because he loves throwing raw stuff in pots and pans and putting them over heat, I think cooking is merely one step toward his real goal, which is to feed people. With all due respect to the miracles Jesus performed, give Michael a few fish and a little bread, and he'd not only feed multitudes with it, he'd season it and turn it into the best dinner anybody ever ate. Plus he'd give them dessert.

When I pulled my Bronco into its spot, Michael and Paco paused with their arms full of groceries and watched me slide out of the driver's seat.

I said, "Have I missed a hurricane warning?"

As soon as I said it, I regretted it because it's not cute to joke about hurricanes in Florida. Especially not in the middle of hurricane season.

Michael said, "I just stocked up on staples. We were running low."

Behind Michael's back, Paco rolled his eyes at me because he and I are pretty sure Michael has enough staples to last at least ten years.

I leaned over his car trunk and hoisted out a bushel basket of green beans. "Yeah, I've been worried about our green bean supply."

Paco grinned and headed toward the back door of their house.

Michael said, "I got those at the farmers' market out on Fruitville. Got some sweet corn too. It's all organic." He got a creative light in his eyes just at the thought of what he could do with those green beans and ears of corn.

We all moved across the sandy yard to the house's wooden deck and into the kitchen, where Ella Fitzgerald was impatiently waiting. She ran first to Michael for a quick cuddle and reassurance that he was going to be home for a *long* time, and then to Paco to get her ears ruffled. Only then did she deign to wind around my ankles and tell me hello.

Ella is a true calico Persian mix given to me as a kitten by a woman leaving the country. If Ella had never met Michael and Paco, she would have been happy with me, but one look at them and she swooned into their arms the same way most females dream of doing. It probably had as much to do with the smell in their kitchen as their looks. My kitchen smelled like tea bags and bottled water. Michael's kitchen smelled like love.

While Ella watched from her accustomed stool at the big butcher-block island in the center of the kitchen, I helped put away a few groceries so I wouldn't look so much like a taker instead of a giver. Then I kissed the top of Ella's head, promised Michael I wouldn't be late for dinner, and left them with their organic booty.

I didn't tell them about the young men coming in Big Bubba's house looking for a girl named Jaz, or say anything about Hetty Soames hiring Jaz to help her with the new puppy she was raising. For one thing, I was too tired to go into it. For another, Michael tended to get downright paranoid at the first hint of me being involved in anything out of the ordinary. Not that I blamed him, since I'd got tangled up in some fairly bizarre situations in the last year. None of them had been my fault, but Michael thought I was entirely too willing to stick my nose into places it had no business being stuck. That had never been true, of course, and wasn't true now, but I knew Michael wouldn't see it that way.

It was strictly to spare him unnecessary worry that I kept quiet about everything that had happened that morning. I thought it was very thoughtful of me.

A long covered porch runs the length of my apartment, with two ceiling fans to stir the air, and a hammock slung in one corner for daydreaming. There's a glass-topped ice cream table and two chairs next to the porch railing where I can have a snack and look out at waves curling onto the beach. Accordion-pleated metal hurricane shutters cover french doors and double as security bars. As I climbed the stairs, I punched the remote that raises the shutters, and yawned while the shutters folded themselves into the overhead soffit.

Pushing through the french doors, I stepped into my minuscule living room where my grandmother's green flower-patterned love seat keeps company with a matching club chair. A one-person eating bar separates the living room from a narrow galley kitchen, and a window above the sink looks out at trees behind the apartment. To the left of the living room, my bedroom is barely big enough for a single bed and a slim chest of drawers that hold photographs of Todd and Christy. An air-conditioning unit is set high on the wall under narrow rectangles of glass to let in light.

I flipped the switch to start the AC and headed down the short hallway to my cramped bathroom, pausing at an alcove in the hall to shed my Keds and cat-hairy clothes and toss them in the stacked washer/dryer. I hate wearing sweaty shoes, so I buy Keds the way Michael buys organic produce. I always have several dry pairs waiting, some damp just-washed pairs on a rack above the washer, and some in the washer.

Mexican tile was cool under my bare feet as I padded into the bathroom and turned on the shower. As soon as the fine spray of warm water hit me, I went into a blissful zonked-out state. I must have had a previous lifetime when water was scarce, because every time I'm in a warm shower all my pores start singing hymns of thanksgiving. After air, I think water is God's best gift to us.

When I was squeaky clean, I slicked back my wet hair, pulled on a terry cloth robe, and fell onto my night-rumpled bed to sleep for a couple of hours. I woke up dry mouthed and a little chilled from sleeping under the AC, so I padded barefoot to the kitchen and made myself a cup of tea. Carrying it in one hand, I flipped on the CD player on the way to my office-closet and let its sly little robot shuffle through a stack of music and surprise me. Smart robot that it is, it selected Billie Holiday's voice to wrap around me while I took care of the business part of pet sitting.

My office-closet is the only expansive feature of my apartment. I don't know why my grandfather made it so big, but it's a good thing he did. It's square, with two entries. One wall has shelves for my shorts and Ts and the other wall has a desk where I take care of pet-sitting business. A floor-to-ceiling mirror on the wall between the two entry doors magnifies the light and makes the room look even bigger than it is. My meager collection of dresses and skirts hang on the back wall. I don't dress up much.

My answering machine had a few calls to return, mostly regular clients letting me know when they would need me to take care of their pets, and I made quick work of calling them. Then I got out my big record-keeping book that I always have with me when I make client calls and transferred notes to individual client cards. I take my pet-sitting duties as seriously as I took being a deputy. In some ways, they require the same skills. You have to be smart enough to tell the difference between a situation that requires force and one that requires diplomacy, you have to be quick to respond to unexpected situations, and you have to be patient if somebody upchucks on you.

My clients like the fact that I've been a law enforcement officer. Knowing that I can use a gun or disarm a criminal makes them feel more confident about letting me come in their houses while they're gone. I don't know how they feel about my crazy time after Todd and Christy were killed. If they know about it, they're all kind enough not to mention it.

When I finished with my record keeping, I got dressed and took a banana out to the porch and ate it while I looked at distant sailboats on the Gulf and thought about how glad I was that I wasn't in one. The thing about water and me is that I love having it fall on me in a warm shower and I love looking out at the Gulf's waves and frothy surf, but I'm not crazy about getting *in* the Gulf. Not in the flesh or in a boat. The Gulf is too big and powerful for me to control, and that makes me uneasy. Not that I'm a control freak or anything. But if I were given a choice between shooting off into outer space or diving to the bottom of an ocean, I'd take space. At least you can see where you're going in space, and it's damn dark at the bottom of the ocean. Besides that, freakish critters live down there, pale things that never see the sun and have weird mouths shaped like flowers. I figure space aliens are similar to us, but sea creatures are bound to be slimy and cold.

Having reminded myself of my deep respect *for* but

aversion *to* deep water, I went back inside and got my backpack and car keys. It was time to make my afternoon rounds.

Later, I would look back on that afternoon and marvel at how innocent I'd been. While I dithered about scary deep-sea creatures I would never meet, scarier beings were on land and headed my way.

# 5

Summer on the key is so hot that going outside between ten in the morning and four in the afternoon is somewhat like crawling inside a pizza oven. By August, the only people who don't illustrate the meaning of "redneck" are shut-ins or nighttime workers who sleep during the day. The only thing that keeps the key from spontaneously combusting in August are the occasional rain showers which, along with sending people running from tongues of lightning, soak the vegetation and cause steam to rise from the ground. August in Florida is God's way of reminding us who's in charge.

Maybe we're just perverse, but the locals love the heat. We use it to keep visitors away. When out-of-state relatives phone to say they're thinking of coming to see us, we say, "Oh, gosh, you don't want to come now! Oooowee, you can't imagine the heat! It's just absolutely miserable, not to mention the sand fleas and mosquitoes. Wait until October or November when it's cooler."

If we're convincing enough, they'll stay away. We

already have red necks from the sun and white eyes from fear of hurricanes. Add company to entertain, and it's just too much.

The sky was clear that afternoon, and heat was rising from the ground in visible shimmering waves. Even cats who never left their air-conditioned homes moved more slowly, as if they felt the need to conserve energy. None of my charges had peed on a houseplant or shredded paper into confetti for me to pick up. When I left them, every pet's tail was raised in approval. To a pet sitter, a raised tail means "Brava! Encore!" I try to be modest about those raised tails, but I'm secretly proud.

On the way to Big Bubba's house, I saw Hetty and Ben on the sidewalk chatting with a man and his Beagle. I tapped my horn and waved, and Hetty gave me a big grin. Ben looked hard at me as if he were memorizing my car. Service dogs are so smart, he might have been.

At Big Bubba's house, sounds of gunshots, sirens, and screaming women blared from his TV, and he was pecking the heck out of a silver bell hanging in his cage. I turned off the TV and looked anxiously at him, hoping he wasn't freaking out from being left alone for so many hours. African Greys react to living behind bars the same way humans do. Leave them in solitary confinement too long and they become self-destructive.

Cocking his head to give me that weird one-eyed stare that birds do, he said, "Did you miss me?"

"Desperately. Did you miss me?"

"Al-waaaaays! Al-waaaaays!"

I swear sometimes Big Bubba truly seems to be carrying on a conversation, not just repeating sounds he's heard.

I said, "Your mom probably misses you too. She's in France, you know, eating at four-star restaurants."

He didn't answer, but tilted his head to one side as if he was considering how much a woman would miss him while cruising down a river in the south of France and eating at four-star restaurants.

I took him out of his cage and put him on the floor. He waddled around peering behind the furniture like a suspicious hotel detective looking for unregistered guests. To replace the sunflower seed I'd sent off with Deputy Morgan, I filled a clean jar with seed from a big bag in Reba's pantry. Then I scraped poop off Big Bubba's perches, disposed of all the seed hulls and knobs of dried fruit on his cage floor, put down fresh newspaper carpet, washed his food and water dishes, and gave him fresh seeds and fruit. I knew he would immediately set to work throwing nuts and apple slices into his water dish to make it yucky, but I gave him clean water anyway because that's how I like it.

Until he was free of the allergy to red tide, I didn't want him to do any strenuous exercise, but I made him do about three minutes of wing flapping. That entailed having him sit on my arm while I moved it rapidly up and down, which meant that I did three minutes of wing flapping too. Then I chased him around the house until I was winded and he was squawking in parrot hilarity.

A pet sitter's life is just one exciting moment after another.

Pet birds need at least twelve hours of dark silent sleep every night, so the last thing I did was tell him good night and drape his cage with a lightweight dark cover. With him tucked in, I went back down the front steps to the

Bronco. I looked, but I didn't see any ghostly faces peering at me through the dark trees. Maybe Jaz had left town. Maybe she wouldn't show up at Hetty's the next day. Maybe those scary boys had left town too.

That's what I told myself. If I'd been able to, I would have thrown a light cover over myself like Big Bubba's so I wouldn't have to see reality.

When I got home, the sun was a golden balloon lightly bouncing on the distant horizon, sending a glittering path across the tops of waves to the shore. Michael and Paco stood on the sand watching it, Michael with his arm slung loosely over Paco's shoulder. I scurried over and stood on his other side so he could hug me too, and we all waited in awed silence while the sun did its daily flirtation with the sea. Like a coy virgin, it hovered just out of reach, seeming at times to pull upward a bit and then dip slightly toward the lusting sea. Behind it, translucent bands of cerise and violet danced with streaks of turquoise and sparkling yellow. Just when it seemed the sun would hold itself aloof forever, it abruptly changed its mind and fell into the sea's open arms. Within seconds, it was lost in a watery embrace, and all that was left were rainbow sighs of contentment.

Michael gave me and Paco a little squeeze and we all turned and trooped toward the wooden deck. Michael's prized steel cooker was smoking and all the extra little gizmos for baking and boiling things were occupied with good-smelling somethings.

Next to Paco and me, Michael loves that grill beyond anything else in the world. He can get rhapsodic pointing out its little side extensions on which you can cook something in a pan—boil potatoes, maybe—while the stuff on the rack grills. And the warming oven below the grill seems miraculous to him. He just loves to warm dinner rolls down there and never fails to mention when he does. Men and outdoor cookers are like men and cars, a mysterious love affair women will never understand.

Michael said, "Ten minutes, tops."

I said, "Gotcha," and raced up my stairs two at a time, punching the remote to raise the shutters as I went.

If there's ever a reality TV show that gives prizes for the fastest shower takers, I'll enter that sucker and win. The trick is to peel off clothes on the way so you're already naked when you turn on the water. A squirt of liquid soap on a sponge, a slick up one side and down the other, turn around to rinse all areas, and that's it. Two minutes tops. Then a quick foot dry to keep from sliding on tile, a fast comb through wet hair and a slick of lip gloss—another two minutes—before a gallop to the closet for fresh clothes while towel-patting exposed damp skin. In nanoseconds I was stepping into clean underwear and pulling on cool white baggy pants and a loose top. No shoes, but I took a second to slide a stretchy coral bracelet on my wrist.

I left the shutters up and clattered down the stairs to the deck where the table was already set for three, with a shallow bowl of gazpacho on each plate. Paco was pouring chilled white wine into two glasses and iced tea into a third. The glass of tea meant Paco would be leaving later on some undercover assignment. I didn't comment on it. He's safer if we know nothing about his work, but it's impossible not to know some things.

Paco gave me a quick once-over the way men do and nodded in silent approval. Cats and dogs wave their tails to applaud, men nod and twitch their eyebrows.

From his beloved grill, Michael said, "Good timing, Dixie. Heat's just right."

I went over to a redwood chaise where Ella Fitzgerald was surveying the scene. She wore a kitty harness with a long thin leash attached to one of the chaise legs, and she gave me a glum look when I stooped to kiss the top of her head. Paco had bought the harness and leash after Ella had bounded into the woods behind the house and he'd spent several anxious hours looking for her.

Paco said, "The princess is pouting."

I said, "She'd pout a lot more if a big critter got her in the woods."

Michael said, "We'll eat the gazpacho while dinner cooks."

Like an artist setting paint on a canvas, he laid thick tuna steaks on the grill, then gave us the kind of beatific smile that only a great chef bestows when everything is going exactly the way he planned.

Paco and I didn't need encouragement. We hurried to slide into our seats and had our spoons ready by the time Michael joined us. Michael's gazpacho is absolutely the best in the world, with everything fresh from the farmers' market and all the flavors blending like an orchestral creation. For a few minutes, the only sounds were the clicks of our spoons against the bowls and my soft whimpers of pleasure. There had been a time when I made those same noises when I made love. But that had been a long time ago.

Paco said, "Gazpacho is what, Spanish?"

Michael did a facial shrug with his eyebrows. "I guess. Or Portugal. Someplace like that."

Paco said, "Did you ever think how different cultures get connected through food? We're having gazpacho, somebody in France is eating nachos right now, some Russian is eating pizza. That's pretty cool."

Michael said, "Sauerbraten with potato pancakes. Some red cabbage." He had obviously lost track of the idea and was imagining menus.

Paco said, "I've always had a fantasy of going to Greece and meeting distant relatives. We'd sit and talk and they'd feed me roast lamb and stuffed grape leaves and kibbe, and I'd come home feeling as if my boundaries had been extended."

I said, "I don't think kibbe is Greek. It's Lebanese."

Michael said, "You hungry for lamb? Why didn't you say so? I'll make you some."

Paco grinned. "No, doofus, that's not what I meant. I'm just talking about how food connects us to thousands of relatives we've never met. They're all over the world, but we eat the same food they eat. You have relatives in Norway, probably in England too, or God knows where, and I probably have Cypriot cousins. If one of my Greek ancestors married an Irish woman and moved to Russia, I may have Greek-Irish-Russian relatives. Heck, we're probably all related to one another in some way."

We all fell silent at the enormity of the idea. My gosh, everybody in the world could be distant relatives of one another. Boy, talk about a family tree!

When the gazpacho was all gone, Paco gathered the

bowls while Michael checked the tuna steaks and peered at the stuff on the grill's side cookers. I didn't do diddly, just sat there like royalty and let two gorgeous men wait on me.

The tuna was cooked to perfection, and the side stuff turned out to be some of the corn and green beans Michael had got that morning. There was also mango-and-papaya salsa for the tuna. All in all, a dinner fit for royalty.

We chatted idly while we ate, but nothing important. Michael said the latest news report said the red tide had drifted away from us, so the fumes weren't a problem anymore. I said Big Bubba would be happy about that because he preferred his outdoor cage. Paco asked who Big Bubba was, so I told him about Reba being in France eating at four-star restaurants. We all agreed that four-star or not, she probably wasn't getting food as good as what we were eating.

They didn't ask me if I'd had any scary encounters with strangers, and they probably didn't even wonder if I had. I mean, why would they? I didn't ask Paco why he'd been home all day, or when he would be on duty again, but I did wonder. Loving people means you let them have certain secrets they don't share with you.

After dinner, Michael and I cleared the table while Paco took a little plate of tuna to Ella. She was still sulking, so he had to sweet-talk her until she condescended to hop from the chaise to the deck floor and eat his peace offering. Michael and I grinned at each other because Paco deals with the dregs of humanity without showing a shred of sympathy, but guilt at cramping Ella's style with a leash had reduced him to pleading with her to eat twenty-dollar-a-pound tuna.

In the kitchen, I loaded the dishwasher and helped Michael stow leftovers in the refrigerator. Then I hugged him good night and headed for bed, with a detour to tell Paco and Ella good night. Paco had stretched out on the chaise and Ella was sitting on his chest purring at him, so I guess she'd forgiven him for trying to keep her safe.

Upstairs, I lowered the storm shutters, checked phone messages, brushed my teeth, and shed my clothes. By nine o'clock, I was in bed with a book. By ten o'clock, I'd turned out the lights and was asleep. When you get up at four A.M., bedtime comes early.

In my sleep, I heard the subdued purring sound of Paco's Harley, and knew that he was headed for some undercover job.

It was after one when I woke to the sound of somebody banging on the hurricane shutters and screaming my name. I shot out of bed in a momentary panic. It took a few seconds to get my bearings and recognize the voice hysterically shouting my name.

# 6

The thing about going crazy, really, truly crazy with no more pretending that you're even a little bit sane, is that once you've been there you don't have to wonder anymore what it's like. Crazy is a dark ugly town. Stay there long enough and you'll learn all the roads, all the houses and gas stations, until you figure out that crazy is just an alternate territory. You can live there if you want to, or you can leave. It's your choice. There's a kind of strength in that, a weird kind of power that people who've never gone crazy don't know about. When you leave crazy and come back to normal, you feel a special closeness to people who were loyal to you while you were there—like the woman calling my name.

Sleep dazed, I grabbed a robe to cover my naked self and ran to open the door to the woman who'd been my best friend all through high school. Maureen had been a total airhead then, but fun. Her father had abandoned her the same way my mother had abandoned me. Being the kids whose parents hadn't loved them enough to stay with them had drawn us together like orphaned lambs huddled away from the herd. In our senior year, Maureen had fallen in love with a sweet guy named Harry Henry. Everybody had expected them to marry, but right after we graduated Maureen had broken Harry's heart by marrying a rich old man from South America.

She and I lost contact after that. I went to college for two years and then to the police academy. Maureen learned to travel in private jets and hang out with movie stars and European princesses. By the time I married Todd, a fellow deputy, I was deep in the hard-edged world of law enforcement, and Maureen was deep in the soft world of luxury. She sent me a baby gift when Christy was born, but we no longer saw each other.

But after Todd and Christy were killed and I fell into a bottomless pit of crazed agony, Maureen had shown up one night with a tremulous smile and a bottle of Grey Goose. She had only come that one time, but I'd always been grateful for it. With Maureen, it hadn't been necessary to pretend to be strong or rational. I could be what I truly was, broken and empty and full of fury. And baring my true self had helped me find the thread that would eventually lead me back to sanity.

Now it was Maureen screaming into the night for my help.

I ran barefoot to hit the electric control to raise the metal shutters. I saw Maureen's feet step back a bit as the shutters folded into the soffit above the door. Her feet were bare like mine. Even sleep stunned and addled, I knew her naked toes were an especially bad omen.

When the shutters were head-high, I opened the glass-paned french doors and Maureen hurled through. She was sobbing so hard I couldn't make out what she was saying, just that somebody was gone.

Clutching at me like a drowning person, she said, "You have to help me, Dixie! Please!"

I held her tightly for a few minutes and talked to her the way I talk to agitated animals who need calming. When her convulsive shuddering had calmed to tremors, I led her to the couch and sat close beside her. She wore white gauze pajamas and carried a pouchy brown leather bag. Even without makeup and with her brown curls in a tumble, she was still as beautiful as she'd been in high school. She also still smelled of tobacco smoke.

I said, "Mo, what's happened?"

Wild-eyed, she choked, "They've taken Victor. Oh, my God, Dixie, they've taken Victor!"

I had to dig into my memory bank to remember that Victor was her husband's name.

"Who? Who took him?"

She waved her hand in front of her face as if she were erasing the air. "I don't know. Somebody who wants money. They say they'll kill him if I don't give it to them."

"When? When did they say that? How?"

"Just now, tonight. They called and told me. They want a million dollars in small bills. They want me to leave it in the gazebo tomorrow night. If I don't, they'll kill Victor."

She spoke as if I was familiar with her private little sunset-viewing house. Actually, I'd only been in it once when she'd invited me to her house for lunch. She hadn't been married long, and her cook—boy, had I been impressed that she had a cook!—had prepared a tasty little spread that we'd eaten in the gazebo. Her husband had come home while I was there and spoiled it. He'd been stiff and cold and looked at me as if I were a smelly bug. I'd left in a hurry and was never invited back.

I said, "We have to call the sheriff's department. They know how to handle things like this."

"No! They said if I called the police they'd kill him for sure. You have to help me, Dixie!"

It occurred to me that Maureen might think I was still a deputy.

I said, "Mo, I'm not a deputy anymore, I'm a pet sitter."

Her eyes registered mild surprise. "You always were crazy about pets."

Maureen never had been very interested in what other people did. In high school, that was a trait that had kept her from being nosy and gossipy. It had also kept her from being discriminating.

I said, "Do you know anybody with a grudge against Victor?"

She gave me a round-eyed stare. "*Everybody* has a grudge against Victor. It's his business. You know, all that oil-trading stuff is cutthroat. Men in that business make enemies."

I could tell by the way she said it that she didn't have a clue what Victor's business dealings were like, or even how he carried them out. Maureen was sweet and cute, but *smart* would be the last adjective anybody would use to describe her.

I said, "I didn't realize Victor was that important. To kidnappers, I mean."

"In his own country he is. Victor Salazar is a big name there."

It was creepy to see how quickly she trotted out his importance, as if it justified his kidnapping.

I said, "Mo, I know people in the sheriff's department. Let me—"

"I'm not going to the cops, Dixie. I can't take that chance. Victor says this happens all the time in South America. That's why he keeps such a tight watch on me. He always told me if he got kidnapped to just pay up. That's what I'll do too. I have to handle this myself."

I said, "Tell me exactly how this happened. When did you last see Victor, and when did you get the call?"

She opened her bag and pulled out a pack of cigarettes, then saw the look on my face and put them back.

She said, "I saw him about three thirty this afternoon. He left to go meet some old buddies from South America. Venezuela, I think, or maybe Colombia. Could have been Nicaragua. One of those places. He said they'd come here on vacation and they were all getting together for a five-day camping trip, just those guys, catching up on old times, fishing, boating, you know, guy things."

For the life of me, I couldn't imagine Victor out in the woods camping. Or fishing. He had seemed more the type to sit in a deck chair on a megayacht and look at the little people through narrow glasses too dark to see his eyes.

I said, "How long after he left for the camping trip did you get the phone call?"

"I don't know, several hours. The call came after midnight. I was already asleep, but I thought it might be Victor calling so I answered. When I heard that voice I got so scared I couldn't breathe."

"Tell me again what the caller said."

"It's still on my machine, I can play it for you, but I played it so many times I have it memorized. It was a man, and he said, 'Mrs. Salazar, we have your husband. If you want him returned alive, put a million dollars in small bills in a duffel bag and leave it in your gazebo at midnight tomorrow. Do not call the police or tell anybody. We'll be watching you, and if you talk to anybody, we will kill your husband and feed him to the sharks.' "

"And then what?"

She looked confused. "I guess the sharks would swim away."

"What else did the man say?"

"That's all. The line went dead then."

I took a deep breath. It was now after one o'clock. Maureen had got the call, freaked out, replayed it several times, then pulled herself together and come to me.

I said, "What do you know about the men Victor was meeting?"

She shook her head. "Not a thing. Victor never said their names, and they didn't come to our house."

"Did he say where he was meeting them? Was he going to leave his car someplace and go with them, or were they going to ride with him? And where exactly were they going to camp?"

I was piling too many questions on her at once, and she waved both hands in front of her face like a besieged child. "I don't know, Dixie! He just said they were going to hike in the woods and do some fishing."

"You didn't ask where he was going?"

"Victor didn't like to be asked questions about his private business."

Something about that sentence caused a camera shutter to click in my brain, but I didn't look at the photo it took. Maureen was an old friend, and my job was to help her, not to analyze every word she spoke.

I said, "When the call came, was there a person you could talk to, or was it all a recording?"

She looked surprised. "I think it was a person."

I didn't want to bring up the possibility that Victor had already been killed. But I was pretty sure pros demanded proof the abducted person was still alive before they made any money drops.

I said, "Maureen, this could all be a scam. It happens all the time in other countries. People get a call that their child or spouse has been kidnapped, and they get so scared they give the kidnappers whatever they ask for. Then they find out there hasn't been any kidnapping at all. This could be a hoax too. We don't know if the call you got was truly from kidnappers. It could have been from somebody who knew Victor was going to be gone and decided to get an easy million dollars."

"I think it was real, Dixie."

"But what if it wasn't?"

"Then I lose a million dollars and my husband comes home when his camping trip ends. Either way, I get my husband back. I'm not going to nickel and dime when it comes to my husband's life."

I suppose that's why kidnapping wealthy businessmen is so popular in certain circles. To people who don't mind losing a million here and there, being kidnapped probably seems no more than an inconvenience.

I said, "If they're watching you like they said they were, they know you came here."

She shook her head. "Nobody saw me leave. Nobody followed me."

Maureen wouldn't have noticed if a convoy of trucks had followed her, and the entire conversation gave me the same weariness I'd always felt in high school when she showed me the inside of her brain. Even then, talking to her had been like zooming to the moon expecting to find life and instead finding a For Rent sign.

I said, "Mo, not to put too fine a point to it, but I'm not crazy about being involved in something like this. If you're not willing to go to the sheriff, I can't help you."

She raised her head and looked at me with the direct gaze of a child. "If it were *your* husband that had been kidnapped, I'd help you."

Heat traveled to my face and I looked down at my hands. Remembering how she'd come to me when I was so wild with grief, I felt ashamed.

I said, "Can you lay your hands on a million in cash by tomorrow?"

She shrugged. "Sure."

She seemed surprised at the question, as if everybody had a million in cash lying around the house.

"Tell me again how they want it delivered."

"At our gazebo. You know, down on the boat dock? I guess they'll come get it in a boat. They said to put the money in a duffel bag."

"What do you want me to do?"

"Just go with me. That's all I ask. Just walk down that path with me to the gazebo. I'll come here and pick you up and take you back to my house, and then we'll go together to take the money. Please, Dixie?"

Her hair had flopped over her eyebrows so that her big puppy dog eyes pleaded with me from under a mass of curls. A girlish barrette with a bright red plastic flower on one end had come loose, and the flower dangled like a reject.

She said, "I can't do it alone. Just the thought of that walk in the dark by myself with that money makes my knees buckle. I'd be so scared I'd faint right there on top of the bag."

If any other woman had said that, I would have thought she was being overly dramatic. But Maureen had never been capable of handling ordinary things other people take for granted. In the state she was in, she would probably drop the duffel bag in the water or somehow screw the whole thing up.

Every ex–law enforcement bone in my body said we should notify the police and probably the FBI as well. But what if I was wrong? What if notifying the police caused Victor Salazar to be killed? Victor had apparently half expected to be kidnapped for ransom someday, or at least he'd known it was a good possibility, and he'd given Maureen instructions to pay the kidnappers and be done with it. Maybe it was smarter for Maureen to pay up and be quiet.

The bottom line was that it wasn't my decision to make. It was Maureen's husband who had been kidnapped, not mine. Maureen was the one to decide how to handle it, not me. All she wanted from me was to lend her support in doing what she had decided to do.

And over and above everything else was the fact that Maureen had been a good friend to me at the lowest point of my life.

I said, "What do you have to do to get the money?"

She looked puzzled. "It's already mine. I don't have to do anything to get it."

"I mean is it in your house, or at the bank, or where?"

She looked wary. "I'm not supposed to tell. Victor never wanted me to tell about the money."

The little camera shutter clicked again, but I ignored it again.

I said, "I only ask because I want to be sure you'll be safe carrying all that money if you have to go to the bank to get it."

"I don't have to leave the house to get it."

Okay, so she and Victor had a home safe stocked with at least a million dollars in cash.

"Is the money you have in small bills like they want, or will you have to have hundred-dollar bills changed?"

She watched my mouth while I talked as if she could memorize what I said more easily if she read my lips.

She said, "The money is in twenties."

Softly and carefully so I wouldn't spook her, I said, "Maureen, do you know the combination to your safe?"

She looked proud. "Two-four—"

"Don't tell me! I just wanted to make sure you knew it. Now, do you have a duffel bag to put the cash in?"

She frowned. "How big do you think it has to be?"

Now it was my turn to frown. How many cubic feet

of space did a million dollars in twenty-dollar bills take up?

I said, "Bigger than a carry-on, but not as big as one of those long things with wheels."

She nodded. "I bought a hot pink bag like that in Italy. I'll use that."

"I guess hot pink is as good as anything."

Maureen looked thoughtful, and I knew damn well she was imagining what she would wear for the money drop. My guess was that it would be something that matched the hot pink duffel bag.

Somehow that made my promise to help her seem more sensible. Expecting this child-woman to carry out a kidnapper's instructions by herself was like expecting a kitten to walk a tightrope over the Grand Canyon.

# 7

At five fifteen the next morning, I stepped through my french doors like a sleepwalker. It had been almost two o'clock when Maureen left, so I'd slept an extra hour and got up fuzzy brained and blurry.

While my metal shutters scrolled down over the doors, I stood at the porch railing and breathed in the clean salty air. The sky was paler than it usually is when I begin my day, with no fading stars in sight, and faint hints of impending pink at the edge of the horizon. The sea was still asleep, dark and glossy and faintly sighing. A few early-rising gulls ambled at the shoreline, and an occasional hesitant cheeping sound came from the trees, but all the other shorebirds and songbirds were still snoozing. Lucky them.

Yawning, I slogged down the stairs to the carport, where my Bronco was parked between Michael's clean sensible sedan and Paco's dented truck. Paco's Harley was gone.

When I got in the Bronco, a great blue heron sleeping on the hood gave me a snarky look, then spread its wide wings and flapped away. I gave him a snarky look back. He should have been grateful for the extra hour I'd given him. Same thing with the parakeets who exploded in hysterical frenzy from the oaks and pines as I drove down the winding lane toward Midnight Pass Road. I usually try not to wake them, but I felt so grouchy that I didn't even slow down.

I definitely don't do well on less than six hours' sleep.

Morning and afternoon, my first call is always to run with Billy Elliot, a rescued Greyhound whose human is Tom Hale. Some retired Greyhounds are like some retired humans—they'd rather stretch out on the couch than walk around the block, and they wouldn't run if you begged them. Billy Elliot, however, is like one of those wiry old guys who were track stars in college and still get up every morning and jog two or three miles before breakfast. He has to run or he gets nervous and twitchy, and he wants his runs to be hard and full out. If he had his way, he wouldn't wear a collar and he wouldn't have a blond woman attached to the leash trying to keep up with him. He's polite about it, but I know he considers me a necessary nuisance. I feel that way about some people too, so I don't take offense.

Tom would have been happy to run with Billy himself, but Tom's life had taken a nosedive a few years before when he was ambling down an aisle in a home improvement store and a display of wooden doors fell on him and crushed his spine. He's still a top-notch CPA, and he and I trade services. I go to his place twice a day and run with Billy Elliot, and Tom does my tax returns and handles anything connected to money for me.

Tom and Billy Elliot live in the Sea Breeze condos on the Gulf side of the key. As soon as I used my key and unlocked his door, I smelled fresh coffee. Tom was up and waiting for me in the living room. Tom has big round black eyes and a mop of short black curls. In his striped cotton robe and wire-rimmed round glasses, he looked like a grown-up Harry Potter.

As Billy Elliot bounded to me for his morning smooch, Tom said, "Is something wrong?"

That's the problem with being the kind of person with a schedule so consistent that people could set their clocks by me. Be an hour late, and people notice.

Avoiding his eyes, I said, "I overslept. Forgot to set my alarm." My head felt like mice had crawled in and built a furry nest, and my tongue tasted like birdcage carpet.

"Huh." Somehow he managed to sound like he didn't believe me but wouldn't press me for the truth. That made me feel vaguely guilty because Tom only pries when he thinks I need a friend.

I clipped the leash to Billy's collar and hustled him out the door without saying anything else. On the way to the elevator, Billy Elliot ecstatically whipped his long tail side to side while I clumped along like a malfunctioning robot. Downstairs, we whisked through the lobby and out to the parking lot.

Cars park in an oval around the perimeter of the lot, and there's a shrubby area in the center. Between the cars and the green stuff, an oval drive makes a perfect racing track for Billy Elliot. As soon as he'd lifted his leg on several bushes and provided poop for me to collect, he tore off around the track while I ran desperately behind him. Since we were running later than usual, a few other dogs and their humans were on the track too, most of them walking sedately. We passed them all. As we did, Billy Elliot turned his head and grinned hugely at each one.

When we'd made three rounds of the track and I felt little hairline cracks opening in my skull, Billy Elliot allowed me to pull him to a brisk walk back to the lobby.

Upstairs, Tom was still in the living room. He said, "Want some coffee?"

My dead brain made a feeble beep. It needed caffeine bad. But if I had coffee, Tom was bound to quiz me about being late, and even on my best days I'm no match for Tom's quick mind.

While I tried to decide, he said, "Looks like it's going to be a nice day. But we could use some rain."

I said, "Could we talk about this later? I'm sort of stupid right now."

Tom studied me as if I were a tax form. "What's wrong?"

"Nothing. I'm just not up to talking about anything deep."

"The weather isn't all that deep, Dixie. Not as a topic of discussion, anyway. Now it can get deep as a reality. You take a twenty-eight-foot tidal surge, now that's deep."

He just can't help himself.

I stooped and unsnapped Billy Elliott's leash.

Tom said, "You don't look like you slept last night."

"Had a surprise visit from an old friend and we yakked too late. You know how you lose track of time like that."

I tried to make it sound like two goofy women having a good time gassing about old times, not like two women planning to deliver a million dollars in ransom for a kidnapped husband.

He gave me an understanding look. I hate understanding looks.

He said, "You don't have to tell me what it is, but you're stressed about something."

Like I said, Tom is sharp.

Looking at his kind eyes caused the memory of Jaz and the young men who'd come in Big Bubba's house looking for her to come crashing back, along with my promise to stop at Hetty's house that morning to see if Jaz had showed up. Maureen had driven them clean out of my head, but now they were back.

I went to Tom's kitchen, poured myself a mug of coffee, and went back to the living room.

I said, "Some hood types came in a house where I was taking care of a parrot yesterday, and Lieutenant Guidry thinks they may be part of a gang that killed a guy night before last. Evidently it was a robbery that ended up a homicide."

"Are you afraid they're after you?"

"I'm afraid they're after a girl I met yesterday morning at the vet's. She was there with a hurt rabbit when I went to pick up Big Bubba. That's the parrot. Congo African Grey, talks a blue streak. When the boys came in, they said they were there for Jaz. That's the girl's name. The man with her called her Rosemary, but she said her name was Jaz. Hetty Soames hired her to work part-time, so now I'm concerned about Hetty. She's raising a new pup for Southeastern."

Tom raised his coffee mug to his lips and took a long drink, his eyes glued to mine the entire time. When he lowered the mug, he didn't look as fresh as he'd looked when I first arrived. I have that effect on people sometimes.

He said, "You think the guys will go to the woman's house looking for the girl?"

"Hetty gave Jaz her address, and if Jaz is part of a gang, she might tell the boys and they'll go there to burglarize the place."

Tom nodded his head very slowly, sort of like a metronome ticking off beats.

He said, "I knew a girl called Jaz one time. Short for Jasmine."

That made sense. The girl looked like she might be named Jasmine. For sure she looked a lot more like a Jasmine than a Rosemary.

Tom said, "This all happened in the last twenty-four hours?"

"Less, really. The sheriff's department has put extra patrols in the neighborhood and I'm going to stop by Hetty's this morning after I see to Big Bubba. Hetty lives alone, and I'm uneasy about the whole thing."

He blinked up at me. "Does it change anything?"

"Does what change anything?"

"Being uneasy. Does it change anything?"

"I guess not."

"Then how about letting the sheriff's department take care of their job and letting Hetty take care of herself, and letting what's her name, Jasmine, do whatever she does."

I drained the last of my coffee. "You mean like mind my own business?"

"Something like that."

"I try to do that, Tom, I really do. I don't go around carrying a sign that says, 'Tell me your problems,' but somehow everybody who has one ends up on my doorstep."

Saying *doorstep* made me think of Maureen and what I'd promised to do that night. I hurried to the kitchen and put my mug in the dishwasher, then told Tom and Billy Elliot goodbye.

I said, "Thanks for listening to me, Tom. And you're right. I'm putting it out of my mind right now."

I doubted that he believed me, but at least he didn't know about Maureen. If I'd told Tom about our plan to stuff a million dollars in a duffel bag and give it to kidnappers, he'd have given me the lecture of a lifetime, even worse than Michael's would be if he found out about it. Michael would be incensed that I was throwing away my good sense, Tom would be incensed at the idea of throwing away a million dollars.

The rest of the morning went smoothly, and I managed to shave off a few minutes of each visit. Big Bubba would be my last pet call of the morning, but before I went to his house I stopped at Max King's to give an antibiotic to his cat, Ruthie. That was my sole purpose, to give Ruthie a pill. I'd done it for the last two mornings and would continue until all the pills were gone. Even though I charged my usual fee for about five minutes of work, Max thought it was worth every penny.

A retired air force colonel, Max was originally from the Bahamas, and still had a hint of island music to his voice. He looked a bit like Sidney Poitier and had a smile that made people want to give him whatever he wanted even before he asked. What he wanted was his wife back. He had become so depressed after she died that his two daughters had decided he needed a kitten, and had made a special trip to Florida to take him to the Cat Depot. Max hated cats, but his daughters had talked him into going with them anyway. The Cat Depot rescues abandoned cats, and Max had lost his heart to Ruthie.

Scottish Folds are medium-sized cats with soft chirpy voices and a curious tendency to sit in Buddha positions or flatten themselves on the floor like little bear rugs. They're all born with straight ears, but when they're about three weeks old their ear tips fold forward. A few kittens stay straight eared, but whether their ears are folded or not, they are incredibly sweet cats. Insisting that a Scottish Fold do something it doesn't want to do is guaranteed to make anybody feel like a vicious ogre.

Ruthie was about a year old now, and she'd developed a nasty urinary tract infection. The vet had prescribed amoxicillin every twenty-four hours. Easy for the vet to say. Ruthie was mellow and affectionate, but she was still a cat, and trying to get a cat to swallow a pill can cause strong men to break down and weep.

Hide a pill in a cat's food, and the cat will daintily pick up every crumb and leave the pill. Force a pill into a cat's mouth and hold its jaws closed so it has to swallow, and it will shift the pill to its cheek and spit it out as soon as you take your hand away. Try to strong-arm a cat by swaddling it in a towel and poking a pill down its throat, and it will spit at you while it spits out the pill.

Max was a man of keen intellect, strong character, and the commanding presence of a man accustomed to having people jump when he gave an order. But when he'd tried to give Ruthie her pill, he'd ended up with a broken lamp, a scratched arm, several wet tablets that Ruthie had spit out, and a note of desperation in his voice when he called me for help.

When I rang his bell, he opened the door with Ruthie in one arm. Even in the uniform of a Florida retiree—shorts, knit shirt, and flip-flops—Max still managed to look like somebody who should be saluted. He gave me his best Sidney Poitier smile and said, "I knew it was about time for you to come, so I thought I'd make sure she didn't hide."

I would have spent all morning searching for Ruthie just to hear Max speak in that warm molasses voice. That man could stand in a supermarket aisle and read his shopping list out loud, and every woman in the store would offer to cook his dinner.

Feeling very white cracker, I followed him to the living room, where I sat down in one of Max's big comfy chairs. The prescription bottle of amoxicillin was on a table beside the chair. Max gently deposited Ruthie in my lap, shook out an amoxicillin tablet that he laid on the table, recapped the bottle, and took a chair opposite me. He moved with the respectful care of a medical student in a surgical theater.

Ruthie looked up at me with the wide round eyes that give Scottish Folds such innocent expressions. Speaking softly to her, I maneuvered her into an upright position with my right hand supporting her chest and my left hand cupping the back of her head. Her hind feet were on my lap. Very gently, with my fingers under one side of her jaw and my thumb under the other, I lifted her from the head so her hind feet momentarily left my lap. She immediately went limp. At the same time, I reached for the pill with my right hand and pushed it into her open mouth—too far down to spit out. Then I lowered her so her hind feet were once again in contact with my lap. After she swallowed a couple of times, I lowered her front feet too. She gave me a look of sweet forgiveness and hopped to the floor.

Mother cats use that same back-of-the-neck lift when they move their kittens because it makes the kittens momentarily immobile. A grown cat shouldn't be handled that way more than a second or two, and very large cats probably shouldn't be lifted that way at all. But when there's a need to get medication down a cat, it's a better method than fighting with them.

As Ruthie leaped into Max's lap for his masculine stroking, I got to my feet.

I said, "I'll let myself out. See you tomorrow."

Max was too preoccupied with telling Ruthie what a good girl she was to do more than give me a nod. Tough young men are pushovers when it comes to pretty girls. Tough old men are pushovers when it comes to their pets.

# 8

Before I went to Big Bubba's house, I stopped by the Crescent Beach Grocery to get fresh bananas for him. Big Bubba liked his bananas a little greenish, so I got fresh ones every couple of days. He wasn't so picky about other fruit, but he really hated a mushy banana.

I hurried to the 10 Items or Less lane, where a young man was paying for a single bunch of cilantro. The checker, a pretty young woman with dark curly hair, handed him change.

She said, "Weren't you in here just a few minutes ago?"

He grinned. "Yeah, my girlfriend sent me to get stuff for a Mexican breakfast. You know, huevos rancheros and salsa. I got parsley instead of cilantro, so she made me come back."

The checker said, "Oh, yeah, you have to use cilantro for salsa. I had to learn that when I came to this country."

He said, "Where are you from?"

"I'm from Lima, Peru. Are you from Mexico?"

"No, I'm from Taiwan. We don't eat huevos rancheros in Taiwan."

She laughed. "We don't eat it in Peru, either, but I love it."

He hurried away with his cilantro and I took his place with my bananas, happily feeling like a grain in the leavening that keeps the world from being tediously dense.

As I drove down the tree-lined lanes to Big Bubba's house, I kept a sharp eye out for a glimpse of Jaz. But the only person I saw was a suntanned man in a convertible with a kayak in the passenger seat. The man and the kayak looked equally carefree. I waved at the man and he waved back. The kayak just stared straight ahead.

When I removed the night cover from Big Bubba's cage, he was so happy to see me that he almost fell off his perch.

He hollered, "Did you miss me? Get that man! Go Bucs!"

I laughed, which made him laugh too—a robotic *heh heh heh* sound—which made me laugh harder, so for a minute we sounded like a crew member of *Starship Enterprise* entertaining a wily Klingon.

I took him out of his cage and let him run around on the lanai while I cleaned his cage and put out fresh fruit, seed, and water for him. Ecstatic to see sky and treetops and hear his wild cousins calling, he flapped his wings and shouted like a kid at recess. After I had his cage nice and clean, I filled a spray bottle with water and gave Big Bubba a shower on the lanai. Big Bubba loved showers, and he fluttered his feathers so enthusiastically that I ended up almost as wet as he was.

After Big Bubba had run around on the lanai some more to dry, I put him back in his indoor cage. Under ordinary circumstances, since the red tide toxins had abated, I would have put him in his big cage on the lanai. But lanai screens are dead easy to cut, and I was afraid those young thugs might come back and steal him. We don't usually have to worry about things like that on the key, and I resented having to think about it.

I turned on his TV and left him carefully pulling his feathers back into their zip-locked position, drawing each feather through his beak to oil and smooth it. He was so intent on making himself sleek again that he didn't even say goodbye.

My cell rang as I was getting in the Bronco. With no preamble, Guidry said, "Where are you?"

I gave him Reba's address, and he said, "Stay put. I'm in the area."

Three minutes later, his Blazer pulled up at the curb. Except for a certain pink tinge to his eyes that said he'd also missed some sleep, he looked as calm and collected as always. Natural linen jacket, pale blue open-collared shirt, dark blue slacks, woven leather sandals, no socks. Guidry's clothes are always wrinkled just enough to say they're made of fine fabrics woven by indigenous artisans, and he wears them with the casual ease of one who's never known the touch of chemically created threads.

Conscious of being sweaty, cat hairy, and damp from parrot bathwater, I waited while he pulled a sheet of mug shots from a manila envelope.

He said, "You recognize any of these guys?"

They were all young men, all with various looks of sulky

rebellion. Three of them looked like the guys who'd come in Reba's house looking for Jaz.

I touched their faces. "I can't swear to it, but I think they're the ones who came in on me."

"Okay." He put the pics back in the envelope.

I said, "Well?"

"One of them is the guy whose prints were on the jar. An eighteen-year-old from L.A. named Paul Vanderson. He and the other two have records going back several years. They're out on bail right now, charged with killing a sixteen-year-old in a drive-by shooting in L.A. The fingerprint people were able to match Vanderson's latents to some that were in the house where the homicide occurred here in Sarasota. With that confirmation, they compared latents in the house to the other two names, and they matched too. Good job getting the prints, Dixie."

I preened a little bit. If I'd had any, I would have pulled some feathers through my beak.

I said, "So what do you do now?"

"We look for them. When we find them, the LAPD will want them first. Their drive-by shooting trial is next month. If they're convicted of that, they'll spend the rest of their lives in prison. If they're not, they'll still have to stand trial for the homicide here."

Thinking how close I'd been to human beings capable of such mindless violence made my temperature drop.

Guidry said, "The girl is the first link to them, so that's where I'll start. You said the woman's house where the girl is working is around here?"

"Next street over. I'm going there now."

"I'll follow you."

I got back in the Bronco and moved toward Hetty's house, acutely aware that Guidry was behind me. I wondered what he thought about seeing me, or if he was thinking of me at all. Probably wasn't, since he was there as a homicide detective investigating a murder, not because he wanted to see me. I felt like an idiot for even wondering about it, but that didn't make me stop.

Being somewhat involved with a man was like being in a foreign place, an alien world in which I didn't speak the language or know the local customs. With Todd, everything had been gradual and easy, moving from friendship to lovers to marriage in an easy arc that felt familiar and right on every level. But that had been before I knew how love can grow so that losing it is an amputation, how forever after you have the phantom other still attached. I had let my anguish go, but I would never be a fully individual self again. Todd would always be a part of me, like my DNA.

Nevertheless, I remained exquisitely conscious of Guidry's eyes on me, and I was absolutely certain that his feelings about me were as conflicted as mine were about him. He'd had a wife once who'd betrayed him. Perhaps it was difficult for him to trust again. He had a comfortable life as an uncommitted man. Perhaps he wanted to keep it that way.

At Hetty's driveway, I pulled into it and turned off the motor. Before I got out of the car I ordered myself to put every thought about Guidry out of my mind. We were here to keep Hetty safe and to get information about Jaz, not for me to trip over some maybe romance that was no more substantial than a moonbeam. With my mind firmly made up, I slid out of the Bronco to join Guidry.

# 9

Carrying the manila envelope with the mug shots in it, Guidry looked at Hetty's house with the quizzical expression of one who couldn't decide if he was seeing sweet sentimentality or sly irony. I rang the doorbell on the magenta-painted door, and watched Guidry tilt his head to look up where pale pink walls of the sheltered enclosure met a dark shade of burnt orange at the ceiling. The overhead light had a globular shade as starkly white as the low iron Victorian bench beside the door. The bench held a golden yellow basket from which red impatiens spilled. Hetty dresses in cool neutrals, but since she's an exceptionally brave and confident woman, she surrounds herself with color.

I heard faint footsteps that stopped for a few seconds before Hetty answered the door, and I knew she had taken those seconds to look out the peephole. I was glad she was taking precautions. After my experience at Reba's house, I thought it was smart to be extra careful. She opened the door with Ben close beside her feet. Ben tried to wriggle through the opening and she knelt to hold him in place.

I said, "Hetty, is Jaz here?"

With both hands firmly holding Ben, she looked at Guidry with a suspicious glint in her eye. "Why?"

Guidry pulled out his wallet and politely exhibited his creds. "Lieutenant Guidry, ma'am, with the Sarasota County Sheriff's Department. We're investigating a murder and there's a possible link between some of the suspects and a girl calling herself Jaz. Dixie told me she might be working for you. If she's here, I'd like to ask her some questions."

Hetty said, "A murder? You think Jaz had something to do with a murder?"

"I think she might know people who had something to do with a murder. She's not in any trouble."

I felt like hollering, "Don't believe him! He's a homicide detective! He'll tell you any lie that works. If Jaz is in a gang that killed a man while they robbed him, she's in big trouble."

On the other hand, I didn't want Hetty to be mixed up with a girl who might be in a gang of thieves and killers, so I kept quiet.

Guidry said, "Is the girl here, Ms. Soames?"

She cut her eyes at me when he said her name, because obviously I was the one who'd given it to him. But then good sense made her give a resigned sigh, and she rose to a stooped position with one hand on Ben's collar and gestured us inside.

"I have coffee in the kitchen." She led the way through her toffee-colored living room, then the dining room with its pale lavender walls, chalk-white trim, low-hanging wire chandelier for real candles, and its vibrations of laughter and smart conversation.

Every time I walked through that room, I vowed if I ever had another house, it would have a dining room just like Hetty's. Not that I had plans for another house. My spartan apartment suited me just fine. Just *if* I ever did. Like if my apartment got too little for some reason. Not that I thought it would, but still.

Hetty's big square kitchen showed more of her cavalier approach to color. Cherry red walls, yellow cabinets, and white countertops. A round, pedestaled table painted glossy purple, with black mule-eared chairs grouped around it. A kindergarten kid with a fresh box of crayons might have used those colors, but probably not with the same sophisticated effect.

Winston sat in one of the black chairs. Jaz sat in another, with an empty plate and a glass of milk in front of her. The plate had yellow vestiges of scrambled eggs on it.

When she saw me, the girl seemed to freeze. When she saw Guidry, she rose from her chair halfway between flight and indecision.

Hetty said, "Jaz, you remember Dixie from Dr. Layton's office? She's a friend of mine. She likes pets too. Actually, she's a pet sitter." Hetty's voice was too high.

Jaz looked at Guidry and her eyes grew more wary. Even in wrinkled linen and sandals on his bare feet, Guidry had the aura of a cop.

Guidry said, "Jaz, I'm Lieutenant Guidry of the Sarasota Sheriff's Department. I'd like to ask you a few questions."

Jaz shot a hostile glare at Hetty.

Hetty said, “It’s okay, Jaz. He just needs some information.”

Guidry opened the manila envelope and laid the mug shots on the purple table. From his chair, Winston peered at them.

Guidry said, “Do you know any of these guys?”

One glance at the shots, and the girl went pale, with an involuntary jerk of her hand that knocked over the glass of milk. I grabbed the glass before it rolled off the table. Hetty scurried to get paper towels, and Ben ran to lap up milk splashing on the floor. With a quiver of disapproval, Winston jumped from his chair and ran out of the room.

Stricken, Jaz said, “I’m *sorry*!”

Hetty said, “No matter, it’s just spilt milk.”

Something about Jaz’s apology for knocking over the milk seemed so ordinary that it surprised me. Being genuinely contrite for making a mess didn’t seem to go with knowing gang members. It was more the way I would have reacted at her age.

In seconds, her face tightened into a closed mask.

After the milk was blotted up, paper towels were deposited in a wastebasket under the sink, and Ben was brought to heel by Hetty’s feet, Guidry said, “You know who they are.”

It wasn’t a question, but Jaz shook her head.

“I never saw any of them before. Who are they?” Her eyelids fluttered with the effort of sounding clueless.

Guidry said, “A man was killed night before last during a break-in and robbery. We have evidence that points to these young men as the perpetrators.”

She shrugged, and her face took on the look of bored adolescence painfully putting up with stupidity from adults. "So why are you telling *me*?"

Guidry studied her for a moment, then spoke very softly.

"They've been looking for you. Asking about you by name."

I've seen kittens inhale in a startled jerk when something frightens them. A quick intake of breath and then they turn tail and run. Jaz made the same involuntary inhalation, and her eyes grew wide and trembly. She had been shocked and frightened just by seeing the boys' pictures. Hearing they were asking about her had frightened her even more.

"I don't know anything about a robbery, okay? And I didn't have anything to do with anybody getting killed! Leave me alone! Just leave me alone!"

Sobbing, she turned to run, but Hetty caught her in a protective hug and held tight.

Over her head, Hetty said, "Lieutenant, I don't think Jaz has anything to tell you."

Guidry said, "The man you were with yesterday claimed to be your stepfather. Is he?"

With her face buried in Hetty's bosom, Jaz moved her head up and down. "Uh-huh."

"Mind giving me his name, and where the two of you are staying?"

Jaz turned her head and glared at him. "Why don't you mind your own business!"

With a half grin, Guidry said, "Actually, this *is* my business. I just need a name and address."

"We don't live here."

"Okay, where do you live?"

"It's a *secret,* okay? I'll get in a lot of trouble if I tell you that."

For a moment, the kitchen went silent with all the possible implications of what she'd said. In that instant, Hetty loosened her grip, and Jaz spun away from her and tore out of the kitchen. The back door slammed against the wall as she wrenched it open, and then we heard the slapping sound of flip-flops on the paved walk around the side of the house.

Hetty put her fists on her hips and glared at Guidry. "That girl needs help, she doesn't need to be bullied!"

Ben reacted to the anger in Hetty's voice and yipped, which made Hetty squat beside him and stroke him calm.

Guidry sighed and picked up the mug shots from the tabletop. Sliding them into the envelope, he let a couple of beats go by before he spoke.

"Ms. Soames, some young men robbed and killed a man in his home here in Sarasota. We believe the same young men broke into another house yesterday where Dixie was. It was here in your neighborhood. They told Dixie they were looking for a girl named Jaz. Not too many girls named Jaz, so it's a pretty good bet that she knows them. We have identified them as members of an organized gang who are under indictment for murder in L.A. We need to find them, and Jaz is the only link we have. Since she's underage, we need to talk to her stepfather."

Chastened, Hetty said, "I don't believe Jaz is a bad girl, Lieutenant."

"Good girls can get mixed up with gangs too, Ms. Soames."

Hetty looked close to tears, and Ben made a quick puppy grunt of sympathy.

Guidry said, "When you made arrangements with Jaz to come work for you, did you get permission from her stepfather?"

Hetty's face reddened and she avoided Guidry's eyes. "There wasn't time. I wrote my name and address for Jaz and gave her my phone number, but then he dragged her out without saying anything to me."

Guidry said, "So he may not know she followed through on it?"

He was being tactful, but he was really asking if Hetty thought Jaz had sneaked away to see her.

With a note of asperity, Hetty said, "I don't encourage children to disobey their parents, Lieutenant. But Jaz doesn't actually seem to *have* a parent, at least not one who takes care of her. Her stepfather seems a hard, uncaring man. I don't believe there's a mother at all."

"Why don't you think there's a mother?"

Hetty waved her hand at the table. "I gave her cookies when she got here and she gobbled them down so fast I asked her if she'd had breakfast. She said she hadn't had anything since lunch yesterday, so I scrambled her some eggs and she wolfed them down too."

Hetty seemed to take it for granted that if there were a mother in the house, she would have fed Jaz. She would have been shocked to know there had been lots of times when my mother had been too drunk to feed me and Michael.

Guidry said, "Any signs of abuse?"

"Not physical abuse, but emotional abuse is just as bad. Her stepfather seems like a verbal bully."

In case Guidry had forgotten, I said, "And he has that underarm holster. He almost went for his gun when Big Bubba yelled at the vet's office."

Guidry said, "And yet he took an injured rabbit to the vet."

Hetty and I looked at each other with the same *Oh, I forgot about that!* expression. Now that Guidry had reminded us, it did seem incongruous.

Guidry tapped the envelope on the table. "She didn't say where she lives?"

"No, but I think she walked here, so it must be nearby."

"If she comes back, would you call me?"

Hetty met his eyes with an unblinking challenge. "No, I won't. But I'll do my best to find out where she lives and what her stepfather's name is."

Guidry chewed on the inside of his cheek for a second and then nodded. "You might be able to get more out of her than I can. Just don't get any ideas that you can save her by keeping her secrets. If she's involved in gang activity, you'll be obstructing an investigation if you protect her. If she's not involved, you can help her to your heart's content, but I still need to talk to her stepfather."

With a brisk nod to me, he extended a hand to Hetty. "I appreciate your help, ma'am."

Hetty allowed her hand to be swallowed in his for a moment, but I could tell she wasn't squeezing back.

Guidry said, "I'll let myself out."

Hetty and I listened to the subdued closing of the

front door and then we both dropped into chairs at the table.

Hetty said, "I just don't believe that girl would be in a gang."

I thought about the naked fear in Jaz's face when she'd heard the boys were looking for her. She might not be in their gang, but she knew who they were and she was afraid of them. I thought about the tattoo on her ankle. Could it be the emblem of a rival gang? But if it were, that had to mean Jaz was also from L.A. If so, what was she doing here? And why did her stepfather carry that gun?

Hetty said, "She's such a scrawny, needy little thing."

"I know, but don't put yourself in danger. Do what you can to help her, but don't endanger your own safety."

Even as I said it, I wondered if there was a bigger hypocrite in the entire world than I was. At midnight, I would be walking with Maureen down a dark path leading to her private little gazebo by the water's edge. One of us would be carrying a duffel bag stuffed with a million dollars, and somewhere in the darkness kidnappers would be watching us from a speedboat.

A bell rang in my head, the kind you hear in a prize fight when one boxer is stretched on the mat for the count. The kidnappers had threatened to kill Maureen's husband if she told anybody he'd been kidnapped. If they saw two women with a duffel bag, they would know she had told. Maureen wasn't the smartest person in the world, but she was smart enough to figure that out. She didn't intend to go down that path with me, she intended for me to go alone.

When I left Hetty, I almost stumbled going down the

drive to the Bronco. There comes a point when offering a helping hand to somebody in need becomes an act of rank stupidity, and I thought I might have reached that point. Like an automaton, I got in the Bronco and headed for the Village Diner. I wanted to eat everything in sight the same way Jaz had devoured the breakfast Hetty had made for her. Girls who don't have good mothers are always hungry for a savior's food.

# 10

At the diner, all the talk was about the heat. Across from me, three men were counting out bills for their tab and saying how it seemed hotter than any other summer they could remember. One of them took a scientific tack.

"It used to be that ninety degrees meant ninety degrees, but now ninety degrees is really about a hundred and five."

One of his friends said, "That's right. The Gulf is hotter now. Has something to do with sandstorms in Africa. One of the deserts. Sahara, maybe."

As they slid out of their booth, the third man said, "Nah, it's that damn Al Gore."

A bus girl cleaned their table so a man and woman could take their place. Judy came with her coffeepot and took their order. The man asked for key lime pie.

The woman said, "Does the lime pie have milk in it? I'm lactose intolerant."

Judy said, "It has condensed milk."

The woman scowled as if the milk were Judy's fault. "I've never been so hot in my entire life, and I was looking forward to key lime pie."

Judy said, "We have some nice apple pie."

"But apple pie needs cheese or ice cream with it, and I'm lactose intolerant. I don't want real coffee either. I'll just have some decaf."

"Do you take cream?"

"Yes, please."

Judy swiveled to pour more coffee in my mug. Under her breath, she muttered, "It's not the heat, it's the stupidity."

I tackled my eggs and fries with more speed. If I had to listen to any more dumb talk, I might cram it all in my mouth at one time and choke myself to death.

On the way home, I stopped at a red light and watched a skinny man I thought might be Paco in disguise. He was pushing a beat-up old bicycle across the street. He wore faded jeans and an oversized green plaid shirt buttoned to the neck. His sleeves were buttoned at the wrist, and he wore a dirty bandanna tied over dusty, gray-streaked long hair. He felt my gaze and turned and looked vacantly at me. It wasn't Paco, it was just a burned-out old stoner pushing his bike across the street.

When I got home, Paco's Harley was still gone, and Michael was on the deck bent over the table with his back to me. Ella was harnessed and watching from a chaise. From the way she was sitting it looked as if she was gathered to jump and run at a moment's notice.

I went over to see what Michael was doing. A seagull stood on the table. The gull had a string of seaweed attached to his foot and Michael was gently untangling it. As if he knew he'd come to no harm from Michael, the gull stood quietly until his foot was free. Then he lifted from the table with a quick flutter of wings and flew straight toward the sea.

I said, "What are you, a gull whisperer?"

He grinned. "I have the touch, little sister."

His smile didn't reach his eyes or erase the strain around his mouth. Paco had left before midnight, and he wasn't home yet. Neither of us would mention it, but Michael and I both knew how dangerous Paco's undercover work was.

I said, "I'll bet you're famous in the seabird world. They probably get together and talk about the big guy that gives them choice fish heads."

He shrugged. "We all take fame where we find it."

I winced, because my fame was mostly from going nuts while cameras rolled. That, and killing a man.

Without really intending to, I said, "Michael, do you suppose Mom is still drinking?"

Old bitterness made his voice sharp. "Why're you thinking about her?"

I'd obviously touched a nerve. Michael had been the one who'd had to grow up too fast so our mother could stay a child. If I told him how Jaz's hunger had made me remember how he'd taken over the job of protecting me because our mother couldn't be depended on, I'd have to tell him about the young thugs who had come in Big Bubba's house. He was worried enough about Paco, I didn't want to give him something else to worry about. So I went in another direction.

"You remember Maureen Rhinegold? My best friend in high school?"

"Tall, hot bod, big curly hair, big boobs?"

"Yeah, her. She came to see me last night. I guess that made me start thinking about Mom. Maureen's dad was an alcoholic too."

Michael studied me for a moment. "I heard her when she came."

I looked toward the sea where the rescued gull was now indistinguishable from all the others. "I guess you heard her yelling at the door."

He nodded. "Woke me up. I came outside to see if anything was wrong, but you'd let her in so I figured it was okay."

More than likely Michael had already been awake worrying about whatever undercover job Paco was doing.

I said, "She was upset. Wanted somebody to talk to."

He stayed poker-faced, which told me he knew there was something I didn't want him to know.

He said, "I didn't know you two saw each other anymore."

I shifted uneasily. "We don't, but we were close once. Some friendships just stay close no matter what."

He didn't seem impressed. In fact, he looked a bit annoyed.

He said, "I remember Maureen Rhinegold better than you think I do. She's the flake who got you to write all her term papers. She's the one who gave you weed to smoke. She's the one who dumped Harry Henry when some old guy waved money at her. I never could see why you put up with her."

I smiled and patted his big shoulder. Bless his heart, he still thought Maureen had been the one who'd got the weed he'd caught us smoking. Besides, while it was true that I'd written Maureen's papers, she'd helped me too. Once she'd spent hours helping me build a diorama for a history class. Even used her favorite purple nail polish to paint a roof on a teensy building.

I said, "Considering the way Harry Henry turned out, it was probably smart of her to dump him."

As soon as I said it, I felt guilty. In actual fact, I liked Harry. And it wasn't like he'd turned to crime or anything, he'd just become a genial beach bum.

Michael said, "She's still a bad influence, Dixie."

I couldn't keep from laughing. He sounded exactly the way he'd sounded when he was seventeen and I was fifteen, and he'd told me he'd kick my butt clear to Cuba if I ever smoked pot again.

I said, "Michael, I'm a big girl now, and nobody influences me. I think for myself."

Boy, was that a bunch of crap! I could almost hear the echo of my own voice promising Maureen I'd go with her to deliver Victor's ransom money.

Michael walked to the chaise and picked Ella up. He'd apparently decided not to press the subject, which should have made me glad but actually made me a bit nervous. Maybe if he pressed me, I could use him as an excuse to tell Maureen I'd changed my mind.

He said, "Want a brownie? I just made some."

"No thanks, I just had breakfast. I didn't get much sleep last night, so I'm on my way to bed."

With Ella's leash trailing over his shoulder, he gave me

a half wave and went inside his house. I headed for my stairs and a nap. Maybe the world wouldn't look so uncertain when I woke up.

For some reason, my apartment seemed too quiet, as if it were anxiously holding its breath. In my bedroom, I flipped the switch to start the AC on the wall, and started toward the bathroom. But in the hall I hesitated at the narrow linen closet and opened the door. My linen closet is neat and spare, narrow stacks of a few sheets and blankets, some spare towels for guests in case I should ever have any. On the top shelf, a pillowcase holding the furry red Elmo that Christy loved so much, and an elegant round hatbox that once belonged to my grandmother.

Almost furtively, I reached overhead and got the hatbox and carried it to my bed. As soon as I opened it, I was nine years old and secretly watching my mother on the day before she left us. Quiet as death, I stood outside her nearly closed door while she carefully lifted out the contents of the hatbox. She laid them in a precise row along the edge of the bed. She seemed intent on getting them exactly a certain distance from the edge, occasionally adjusting one, moving it higher or lower until she had them the way she wanted them. Then she went still and looked at them for a long time, finally caressing each one as if it were a loved one's cheek. From my spying place, I held my breath. I didn't move. If I moved, my mother might explode into one of her irrational furies. I didn't know what the objects were, but I knew they were more important to her than I was. After a few minutes, she gathered the objects up and replaced them in the box. When she got up from the bed to deposit the box on the top closet shelf, I melted away.

My mother left us for good the next day—ran off with a man my brother and I had never even heard of. After I knew she was never coming back, I stood on a chair and got the box from its hiding place. I don't know what I'd expected, but it wasn't what I found. Ticket stubs to a Grateful Dead concert she and my dad had gone to in Tampa, the baby bracelets Michael and I had worn in the hospital when we were born, Michael's first lost tooth Scotch-Taped to a card with the date and time he lost it, and a handprint I'd made for her in kindergarten. There was also a photo of her and my dad when they were high school sweethearts.

I'm not sure why I've held on to that box, but every now and then I do exactly what I watched my mother do—lay the things out and caress them. The box is my only inheritance from my mother. It links us in a powerful way that transcends reason.

Putting the box back in its place beside Christy's Elmo, I peeled off my clothes and threw them in the washer in the hall, then clumped naked into the bathroom and turned on the shower.

While I stood under a hot shower, I thought about how Maureen had looked when she begged me to help her. Her big pleading eyes. Her messy hair with that dangling barrette with the red plastic flower.

I imagined myself calling Maureen. I imagined myself saying, "You're going to have to do this without me." Then I imagined her saying, "If it were *your* husband, I'd help you."

While I brushed my teeth I imagined calling her and asking, "Are we still on for tonight?" I imagined her saying,

"We don't have to! Victor's here with me! The kidnappers drove him home and we just handed them the million."

Yeah, right. Like kidnappers delivered COD.

I pulled on a terry cloth robe and fell into bed with a dark cloud hovering over me. From a distant place in my head, a voice sang:

*The one with the scarlet flowers in her hair*
*She's got the police comin' after me*

# 11

After a long nap, I dressed and pulled my narrow bed away from the wall to get at the customized drawer built into its dark side—the one that holds my guns in their special cushioned niches. Every law enforcement agency in the country issues standard weapons to its officers, the standard depending on the city or county's choice. Sarasota police are issued 9mm Glocks, while the Sarasota Sheriff's Department prefers SIG SAUERS. Regardless of the weapon issued, law enforcement officers also qualify for several off-duty guns at their department ranges. Using a gun for which you haven't qualified means big trouble, so sworn officers usually qualify for several models even if they mostly stick to one favorite.

After Todd was killed and I went on indefinite leave of absence, I returned our SIG SAUERS to the department, but I still had our personal guns. I was qualified on all of them, and I had a concealed weapon permit making it legal to carry any one of them.

Some states are picky about guns, but Florida, bless its heart, takes the position that people need to compensate for *something,* even if it's just their own frightening imagination. The state therefore offers the right to tote a pistol to anybody with the guts to stare down howling hurricanes, venomous snakes, rapacious developers, and squirrelly election officials.

Actually, guns and responsible ownership of guns have always been part of my life. When my grandparents first came to Siesta Key, rattlesnakes outnumbered humans, and some of the humans were unsavory types one step ahead of bounty hunters. A rifle was a handy thing to have around for protection against all those varmints, and my grandfather would have thought it ludicrous for anybody to question his right to own one. On the other hand, he would think it equally ludicrous for civilians to claim they needed machine guns or assault weapons for personal protection.

When Michael and I were little, our grandfather would take us out to the country and let us shoot tin cans off fence posts. He'd preach that guns were dangerous weapons not to be left loaded or lying around. On the way home he'd make us giggle with the old Jimmie Rodgers song our grandmother wouldn't let him sing in her presence: "If you don't want to smell my smoke, don't monkey with my gun."

I was always a better shot than Michael because he was too physical to enjoy the precision that shooting requires. Good shooters are precise people, like clockmakers or safecrackers. Either because of my grandfather's training or Jimmie Rodgers's blue yodel or some genetic trait, I was one of the best shooters the police academy has ever had. Michael, on the other hand, doesn't own a gun and thinks armed civilians are ridiculous Clint Eastwood wannabes. I sort of agree with him, except that now I'm also a civilian with a permit to carry a concealed weapon.

My preferred gun is one of my former off-duty guns, a snub-nosed, five-shot, J-frame .38 caliber. It has a stainless steel two-inch barrel and cylinder, and an aluminum alloy frame with an exposed hammer. Its checkered black rubber boot grip is easy to handle and it fits well in my hand. No safety to worry about, no decocking levers to slow me down, no magazines to fail. Only thirteen ounces, it's a sweet, simple, dependable gun.

I doubt that I'll ever go back to being a law enforcement officer, and I have no fear of hordes of murderous aliens—either from outer space or other countries—coming to hurt me. But good shooters like to remain good shooters, and my lightweight .38 has a wicked recoil that can ruin my aim if I get sloppy about practicing. I therefore spend some time every week at the handgun shooting range. They all know me there, and the young man who led me to a vacant booth didn't bother to tell me the rules. He just put up the paper target and left me alone.

If I'm honest with myself, I have to admit I don't practice just to stay a good shot. There's also something about putting on the eye and ear protectors, spreading my feet, and aiming at a fresh piece of paper with a bull's-eye painted on it that gives me a feeling of kick-ass Wonder Woman power. I might get the same feeling if I just put on the Wonder Woman costume, but I don't think so.

I shot with the pistol held in two hands and then in

one, and when I was satisfied that I was still a good shot, I loaded everything up and left the range still feeling like Wonder Woman. I remained Wonder Woman until I remembered that I'd just practiced the art of killing another human being. Because let's get real, that bull's-eye target stands for a human heart, and every shooter knows that.

Enjoying target practice with a gun is probably the way people feel if they own profitable stock in health insurance companies that routinely deny lifesaving surgery or medication. It's better not to dwell on the fact that something that gives us so much pleasure is linked to the increased likelihood of another person's death.

On the way home, I noticed a couple of men I thought might be Paco—a man with a long beard and ponytail leaning against a *Pelican Press* dispenser, and a teen with a purple mohawk in dark shades, baggy jeans, and a huge shapeless shirt—but it was dumb of me to do that. If Paco's disguises were the kind I could see through, they wouldn't be effective, and I knew his were extremely effective.

When I got home, I spent an hour at my desk with client records, then went downstairs to spend time with Michael and Ella. To be strictly honest, I was also drawn by the memory that Michael had made brownies. No matter how grim the world gets, chocolate makes anything more tolerable.

Michael was in his kitchen with several steaming pots on the stove and a look of grim anxiety in the set of his jaw. Ella was perched on her barstool watching him and occasionally licking her lips.

I gave Ella's furry head a kiss, poured myself a glass of

milk from a carton in the fridge, and got myself a brownie. I sat on a barstool beside Ella and watched Michael. Like Ella, I licked my lips every now and then, but in my case it was for the chocolate and milk. I suspected Ella did it from a sublimated urge to lick Michael. She wouldn't be the first female to want to do that.

He concentrated on his pots and pans, giving one a furious stir, grabbing a smoking cast-iron skillet's handle and moving it back and forth like he was trying to shake sense into it, glaring down into a soup pot's innards as if he thought it was hiding something. I had the feeling he had forgotten that Ella and I were there.

Meekly, I said, "What're you cooking?"

His head whipped toward me. "Huh? Oh, just some stuff for the freezer. Corn chowder. Roasted poblano peppers, some shrimp and mushrooms to put in the peppers."

I said, "Hunh."

I looked down at Ella, who was looking up at me with a pleading expression. I guess she thought one human should be able to communicate with another human better than a cat could. She didn't understand how hard human-to-human communication is.

I said, "Have you heard from Paco?"

His shoulders hunched, and he increased the speed of the wooden spoon circling in the soup pot. "He never calls when he's working."

I knew better than to ask if he had any idea what the job was, or where it was, or how long it would last. But I also knew that something about this job was unusual. Otherwise, Michael wouldn't be so closed off.

I said, "Paco's a good cop. He knows what he's doing."

"I know that."

I got up and rinsed my milk glass and put it in the dishwasher. Threw the paper towel I'd used as a napkin into the trash under the sink. It was time to go out on my afternoon calls. Just before midnight, Maureen would come for me, and I would go with her to her house. Then one of us would make the ransom money drop, and I knew which one of us it would be. Just thinking about it made me stop breathing.

Michael gave me a phony smile when I left and Ella tried for a nonchalant wave of her tail, but we were all putting on an act. I told myself that Paco would be home by nightfall, that the money drop would go off without a hitch, and that Maureen's husband would be back in the bosom of his family by morning. I told myself that the next day Paco would be resting up from whatever he'd done, I would go off to take care of pets, and Michael would go to the firehouse happily bearing a big container of corn chowder.

I just had to make it until the night was dark enough to hide the insane thing I was going to do.

At Tom Hale's condo, he was in his wheelchair in the living room reading the real estate section of the *Herald-Tribune*. Billy ran to kiss my knees when I let myself in, and Tom raised his head and smiled hello.

He said, "A friend just left me a bag of fresh-picked mamé sapote. They're in the fridge. Want one?"

Offering a sweaty Floridian a taste of ripe mamé sapote is like offering warm blankets and hot chocolate to somebody just pulled from the icy waters of the Bering Strait.

I gave Tom such an eager "Yes!" that Billy Elliot gave me an injured look. No matter how many legs we have, we all think our needs should come first, and Billy didn't want to wait for his run.

Tom rolled into the kitchen and got a brown paper bag from his refrigerator while I got two dessert spoons and a sharp knife.

Mamé sapote is a fruit about the size of a softball, with a tough leathery skin. The flesh is deep orange in color, with a flavor that's a combination of chocolate and pumpkin and ice cream and delicate spices not yet discovered.

Tom cut a brown globe in halves and handed me one. We spooned its cold sweetness straight from the rind.

Tom said, "I love this stuff."

I said, "Todd and I had a mamé sapote tree in our backyard."

The minute I said it, I wished I hadn't. Remembering that tree made me remember how thrilled we'd been when it first bore fruit. One night we took the fruit to bed to eat while we watched TV. We didn't watch TV long. With our lips coated with flesh from the mamé sapote, we fell on each other like bears after honey, inhaling each other's scent and eating each other's taste. Christy was conceived that night, and Todd had always said that when she was a grown woman he would tell her that I'd been too turned on by mamé sapote juice to take time to put in my diaphragm. Unless he and Christy are somewhere in heaven together, she will never hear that story.

With an effort, I pulled my memories away from that night so my heart wouldn't crack in Tom's kitchen.

Tom said, "I was just reading that a penthouse condo on

Siesta Key sold for seven million dollars. The sellers had to reduce the asking price from eight million because times are so tight right now."

I said, "My heart bleeds for them."

Tom waggled his hand. "It's all relative. To a billionaire, a million is like a hundred to everybody else."

I tossed my fruit rind in Tom's kitchen trash and rinsed my spoon. As I put it in his dishwasher, I said, "I know a woman who has a million in cash in her home safe."

He raised a CPA's suspicious eyebrow. "Legitimate money?"

"Yeah. Her husband's an oil trader, whatever that is."

He grunted, and I went to get Billy Elliot's leash. Billy had waited long enough.

Billy and I ran around the oval parking lot track like banshees on holiday. When Billy was happy and I was pouring sweat, we rode upstairs in the cool elevator. Tom was at the kitchen table working on papers of some kind. Before I replaced Billy's leash in the foyer closet, I went to the kitchen. Tom looked over his glasses at me. Probably thought I was going to ask for a second mamé sapote.

I thwacked the end of Billy's leash against my open palm. "Tom, exactly what does an oil trader do?"

He shoved his glasses up on his nose. "Crude or paper?"

"Crude, I think."

"Then he sells oil, big tankers full. Say he represents an oil producer in Norway. They notify him that they've filled a tanker with oil, and he seeks out a buyer. Maybe the buyer is a refiner in Japan, so he strikes a deal with them and notifies the tanker to sail to Japan. But maybe on the way, a refiner in England wants the oil and is willing to pay more. So he strikes a deal with Japan to sell the oil to England, and notifies the tanker to change course. He can do that over and over, and every time the oil changes owners, he gets a percentage of whatever the selling price is, plus fees from both the sellers and buyers for handling the sale. Traders spend their days looking for people willing to pay more or sell for less. It's a lucrative business, but nerve-racking."

Brilliantly, I said, "Hunh."

He tapped his fingers on the tabletop. "No cash gets exchanged in a business like that. It's all wire transfers."

As if it made a difference, I said, "This oil trader I know is from South America."

"Venezuela is one of the largest oil producers in the world. I think it supplies about a fifth of the world's crude."

"Hunh."

Tom seemed to have run out of things to say about oil trading. I couldn't think of anything to say that might explain why my unnamed friend with an oil-trading husband had a million dollars in cash in her home safe.

I said, "Well, okay then. I guess I'll be on my way."

Tom nodded, his eyes bright with something he wanted to say but was holding back. I gave Billy Elliot a smooch and hotfooted it out of the condo. All the way down in the elevator, I wondered where that money in Maureen's safe had come from. Even for superwealthy people, a million dollars in emergency cash seemed excessive. It also didn't seem likely that she and her husband had pulled it out of a bank account to keep close at hand. But if they hadn't got it from their bank, where had it come from?

For the first time, it hit me that Victor's wealth might

be from something illicit. All I knew about Victor was what Maureen had told me, and Maureen could have lied. Even more probable, Maureen might not know herself. Or care. She wasn't the curious type. All she cared about was what Victor's money bought.

At my Bronco, I got inside and bounced my forehead off the steering wheel a few times.

Out loud, I said, "It's not illegal to pay off kidnappers. And delivering money to kidnappers won't make me a criminal, no matter where the money came from."

But inside my head, a little voice said, "Are you sure about that?"

I wasn't the least bit sure.

The Buddhists say, "Before enlightenment, chop wood, carry water. After enlightenment, chop wood, carry water." I felt enlightened by my conversation with Tom, but now what?

I started the engine and headed for my next pet client. Before enlightenment, empty litter boxes, walk dogs. After enlightenment, empty litter boxes, walk dogs. I'm a professional. I meet my responsibilities. Even if I'm planning to do something incredibly stupid and possibly illegal, I take care of my pets.

But after I'd taken care of all the cats on my list, and before I headed for Big Bubba's house, I drove to the village and parked in front of Ethan Crane's office.

I needed legal advice.

# 12

If I had a lick of sense, I'd have thrown myself at Ethan Crane the moment I met him. By any woman's criteria, Ethan is high on the desirability list. He's honest. He's sharp. He cares about things that people should care about, like the environment and the community and dogs. Add all that to the fact that he looks like an underwear model and you have one of the world's best men. Add to that the fact that he and I had a strong attraction from the first moment we met, and you have the world's most stupid woman, because I kept turning him away. And the worst of it was that I turned him away because I was even more drawn to Guidry, who wasn't half as direct as Ethan about wanting me. Not even a fourth as direct, as a matter of fact.

The last time I'd seen Ethan, he'd made it clear that the next move was up to me. He'd also made it clear that he wasn't offering a commitment, but an invitation to explore what we felt for each other and see where it led. I had left vowing to myself that I wouldn't give him any more mixed messages. I wouldn't make any excuses to see him again unless or until I was able to do so without bringing any emotional baggage with me. And yet here I was, baggage and all, coming to him for advice.

Ethan's office is in the oldest part of Siesta Key's business district. His stucco building is as old as the streets, with corners rounded and walls pitted by age and sandy sea breezes. The flaking gilt sign on the front door originally named Ethan's grandfather, ETHAN CRANE, ESQ. Ethan hasn't seen fit to modernize either the sign or the building, so stepping into the minuscule foyer and ascending the worn stairs to the second floor is like stepping back in time to a century when people were more civil and formal. Just the odor of furniture polish and old law books and leather chairs makes me want to live up to a higher standard of conduct.

Ethan's door was closed, and his secretary was busy at a computer in a side office. She wasn't the same secretary I'd seen at his office before. The other woman had been older and dignified, probably another inheritance from Ethan's grandfather. This one was middle-aged and plump, with severe sticking-up hair dyed the color of eggplant. When I stopped at her door, she gave me a scathing once-over.

I said, "I'm a friend of Ethan's. Is he busy?"

She wore dark ruby lipstick on oversized pillowy lips, and when she pursed her lips the effect was a bit alarming. Like they might have suctioning ability that could vacuum me in.

She said, "Does it look like he's not busy?"

The woman obviously saw herself as Ethan's protector,

there to guard him against door-to-door salesmen, scam artists, and women with cat hair on their shorts.

I said, "Sorry, I should have called before I came."

Her big lips did that scary thing again. "Yes, you should have."

She had the charisma of tofu.

I said, "So I guess after I leave, you can just tell Ethan that a good friend was here and left because he was too busy to see me. Better yet, I'll tell him myself and save you the time."

Some of the air went out of her lips, and her eyes narrowed. With a glance at a light on a phone setup on her desk, she said, "He's on the phone. When he's off, I'll let him know you're here."

I gave her a phony smile and she gave me one back. I had won this round, and we both knew it, but sportswomanship kept me from gloating. Thus do women communicate with one another, our little versions of power plays that remain largely invisible to men.

She went back to whatever she was doing on her computer, and I leaned against the doorjamb and waited. From where I stood, I could see the yellow light on her phone board, and when it went out I cleared my throat and pointed.

I got an evil glare, but she punched a button and spoke into an intercom. "Mr. Crane, you have a visitor. She says she's a friend."

It was clear from her tone that she didn't believe he could have a friend like me. She didn't seem to realize that since she hadn't asked for my name, there wasn't much he could do but see me. I wondered how long it would take Ethan to fire her.

In a few seconds, Ethan opened his office door. When he saw me, he looked pleased. I was sorry the pillow-mouthed woman couldn't see his expression from her desk.

Ethan is tall and lean, with high cheekbones, smoldering dark eyes, and glossy black hair from Seminole ancestors. He had on lawyer clothes—dark pin-striped trousers, crisp white shirt with onyx cuff links, a dark rose-hued tie.

He said, "Dixie! What a nice surprise."

He beckoned me into his office and stood aside as I entered. I thought about kissing his cheek and decided not to. He seemed to have the same internal debate, so there was a moment of eye contact at the door that asked questions for which neither of us had answers.

He shut the door and waved me to one of his grandfather's old dark leather chairs. Sitting down behind his desk, he said, "Is something wrong?"

I flinched at the question, but it was fair. Every time I had reached out to Ethan, it had been because I needed help.

His suit coat was on a wooden hanger hooked over an arm of a mahogany hall tree, the kind you only see in antiques stores. The tree had an umbrella holder at its base. I imagined the countless times his grandfather had hung his own coats on that hall tree, imagined the hundreds of clients shaking out damp umbrellas and sliding them into the holder. All that solid tradition behind Ethan was part of what made me trust his advice. It was also part of what put distance between us.

I said, "Ethan, is it illegal to pay off kidnappers?"

His eyes widened. "Why do you ask?"

"A friend needs to know."

One of his thick eyebrows lifted, and I felt my face grow hot. *A friend needs to know* has the same ring of truth as *The dog ate my homework*.

I said, "I have a friend whose husband has been kidnapped. She's planning to pay the ransom. Is that against the law?"

"Not in this country. If she lived in Colombia, she'd be arrested if she paid."

"What if the husband is *from* Colombia but lives here?"

"You have a friend whose husband is from Colombia, and he's been kidnapped?"

"I'm not sure where he's from. It could be Colombia." I felt stupid saying it, like a receptionist who had failed to get a visitor's name.

"Kidnapping is such big business in Colombia that the government has made it illegal to pay a ransom."

I said, "But he lives here, and the kidnappers are here. My friend refuses to report it to the police because she can easily pay the ransom, and that's what her husband has always told her to do if he's kidnapped. She just wants to be sure it's legal."

My voice quavered a bit when I said that, because Maureen didn't give a gnat's ass whether it was legal.

Ethan said, "It's dumb, but it's not illegal."

I said, "So I guess actually *delivering* the ransom money to the kidnappers, like putting it where they said to put it, is okay too?"

"I didn't say it was okay. I said it wasn't illegal."

My lips squinched together to keep from asking what I wanted to know. Then I blurted, "Does it matter where the money came from? I mean, if the ransom money came from something illegal, does that change anything?"

"Let me be sure I understand this. You have a friend from Colombia, which just happens to be a huge exporter of illegal narcotics, and he's been kidnapped. By a happy coincidence, his wife just happens to have a bunch of possibly illegally obtained money, and she's going to use it for ransom. Have I got the facts right?"

I didn't answer. The way he'd put it made it sound a lot worse than anything I'd been imagining.

Ethan sighed and leaned back in his chair. "Dixie, what the hell are you mixed up in?"

"I'm not *mixed up* in anything."

"You're going to help deliver ransom money. Possibly dirty ransom money."

My chin jutted out. "I didn't say that."

"But that's what you're planning, isn't it?"

"You just said it was legal."

"I said paying ransom was legal. I also said it was dumb. Whether they get paid with clean money or dirty money, kidnappers aren't nice people. Paying them ransom money isn't like handing cash to somebody at the Taco Bell drive-through."

I stood up. "Thanks, Ethan. I'll pass the information along to my friend. I didn't know anybody else I could ask."

He stood too. "Don't do it, Dixie."

I said, "This is an attorney-client secret thing, right?"

"It's a stupid thing to do."

"It's my friend's husband. Her decision. I'm not really involved."

"That's what people say just before they get into deep shit. Don't do it."

This time I kissed his cheek as I left. His cheek was hard and smooth, with a clean, healthy, testosterone-laden scent laced with a musky aftershave. My hormones all stood up and cheered when my lips touched him. I was a fool to leave without throwing him to the floor and doing delicious things to him.

It was nearing sunset when I finished with all the four-legged pets. Big Bubba would be my last call, but first I swung by Hetty's house to see if she'd heard from Jaz.

She was happy to say that Jaz had returned.

She said, "I was afraid she'd never come back, the way she ran out this morning, but she came back in an hour or two. We made cookies."

Before I could ask if she'd got information for Guidry, she said, "I was afraid to push her, Dixie. She seems so *scared.* Any little thing spooks her. Something has traumatized that child."

I said, "If she's been involved with a gang, that would be enough to traumatize her."

"She's a sweet girl."

"Something is weird about the whole situation, Hetty. Just be careful."

She said, "It's weird, all right. Her name is a secret. Where she lives is a secret. Why in the world would it be a secret?"

All the possible answers I could think of were too disturbing to voice.

I said, "Is she coming back tomorrow?"

Hetty looked guilty. "She may come back later today. She said she would try to."

"Hetty, she knows gang members wanted for murder. Lieutenant Guidry *really* needs information about her."

"I know. I'll try, but I'll have to wait until the time is right. If I push her, she'll leave and I'll never learn anything."

I couldn't argue with that. I also couldn't argue with Guidry's belief that Hetty was probably the only person who could get information from the girl. As a minor who had done nothing wrong, she was not somebody he could take in for questioning. All he had was the fact that she had behaved strangely when pressed for information about where she lived, and that gang members had asked for her by name.

At Big Bubba's house, I put fresh water and a new millet sprig in his cage, along with some apple slices and half a banana. While I did that, he ran around on the lanai and squawked at the wild birds outside. Big Bubba is bilingual, which is more than I can say for myself. They squawked back, so I suspected he was saying rude things in bird language.

After his food and water were replenished and his cage tidied, I got out some of his toys and we played together. When it was time for me to go, he allowed himself to be returned to his cage, and I draped his nighttime cover over his bars.

I wished somebody would put me behind bars before Maureen came that night. I wished they'd drop a cover over me to hide me from the world.

Instead of going home, I called Michael and told him I wouldn't be there for dinner. He didn't sound disappointed. In fact, he sounded as if dinner was the last thing on his mind, which was another indication of his anxiety about Paco. I didn't need to ask if he'd heard from him.

I drove to Anna's Deli and got a Surfer sandwich to take to Siesta Beach. Siesta's powdery white sand is composed of always-cool quartz, and locals believe it has mystic qualities unknown to ordinary beaches. Whether our faith is based on fact or fantasy, I need to shuffle my feet in that crystalline coolness on a regular basis and absorb some of its energy.

I arrived at the beach when a tangerine sun was inches above the horizon. Ribbons of cerise and gold streaked the sky and gilded the edges of baby white clouds. I walked toward the edge of the surf and sat cross-legged to watch. Along the beach, people fell silent and respectful, all of us watching the last quivering moments of resistance before the sun slipped smoothly into the water, sending out brilliant shafts of color.

When the light dimmed and the clouds turned gray, people gathered up their towels and picnic hampers and straggled toward the pavilion while seabirds wheeled overhead. Alone, I listened to a rosy-pewter sea whisper spume-filled messages, then took off my Keds and went down to let the surf wash over my feet.

When I was a kid, I had a fantasy that I could fly and see through walls. Wonder Woman must have started out like that and then grew boobs and got that costume that didn't move when she did. Anyway, in my Wonder Kid fantasies, I always began standing in the surf. I thought the sea foam rolling over my toes brought magical energy, so I'd stand there and let the magic seep into me, rising up my legs and into my skinny torso, and finally through my outstretched arms. Only then could I lift off and rise in the air. I didn't have to flap my arms or kick my legs or anything. All I had to do was think where I wanted to go, and my body went there. In my imagination, I sailed over Siesta Key's streets and watched cars and pedestrians down below. I hovered over my friends' houses and watched their families. I sailed around the firehouse where my father was and looked at him laughing with his fellow firefighters. Sometimes I settled down on the firehouse roof so I could be close to him.

I guess I haven't changed much since then. Feeling the surf tickle my toes still made me feel charged with energy. I don't believe anymore that I can fly, but by the time I walked back to my sandwich, the Siesta symphony of surf, salt, and sand had soothed my soul.

I would help Maureen leave the money to ransom her husband, and I would not have any more nervous quibbles about it. I had made a promise, and I would keep my word. If the money that ransomed Victor was ill-gotten, that wasn't my problem. If paying off kidnappers was a dumb decision, it was Maureen's decision to make, and she'd made it. I was simply being a friend, a sidekick, like Sancho Panza or Tonto.

For the moment, I'd forgotten about friends like Thelma and Louise. It's good that we can't see too far ahead. If we could, we'd never go forward.

# 13

When I got home, Michael and Ella were in a chaise on the deck. Michael was stretched out almost flat on his back, and Ella was sitting upright on his chest with her ears cocked toward the darkening shadows under the trees. She didn't wear her harness and leash, but Michael's encircling hands were ready to restrain her if she decided to investigate the night.

When they heard my footsteps, two heads turned to look at me. Ella flipped the tip of her tail, and Michael tipped his chin.

I said, "I didn't groom Ella today. I can do it now."

Michael said, "I already combed her. I'm getting pretty good at it."

I was disappointed. Grooming Ella is my job, and I enjoy it.

I dropped into a chair and let the evening sounds of whooshing surf and late-hunting seagulls envelop me. One of Michael's hands stroked Ella. She yawned.

If Paco had been home, it would have been a normal end to the day. Except that it wasn't the end of my day, just an end to Michael's and Ella's. In about four hours, Maureen would be here to get me. If I was lucky, Michael would be asleep and never know.

I said, "No word from Paco yet?"

He shook his head, and I could tell from the grim line of his mouth that he didn't want to talk about it.

Overhead, the sky had gone from blue to a murky violet, and early stars were beginning to wink at us. I looked for a hint of rain clouds, but there weren't any. At least I wouldn't have to slog in the rain to leave Maureen's ransom money.

I stood up and brushed at cat hair and beach sand on my shorts. I said, "Well, I'm going to bed."

Michael said, "Yeah, me too. You want me to put Ella in your place when I leave tomorrow?"

He would be going back to the firehouse at eight o'clock the next morning. The fact that he'd asked the question meant he didn't expect Paco to be home when he left.

I said, "If you'd like. Or I can get her when I come home."

Ella looked back and forth at us like somebody watching a tennis match. We didn't like to leave Ella alone too long, so she stayed with me when Michael and Paco were gone. But that wasn't why Michael and I were talking about her. We were doing that to avoid talking about the big gaping hole where Paco should have been. I finally gave them both a smooch and went upstairs for a shower.

After I showered, I stood in my closet and thought about what to wear. A man wouldn't do that. If a man planned to take a bag of money to pay off kidnappers, he wouldn't give a single thought to what he should wear. He'd walk out in the same clothes he wore every day—pants and shirt, shoes, maybe a sweater or jacket. He's a man, what other choice does he have? Women, on the other hand, have a boatload of choices.

I was going to walk down a dark path where chilly sea breezes would blow at me. Bad people would be watching from somewhere in the darkness, only they would think I was Maureen. If they knew I was me, the person Maureen had run to after they'd specifically told her to keep her mouth shut, they would kill Maureen's husband. All of which meant I had to dress right or Victor might end up dead.

I decided on a pair of old black jeans that would blend with the night, and topped them with a hooded navy sweatshirt. I put on my usual white Keds. With all the dark stuff, the white Keds stuck out like Minnie Mouse paws, but they'd have to do. When I checked myself in the full-length mirror in my office-closet, the faded seams on the sweatshirt made chalky lines and my knees shined through the holes in my jeans like yellow traffic lights. Without the hooded top, I would have looked like a silly rich woman wearing falsely distressed jeans. With it, I looked like a desperate woman in truly distressed jeans ready to scrounge food from a Dumpster.

Next, I had to choose accessories. For that, I pulled out my gun drawer and got my freshly cleaned and oiled .38. I dropped five rounds in the cylinder, and slid the barrel under the waistband of my holey jeans. Force of habit made me put another five rounds in a speed loader and stash it in my pocket. Then I went downstairs and got my old department-issued four-C-cell flashlight out of the Bronco. My accessories weren't terribly chic, but I figured I might need all of them while I skulked around in the dark.

I still had a couple of hours before Maureen came, so I lay down in the hammock on my porch and drifted off to sleep. I woke with my heart pounding from the tail end of a dream in which I was a kid and my mother had left my brother and me alone at night. She'd actually done that several times while our father was on duty at the firehouse and unaware, but Michael and I had never told on her. Kids are loyal to their parents, even when their parents aren't loyal to them.

My heart was still pounding when the headlights of Maureen's SUV shot through the darkness. I jumped to my feet, and by the time she pulled to a stop I was already downstairs. I opened the passenger door and crawled in without speaking, then pulled the door shut as quietly as possible. My gun was invisible under my sweatshirt. If Maureen noted the flashlight I carried, she didn't comment.

As I'd expected, Maureen wore a pink jumpsuit that I was sure had a designer label. She looked alert and oddly excited, the way people do when they're leaving before dawn for a long cross-country trip. Her car smelled like tobacco smoke.

I said, "Turn around quietly. I don't want Michael to hear us leave."

She nodded and did an expert K-turn that took us

down the lane with a minimum of engine noise. Maureen always had been good at backing out of tight places.

We didn't speak, but sat side by side like passengers on a bus. When we hit Midnight Pass Road, Maureen turned north, driving past the new condo that had replaced the tacky apartment building where she and her mother had lived. Maureen's mother had been the meanest woman on the planet, hands down, no contest.

I said, "How's your mother?"

"She got married and moved to Georgia. I don't see much of her."

I said, "Hunh."

I tried to consider Maureen's mother from the viewpoint of the adult I was and not the teenager I'd been when I knew her. From an adult's perspective, I decided that being left to raise a daughter by herself might have had a lot to do with her sour disposition.

I said, "Ever see your dad?"

She shrugged. "Just that one time."

And with those four words, Maureen summed up the real reason I had agreed to do what I was doing. She had expected me to understand her cryptic answer, and I did. For a second we were once more two hurt kids who only admitted pain to each other.

I well remembered the moment Maureen had told me about seeing her father. We'd been hiding behind a sand dune on Turtle Beach, trying to get high on a marijuana cigarette a boy had given me during math class. She said her mother had sent her to the 7-Eleven for a loaf of bread, and her father had been there buying a carton of cigarettes. She hadn't seen him since she was about five, but she had recognized him immediately.

Telling it, she'd taken a long drag and squinted her eyes, the way we imagined real users did, and passed the roach to me—we called it a *roach* no matter how long it was.

She said, "He didn't even know me. I'm his own daughter, and he didn't know me."

I sucked on the joint and wiped at moisture in my eyes. With adolescent swagger, I said, "I hope I never see my mother again. If I saw her, I'd turn my back and walk away."

Tears had spilled down my face as I said it. I had pretended it was the weed making my eyes leak, but the truth had been that if I'd seen my mother again I would have run to her and begged her to forgive me for whatever I'd done to cause her to leave.

The other truth was that Maureen had known how I really felt, but she'd let me pretend to be tough. Nobody ever knows us as well as the friends we had before we got old enough to be good actors.

At Stickney Point, we turned east and went over the bridge to the Tamiami Trail, where we turned south. We rode silently for a while, all my nostalgic memories making me think of how crazy Maureen had been about Harry Henry, and how devastated Harry had been when Maureen married Victor Salazar.

I said, "Mo, do you ever see Harry?"

"No! Of course not! I'm faithful to my husband." Her voice was too high.

I turned my head and studied her profile. "I wasn't

implying you weren't. Harry lives here, you live here, you're bound to see him every now and then."

Stiffly, she said, "We live in two different worlds now. I probably wouldn't even know him if I saw him."

It was true that they lived in different worlds, but the key is small, and I doubted that she never caught a glimpse of him.

Maureen and Victor lived on Casey Key, which is south of Siesta Key. Like God on the ceiling of the Sistine Chapel, Casey's outstretched finger touches the south end of Siesta. Even so, to get to Casey by car you have to drive down the Tamiami Trail for a piece, then turn west and go over a bridge. Casey Key's bridge doesn't rise to let boats through like Siesta's bridge does. Instead, the whole thing swivels to the side. It's probably one of the last swiveling bridges in the world.

The bridge leads to a narrow strip of land where some of the world's most famous people have built houses that make Versailles look modest. It's a miracle the little island hasn't sunk from the sheer weight of all the brick and marble.

Maureen's house was at the far south end of the key, built artificially high on trucked-in soil that had been cleverly terraced to give the effect of steepness down to the shoreline. Three stories tall, the house was the color of raspberries. Standing proudly behind a green screen of royal palms, it had lime green shutters. The house and grounds were enclosed by an eight-foot-tall raspberry stucco wall. Lime green iron gates in the wall kept out both the uninvited and those whose color scheme clashed.

At the gate, Maureen did something magic and the gate parted like the Red Sea, its two halves silently gliding wide to allow us entry. I refused to ask her by what remote signal she'd made that happen.

The driveway curved around the side of the house to a six-car garage. One of the garage doors was open, and Maureen slid the SUV inside its lighted interior. The garage was paneled. I wasn't sure, but the paneling looked like teak. Rich people spend money on strange things.

We sat still for a moment and then looked at each other.

Maureen said, "We might as well get this over."

"Yep."

While I got out she went to the back of the SUV and hauled out a good-sized pink duffel bag. It wasn't stuffed so tightly that it didn't bend in places, but it wasn't slack, either. She slammed the SUV door and turned toward the path leading down the terraced descent to the beach. The bag was heavy enough to make her list to one side.

I gripped the bulb end of my flashlight and rested its barrel on my right shoulder, law enforcement fashion. If I needed to, I could bring the barrel down on somebody's head. With my left hand, I pulled the hood of my sweatshirt forward and followed her. Not that I was cold, I just wanted to hide from the eyes I imagined watching us.

Before we stepped into an area where we'd be fully visible from the water, Maureen stopped and looked intently into my face. I knew what she was going to say.

"Dixie, they said for me to come alone. If both of us go, they'll know I'm not alone." She seemed proud of herself for figuring that out.

I stuck out my left hand. "Just give me the damn bag."

A million dollars in twenty-dollar bills is surprisingly heavy. The bag clunked against my left leg as I went down the path. On each terraced level, my flashlight illumined a walkway that curved for a few feet to create a serpentine trek around low-growing flowering plants. I had mental images of a crew of landscapers coming in every few weeks to replace things killed by the salt air. I also had mental images of criminals in a boat somewhere out in the darkness watching me through night goggles. With my blond hair covered, I doubted they could tell that I wasn't Maureen, but I was still careful to keep my face out of the light.

The descent seemed to take forever, but it was probably less than five minutes. At the shore, a long dock stood with its feet in the water. A sliver of lemon peel moon left the sea hidden in darkness, with only occasional glints of starlight reflecting its humped sleep. The only sound was the sea's rhythmic gasps and my own breath. At the dock, three boats nosed the planks like nursing sea creatures—a forty-footer, a twenty-foot pleasure cruiser, and a runabout. At the far end of the dock, a graceful little gazebo made an incongruously delicate note.

Turning toward the gazebo, I strode past the line of boats with what I hoped was the walk of a rich woman. I kept my gaze straight ahead and tried to breathe normally. At the gazebo, I paused and tilted the flashlight to search the interior before I stepped inside. On the one occasion when I'd been there for lunch with Maureen, tall woven chairs with flaring peacock backs had been arranged around a cane table. Around the perimeter of the room, bench seats had been topped by bright colored pillows.

The floor was paler than I remembered, probably bleached by salt breeze, but the peacock chairs and table were still there. The chairs had a strangely shabby look, as if they needed attention, and the pillows that had topped the bench seats were probably stored in the benches. From what I remembered of Victor's iciness, I doubted that he and Maureen had enjoyed many romantic times in the gazebo.

I stepped inside and made a straight line to the cane table. For a second, I couldn't decide whether to leave the duffel bag in one of the chairs or on top of the table. The voice of reason in my head screamed, *It doesn't matter! Just put it down!*

I set the bag in one of the chairs and turned on my heel. I'll bet the guards at Buckingham Palace don't turn any more smartly. For some reason, it seemed important to move crisply so people watching me wouldn't know how uneasy I was.

Heading back across the dock, I told myself that all the kidnappers wanted was money, and I had given it to them. They would come get it and they would be grateful to me. Well, not grateful maybe, but they'd think kindly of me. Not of me, of course, because they thought I was Maureen. And maybe not kindly, because kidnappers probably don't have kind thoughts, but they would dismiss me from their minds, which was good. I hoped they were busy dismissing me from their minds right that moment.

I didn't exactly run, but I definitely crossed the dock in double time and then chugged back up the path as fast as possible. When I got to the top of the path, I broke into an all-out gallop.

I smelled Maureen's cigarette before I rounded the corner of the garage. She was standing in a puddle of light from a security lamp, and when I ran toward her, she tossed the cigarette down and ground it under her heel. I didn't even slow down, just ran straight to the SUV and got inside. I switched off the flashlight and held it in my lap. My hands were trembling and it felt good to grip something solid.

She crawled in the driver's seat. "Did you see anybody?"

I didn't want to talk about it. My jaws were trembling, and I had to clench my teeth to keep them from rattling.

She started the engine and backed out of the garage. "How long do you think it will be before they bring him home?"

I shrugged and tried to stop shaking.

She did that secret magic thing again that opened the gate in the wall. "You think he'll be home when I get back?"

I gave her a jerky smile. "I hope so, Mo."

Maureen was energized, shot through with excitement. I was a wreck.

I felt as if I'd just gone through a rite of passage into an exclusive world, like my first period or my first kiss with tongue. Now I was a member of a club whose members have delivered ransom money to a kidnapper. It was a creepy feeling.

I closed my eyes and leaned my head back for the rest of the drive. Maureen chattered without seeming to notice that I wasn't responding. When we rolled to a stop at my place, I opened my door and slid out.

She said, "I owe you one, Dixie."

I said, "Mo, please don't ever mention this night again. Not to me or to anybody else."

She held her thumb and forefinger together in an O. "You got it, friend!"

I clicked the car door closed and walked away. As I started up my stairs, she backed out and zoomed down the drive loud enough to wake Michael, the seagulls, and all the parakeets.

Feeling as if I were wading through deep water, I went upstairs and dropped my clothes on the floor beside my bed. The clock on my bedside table said it was twelve forty-five, slightly less than an hour since I'd left. I fell into bed as if I were drugged. As I lost consciousness, I reminded myself that even though it had been a stressful night, Maureen would get her husband back.

At least that's what I thought.

# 14

My alarm went off at its regular time, and I got up with a surprisingly clear head, as if my middle-of-the-night tryst with a million dollars had given my nervous system a boost. I was so full of energy that I ran an extra lap around the parking lot track with Billy Elliot, and I spent a few extra minutes with every cat playing spirited games of attack-the-peacock-feather or leap-at-the-flying-dish-towel.

Even pilling Ruthie went faster. Now that she knew what to expect, she seemed to look forward to being lifted from her head. I've found that to be true with most cats. I'm not sure whether it's because they associate the feeling with being kittens carried by their mothers, or if they just think they might as well get it over with. She and I did our act in about a minute flat, and then she ran to Max for praise.

Max said, "I think Ruthie knows you used to be a cop. She's intimidated by authority."

He said it in a joking way, but I suspected he missed being able to intimidate people with *his* authority.

I said, "That's an act she puts on. She's really using me to save face. This way she doesn't have to give in and swallow the pills by herself, plus she gets extra attention from her favorite human."

He looked pleased. "She does follow me around like a dog."

I wasn't surprised. Even when they live with more than one human, Foldies typically become especially bonded with one person.

I left Max and Ruthie admiring each other and sped to Big Bubba's. When I whisked away his night cover he fluttered his wings as if he had as much extra pep as I did. I opened the door to his cage so he could hop out, and he clambered from his doorway to the top of his cage and surveyed his domain like a king. Parrots are like cats in their belief in their own superiority over all other beings.

I left him there and went to the kitchen for his morning fruit. He was still atop his cage when I came back, so I gave him half a peeled banana.

I said, "Would you like fries with that?"

He gave me the one-eyed bird stare and pecked at the banana.

I scraped poop off his perches and washed his dishes. I removed the dirty paper from the bottom of his cage and put down fresh.

I said, "I'm giving you the sports section today. You like that?"

He spread his wings and sailed to the floor. I opened the sliding doors to the lanai so he could go out into the fresh air. Instead, he waddled to the table that held his TV, and pecked at a table leg.

I said, "Not talking today, huh? Well, that's okay. I have days when I don't feel like talking either."

I put fresh seed and water in his cups. I hung a fat sprig of millet from his cage roof.

I said, "How about some Cheerios with your seed this morning?"

He didn't answer, but I gave him some anyway.

He flapped his wings and hopped over the slider groove to the lanai where he stalked around the perimeter like a border guard. Wild birds in the trees immediately began loud insistent chirping, and he squawked bird-language replies that sounded like a military commander ordering his troops to shape up. Max would have been proud of him.

While he shouted to the wild birds, I got out Reba's hand vac and sucked up all the seed shells and fluffy little underfeathers that had fallen on the floor. Then I went out to the lanai and coaxed Big Bubba onto my arm. With his relatives looking on from the trees, I ran around the lanai a few times while Big Bubba raised his wings for balance and hollered with excitement. The wild birds probably thought I was Big Bubba's handmaiden, a servant who meekly provided his every need. They weren't far off.

When I was too winded to run anymore, I carried him inside and let him hop into his cage. Then I turned on his TV and tuned it to the Discovery Channel.

I said, "I've enjoyed our time together, Big Bubba. I hope you'll keep everything we've said confidential."

He cocked his head and fixed me with one eye. He said, "Did you miss me?"

I laughed. "Too late to sweet-talk me now, Big Bubba. But I'll be back this afternoon and we can discuss it."

Big Bubba was my last pet visit of the morning, but before I headed to the Village Diner for breakfast I stopped at Hetty's house. Like before, I heard her footsteps stop behind the door so she could look out the peephole before she let me in. She was smiling when she opened the door, and she invited me inside as if she really meant it. She was wearing an elastic bandage wrapped around one wrist.

Louder than necessary, she said, "I was just telling Jaz that you might stop by this morning."

Ben skittered out of the kitchen, his puppy feet so fast and awkward that he slid on the wooden floor. Jaz swung into the open doorway behind him, a giggle trailing to a stop when she saw me. She wore shorts with just-bought creases in them and one of those barely-there cotton tops that look indecent on any woman over the age of fourteen. Her skin and hair had a new glossy look, as if she'd had a recent bath and shampoo.

Still speaking as if I might have gone deaf since she last saw me, Hetty gestured me through the kitchen door. The kitchen had a faint aroma of bacon, a smell I love more than perfume. It didn't take detective skills to guess that Hetty had made breakfast for Jaz.

She said, "Doesn't Jaz look cute? We went to Wal-Mart last night, all three of us. Ben needed experience in a crowded store and Jaz was nice enough to go with us, and while we were there I saw a bunch of things that were perfect for Jaz. We had a great time."

In other words, Jaz had returned to Hetty's house after sundown, and Hetty had hauled her off to Wal-Mart and bought clothes for her. I wondered if Jaz had gone with her stepfather's permission.

Instead of asking questions, I made female noises about the new clothes. Jaz didn't exactly smile under my praise, but her face lost some of its tension.

In the kitchen, Winston sat at the table like a judge presiding at court. I scratched the top of his head and turned down Hetty's offer of coffee and cookies.

I said, "Hetty, how'd you hurt your wrist?"

She made a mock grimace and waggled it in the air. "Oh, I twisted it this morning lifting a bag of puppy food. It's not hurt bad, just a sprain. Good thing Jaz is here to help me with heavy things."

Jaz said, "And combing Ben."

Hetty looked a mite embarrassed. "And combing Ben too. My goodness, if Jaz weren't doing that, Ben would be a tangled mess."

I bit back a grin. Ben's puppy hair did need combing, but he wouldn't exactly be a tangled mess if he skipped a day. I also suspected that Hetty's injury was mostly talk, a way of making Jaz feel needed and important. Nothing wrong with that. We all need to feel important.

I said, "Good thing you're nearby, Jaz. Where did you say you live?"

The girl shrugged. "A few streets over. I don't know the name."

She was either a really good actress pretending not to know her own address, or a kid who hadn't lived in her house long enough to learn it.

Careful as walking on spilled birdseed, I said, "Is your house on stilts? So you go up tall steps to get to your front door?"

She seemed to consider whether it was safe to answer, then nodded. "How'd you know?"

"Just a guess."

Hetty looked perplexed, wondering how I'd figured out where Jaz lived.

I hadn't the faintest idea where she lived. I had described Reba Chandler's house because the boys had come to Reba's believing it was where they'd find Jaz. It therefore seemed a safe bet that she and her stepfather lived in a house that looked like Reba's.

I was doing so well with my hunches that I tried another one.

I said, "It's really nice of you to help out here, Jasmine." I pronounced it "*Jas*-min."

"Jas-*meen*," she said, then clapped her hand over her mouth.

I tried not to look as pleased as I felt. "I said it wrong, huh? Sorry."

Above her covered mouth, her eyes were wide and frightened.

Hetty said, "No matter how you say it, it's a pretty name."

The girl lowered her hand, but she looked wary. "I'm not supposed to go by that name now."

Hetty's eyes met mine for an instant, both of us keeping our faces still.

I said, "I have a friend named Maureen, but I've always called her Mo. I don't remember why I started calling her that, but Mo fits her better than Maureen. Maureen is sort of formal, don't you think? Mo is friendlier."

She said, "I don't want to be a Rosemary."

Hetty and I exchanged glances again.

I said, "You seem more like a Jasmine than a Rosemary." I was careful to pronounce the name Jas-*meen*.

Stiffly, she said, "That's because I *am* a Jasmine. That's what my mother named me."

Hetty picked up the empty teakettle and carried it to the sink to fill, and Jaz was quickly beside her.

She said, "I'll do that! You'll hurt your wrist!"

Hetty smiled sheepishly and allowed Jaz to fill the pot and carry it to the stove. Jaz looked serious and determined. She and Hetty obviously had a mutual-admiration thing going.

As Jaz settled the pot on the stove, she looked up at the purple clock on the kitchen wall and stiffened. "Oh, my gosh! I didn't know it was so late! He'll kill me if he finds me gone!"

With her face anxiously pinched, she turned and ran out the back door, letting it slam shut behind her.

Hetty said, "What—"

I didn't stick around to hear what she was going to say. Instead, I grabbed my keys and ran to the front door as fast as I could. Unlike Jaz, I pulled it closed behind me before I charged to the Bronco. I was determined to find out where Jaz lived.

# 15

Jaz was already half a block away, running on the sidewalk like a spooked colt. I started the Bronco, backed out of the driveway like Mario Andretti at the starting line, and then slowed so she wouldn't know I was there. She ran toward the bay, following the curves of the street, all spindly legs and determined rush. A couple of cars pulled around me to pass, the drivers probably wondering why I was creeping along so slowly.

The closer she got to the bay, the more I wondered where the heck she was running. There are no private homes on that particular stretch of the bay, only the posh Key Royale resort hotel. An acre of wild nature preserve separates the hotel from private homes, and as Jaz neared its edge I saw a khaki-colored Hummer idling at the curb.

Something about that mountainous Hummer sitting on the street made me uneasy, so I sped up to narrow the gap between us. When I was about twenty-five feet behind her, she ran past the Hummer's right side. As I swerved around the Hummer on the left, Jaz suddenly made a right turn and plunged into the nature preserve. I pulled to the curb in front of the Hummer, but all I caught was a glimpse of her head before she was swallowed by the greenery. Behind me, the Hummer revved its engine and roared toward the bay.

I sat for a few minutes trying to figure out where Jaz was going, but the answer was as obvious as it was unlikely. She could only be headed toward the resort hotel.

Sarasota has almost as many pricey tourist hotels as it has private homes, but the Key Royale caters to the crème de la crème. The Royale's guests crave privacy and seclusion above all else, and they're willing and able to pay top dollar for it. No paparazzi, no nosy reporters, just discreet hotel employees.

Jaz and her stepfather were not wealthy. They were not famous actors seeking a respite from continuous press coverage. They were not politicians or world leaders needing time out of the limelight. But if Jaz was trying to get home before her stepfather found her gone, that home had to be at the Key Royale. Which could only mean that her stepfather was an employee there, and they had been given living quarters.

Okay, it was beginning to come together. The stepfather wore a shoulder holster. If he was an employee at the Key Royale, he must be a security guard there. There was no mother, so he had complete responsibility for Jaz. Since the place was the epitome of exclusive, he practically kept her under house arrest to make sure she didn't spill any secrets about the famous people staying there. He was a first-class jerk, a mean tyrant with no idea how to raise a teenager, a rent-a-cop in a cheap suit, but not a gang leader.

But then why had young men who were gang members in L.A. come to Siesta Key looking for Jaz? And why had her stepfather been so edgy and nervous at Dr. Layton's office? Maybe he was a gang leader who had got a job at the Key Royale as a cover while he was in Sarasota. Maybe he didn't have a record, so his background check hadn't raised any flags when he was hired.

While I sat thinking, the Hummer passed from the other direction. It had driven to the bay and made a U-turn. It was behind me before it caught my attention, and all I could make out in the rearview mirror was the backs of three heads. They could have been the heads of the guys who had come into Reba's house looking for Jaz. Or they could have been tourists. Or frustrated reporters denied entry into the resort. Or simply innocent people who were driving around in a dumb muscle car.

I pulled away from the curb and drove to the Key Royale. At the guardhouse, I pulled to a stop and flashed my most ingratiating smile at a gruff gray-haired man. Gruff gray-haired men are always pushovers for blondes who smile at them. You just have to act like you don't know they'll be pushovers.

I said, "Hi, I'm Dixie Hemingway. I'm a pet sitter here on the key, and I got a call this morning from some former clients who asked me to come look the place over and see if I think their Shih Tzu would like the amenities here. Do you think security would let me do that?"

He frowned and tried to look fierce. "Why don't they

just call and talk to the concierge? He'll even send them pictures of the pet rooms."

I said, "They had a very bad experience one time at a hotel that promised their dog would get nothing but the best. The best turned out to be top-quality fleas, so now they won't take anybody's word unless it's somebody they know and trust."

I said it modestly, so he wouldn't think I was arrogant about being the person these fictional people knew and trusted.

I said, "I'm bonded, you know. Wait, I have an ID card I can show you."

I dug around in my handbag and handed him my laminated membership card that showed I was in good standing with a major pet-sitting association. He looked at it and handed it back to me. I don't imagine he'd ever seen one before, but he acted as if he looked at pet sitter association cards every day. Picking up a big black phone with impressive antennas shooting up a foot tall, he mashed some buttons.

As gruffly as possible, he said, "Lady here at the gate wants to look at the pet-friendly area. She has a dog that got fleas at some other hotel, and she's not taking any chances."

Squawking noises came from the phone. He nodded at it. "Yeah, I checked her ID."

More squawking noises, and he turned the phone off and put it down.

"Drive on in and park in the valet area by the front door. Go to the front desk and ask for Gary."

I gave him a megawatt smile. "Thank you *so* much!"

About twenty years fell off his face when he smiled. "You're welcome, hon. Wouldn't want that dog to go someplace where it'd get fleas again."

Governments should hire blondes to spy on other governments. We can get into places nobody else in the world can go. The only problem is that once we're in, we have to be twice as charming as we were when we talked ourselves in.

I obeyed directions and parked in the valet zone. I brushed off as much cat hair as possible and went inside the hotel. The lobby was surprisingly plain. No gilt, no crystal chandeliers, no murals on the ceiling, no pretension at all. Just clean lines and neutral sand colors.

The desk people weren't snooty either, and if they knew right away that I didn't belong in that rarefied atmosphere, they were nice enough not to show it. When I asked for Gary, a handsome man who looked as if he would be at home anywhere in the world came forward and shook my hand. I hadn't expected a handshake. Since I was there to bamboozle him, it made me feel ashamed.

I said, "Gary, it's so nice of you to let me come in. I'm Dixie Hemingway. I'm a pet sitter here on the key. Some former clients who have moved to Switzerland called me this morning and asked me to look at your hotel for them. They have a Shih Tzu who's like a child to them, and they want to make sure she'll be happy if they stay here. Her name is Sally."

I should have been alarmed at how easily I lied. I almost convinced myself that I had clients who had moved to Switzerland with their Shih Tzu named Sally.

Gary said, "Of course. We take pride in the amenities we have for our pet guests."

He snapped his fingers and a young man in a crisp white uniform stepped forward and stood at attention. He looked like a cruise ship captain.

Gary said, "Don, please take Ms. Hemingway on a tour of our pet-friendly area. And if one of the pet rooms is vacant, let her look at it."

Don said, "Yes, sir," and gave me a respectful smile. These people were all so nice, I wished I really *had* clients who had asked me to check out the hotel. I would have recommended the Key Royale in a minute.

Don said, "This way, ma'am," and strode off in a crisp and manly way. I followed him down a hall to double glass doors that slid open when they saw us coming. We stepped through onto what looked like an outside wide bricked pathway, but all the humidity had been sucked out of the air, and it was cool. Overhead, a clear arched ceiling let in filtered light, and we walked between leafy green and flowering plants. There were even little yellow butterflies flitting around, and they looked happy. For butterflies, a lifetime spent in a cool place with no predators and plenty of sweet nectar to drink is probably their idea of heaven. Sounds pretty good to me too.

Don said, "I'm taking you this way because it's the fastest path to the park area where your dog could exercise. It would have to be on a leash, but it would have plenty of room to run. We provide doggie bags, and our groundskeepers also police the area several times a day."

I said, "It's not actually my dog. I'm just a pet sitter checking out the place for some clients."

Some of the starch went out of his uniform, and he slowed to a less brisk walk.

We left the air-conditioned butterfly garden for a truly outdoor walk toward a parklike area ringed by a curved two-story building that I assumed held rooms and suites.

Don said, "This place really is great for pets. It's not just a hotel come-on."

I said, "You know, I live here on the key but I've never been to the hotel before."

He shrugged. "Most people haven't. I mean, unless you work here, you wouldn't come here."

"Pretty pricey, isn't it?"

He grinned. "Some of the rooms go for five thousand a night. Can you believe that? And a suite for a weekend will set you back twenty thousand."

"Wow. Who has that kind of money?"

"Lots of people. We're always booked."

We reached the grassy park and stopped at its edge. It looked like a very well-tended golf course. The grounds-keepers probably immediately excised any grass that turned yellow from dog pee.

Don said, "Guests who want their dogs in their rooms stay in this building, but some guests prefer their dogs to stay in their own private room. In either case, all the dogs come here to exercise. We get a lot of rabbits from the woods, so even dogs that are well trained have to be leashed. Not many dogs can resist chasing a rabbit, huh? They're not allowed on the beach, either, so if guests want to take their dogs to a beach, we give them directions to Brohard Beach in Venice."

By this time I was so taken with the place that I

couldn't wait to tell my nonexistent clients in Switzerland that a dog beach was only twelve miles away for Sally's enjoyment. But Don had just explained the source of the injured rabbit that Jaz had carried into Dr. Layton's office, which brought me back to the real reason I was there.

I said, "Gee, I'd like to work here. Do they give you guys living quarters?"

"Just the managers. They have apartments on the ground floor."

"What about the security guards?"

He shook his head. "Nah, they go home when their shift is over. There's too many of them to give them all an apartment. We've got plainclothes detectives all over the place."

"What if the managers have kids? Do they live here too?"

Some of his earlier stiffness returned. "You'd have to ask them. I don't know about their private lives."

I was impressed. He was willing to give me some insider stuff, but he drew the line at revealing personal information about other employees.

He said, "Let me show you the private rooms for dogs."

I dutifully went along with him, but all the time my eyes were searching for Jaz. The more I saw, the less I expected to find her. The place sprawled all over the bayfront, with tennis courts and swimming pools and little alfresco dining spots under the trees. The bay itself had speedboats, sailboats, fishing boats, canoes, water skis, and paddleboats for more outgoing guests. But set back from the bay were cottages and villas completely separate from the active areas, and winding all over the place were meandering brick paths that led between buildings. An occasional ground-level sign politely pointed the way to landmarks in case guests became confused by all the options.

Don took me to the special building where dogs and cats could vacation in air-conditioned splendor, with top-of-the-line beds, climbing posts, scratching posts, private TVs, music, and room service. I was positive the imaginary Shih Tzu named Sally would absolutely love one of those rooms, but I still had an eye out for Jaz.

On the way back toward the main building, a small sign announced HONEYMOON COTTAGES, with a female hand sporting a big sparkly wedding ring pointing down a shady path edged with sweet alyssum. The cottages backed up to the nature preserve and their fronts were screened from view by palms and sea grape. Through the foliage, I saw a flight of stairs going up to a narrow porch.

I said, "Ooh! Is this where the honeymoon cottages are? Oh, that would be so terrific, to come to a place like this on a honeymoon!"

I sounded so wistful, I nearly moved myself. For sure I moved Don.

He looked over his shoulder to make sure nobody was watching. "You want to look at them? From the outside, I mean, I can't take you inside."

"Ooh, yes!"

I moved forward so fast Don had to double-step to keep up. The honeymoon cottages were brilliantly situated at angles so no cottage faced another, and no window looked out at another. Each was built in old Florida beach style, tall on wooden stilts, with a flight of steps leading up to a narrow porch. Each had a private single-lane drive. Each was a miniature version of Reba's house.

I said, "Do those cottages have numbers? Like addresses?"

For the first time, Don looked uneasy. He said, "They have names, not numbers."

Of course they did. I should have known. They would be called the Flamingo or the Hibiscus. If Jaz actually lived in one of those honeymoon cottages, she wouldn't know her house number because she wouldn't have one. But what was she doing in a cottage that cost twenty thousand dollars a weekend?

Don said, "We'd better get back to the front desk. They'll be wondering why I'm taking so long."

I said, "Oh, I'm sorry! I shouldn't have asked you to show me those cottages. It's just that women dream, you know?"

He said, "Are you married?"

"I'm a widow."

He colored in embarrassment, and I hated myself. I had never used my widowhood before to get sympathy, and it made me feel cheap. But Don felt so sorry for me now that he'd quit wondering why I'd asked if the managers had children or if the honeymoon cottages had numbers. He probably thought grief had made me weird. He wasn't far off, but in that particular case I'd been more calculating than nuts.

I walked with him back to the front lobby, thanked Gary profusely for providing an escort, promised to highly recommend the Key Royale to my mythical clients in Switzerland, and got back in the Bronco. At the gate, I waved a jaunty goodbye to the guard and mouthed, *Thank you!* He waved back like we were old friends. I should have been contrite to have fooled a nice man, but I actually felt quite proud.

I was positive that Jaz and her stepfather were somehow connected to the Key Royale resort hotel, and that she had described one of the honeymoon cottages to somebody in L.A. as her home.

I still didn't understand why she would do that.

# 16

At the diner, I picked up a copy of the *Herald-Tribune* from a stack by the cashier's stand and dropped it on my table to mark my spot while I washed up. My energy boost was draining by then, and it pretty much completely evaporated when I saw Bambi Dirk standing at a sink in the ladies' room. The fact that her name was Bambi was just another example of how some people's names don't fit them. Bambi Dirk was more like a moose than a fawn, and for a second I wondered if there was some kind of karmic high school reunion going on, a cosmic force that had first drawn Maureen to me and now Bambi.

But where Maureen and I had once shared a special closeness, Bambi and I had shared a special dislike. Actually, she'd hated me like poison and the feeling had been mutual. Bambi had never gotten over the fact that her boyfriend had dumped her for me, and I'd never gotten over the fact that she'd branded Maureen the school slut. All that high school stuff should have been put behind us, but

Bambi and I eyed each other like two cats ready to hiss and pounce. She wore a toad-colored blouse and white shorts so tight in the crotch they were giving her a wedgie. She had put on weight since we'd last seen each other, and I hadn't. That gave me great pleasure.

She said, "Why Dixie, I didn't know you still lived on the key. I heard you got fired from the sheriff's department and left town."

I held my hands under a spray of water and resisted flinging some on her.

I said, "Wrong on both counts, Bambi. I wasn't fired and I'm still here."

Her eyebrows drew together to make a deep vertical groove on her forehead. In a few years, that groove would be permanent and she'd look like an elk. Couldn't happen to a more deserving woman.

She said, "But you're not a deputy anymore."

"I'm a pet sitter."

In the mirror, her face registered disdain. She ran long manicured fingers through her hair. "I guess you've heard what happened to your old skanky friend."

"I have a lot of old skanky friends, Bambi. Which one do you mean?"

"If you don't know, then you live on another planet. It's all over the news."

I jerked a paper towel from its slot, dried my hands, and wadded the towel into a ball. My hand wanted to throw it at Bambi, but instead I tossed it in the wastebasket and turned on my heel, ready to flounce out. But it's hard to turn on your heel when you wear Keds, harder still to flounce in cargo shorts. A proper flounce needs ruffles or at least a billowing full skirt. As flounce impaired as I was, though, I managed to get in the last word.

"Nice to see you're still spreading gossip, Bambi."

The door sighed closed behind me and I stomped down the hall past the men's room, the manager's office, and a public phone. At the counter where people sit if they want TV with their meals, everybody was staring up at the huge screen on the wall. I zipped past them toward the main dining area, and then stopped cold when I heard Maureen's voice. Weak-kneed, I turned to look up at her magnified image on the TV.

She looked good. She looked like what she was, a not-too-bright woman with great hair and a terrific body who had married money. A lot of money. She wore a hot pink short skirt and close-fitting jacket that had a fluff of something feathery around the edge. The camera was too close to tell what shoes she wore, but only very high heels would have given such a forward thrust to her boobs. Her glossy brown hair was made big as China by curly extensions, her trembling lips were sweetly pink, her eyelashes were thick and dark, and her big brown eyes looking into the camera were moist and pleading. Her voice was so soft it would have made a pit viper weep.

"Please, please bring my husband home to me. I've given you what you asked for. You and I know what that was. Now please keep your promise and bring my husband back."

She raised her chin then, like a woman determined to be brave no matter what.

"Victor, if you can hear me, hang on, darling. I love you very much, and I'm counting the seconds until you're home with me."

Bambi Dirk popped from the ladies' room hallway and passed behind me on her way to the front door. When she saw me watching Maureen, she gave me an evil grin.

"Told you," she said.

I didn't answer. I was fresh out of witty comebacks. Besides, what she'd said was apparently true. Maureen was all over the news. Having been all over the news myself one time, that wasn't what bothered me. What bothered me was knowing that Victor's kidnappers had said they'd kill him if Maureen told anybody he'd been taken. Instead of keeping quiet, she'd gone on national TV and blabbed it to the world.

Maureen was dumb, but she wasn't that dumb.

The close-up shot changed to a long view of Maureen's lime green gate and the palatial raspberry mansion behind it. The gate opened to allow some official-looking men to surround Maureen and help her through it. Then the gate swung shut to keep out a crowd of newspeople holding cameras and notebooks, all of them shouting questions.

As the camera followed the little group escorting Maureen to her house, an announcer's over-voice said, "That was a rerun of a press conference called this morning by the wife of Victor Salazar."

While I was thinking, *A press conference?* the announcer's voice continued.

"Mr. Salazar was allegedly kidnapped three days ago, and Mrs. Salazar received a ransom demand from his kidnappers asking for a million dollars in cash to be left at a specific location. Mrs. Salazar says that she complied with the demand, but her husband has not been returned. According to a spokesperson with the sheriff's office, Mrs. Salazar has not contacted them regarding her husband's kidnapping. The spokesperson stressed that people who believe a loved one has been kidnapped should immediately contact their local law enforcement agency for help."

The scene switched to three experts with ponderous faces and even more ponderous opinions about the proper way people should respond to a kidnapping. I doubted that any of them would recommend Maureen's way.

I went to my booth and plopped down on the seat. Judy had my coffee waiting, and I drank it in a little dark cloud. The woman I'd just watched begging for her husband's return must have been up all night getting her hair and makeup right before she called a press conference. The pink suit must have been carefully chosen too, not just to harmonize with the raspberry house, but because a woman in pink looks feminine and vulnerable but with plucky inner strength. People just eat that crap up, and Maureen knew it. I couldn't shake the feeling that Maureen had put on a big phony show for the camera.

For the first time, I wondered if Maureen really wanted her husband back. I had no idea what kind of marriage she and Victor had, but I knew that she loved being rich. If her marriage ended, she wouldn't be so rich, not even after getting the considerable amount the law would allow. But if Victor were dead, she would get it all. You don't have to be a money-grubbing bimbo to know that when money is the goal, all is definitely better than some.

Judy stopped by my side to top off my coffee. "Who're you planning to kill?"

"What?"

"You look like you're plotting to knock somebody off."

I didn't want to tell her I was pretty sure my old high school friend was scheming to get her husband knocked off. For one thing, it was too awful to talk about, and for another, if I was right about what I suspected Maureen was doing, I had played a part in her scheme.

Some truths are so solid there's no point in questioning them. Gravity, for example, or two plus two being four. Luck is another one. Everybody knows that luck surrounds some people. Luck allows a fortunate few to do stupid things and never pay the consequences.

I am not one of those people.

It didn't matter that I'd tried to get Maureen to call the cops and report Victor's kidnapping. It didn't matter that I'd helped her because I felt a debt to an old friend. It didn't matter that my intentions had all been good. The fact was that I'd done something really dumb, and I could feel the icy breath of consequences creeping up on me.

# 17

Everything was quiet when I got home, with that peculiar middle-of-the-day lassitude that mutes both surf and birdcall. Ella was in the living room on the love seat, and we spent a few minutes assuring each other that there had never been anybody else in our entire lives that we loved as much as we loved each other. She purred extra loud to try to convince me that she wouldn't drop me like a hot mouse the minute Michael came home.

I've loved Michael all my life so I understood how she felt. I carried her to the kitchen and gave her fresh water, then headed for the shower. On the way, I flipped on the CD player to let Pete Fountain's sweet clarinet perfume the air.

I usually do my best thinking while water is spraying on me, but this time my thoughts were too scattered to come up with any conclusions. I told myself I should phone Maureen because I was her oldest friend and she was in distress. I reminded myself that fifteen years had passed since we were in high school, that her phone number was unlisted, and that I didn't have it.

I told myself that I was involved in Victor's kidnapping because I'd let Maureen manipulate me into taking that damn duffel bag of money to the gazebo. I reminded myself that she hadn't mentioned me in her staged press conference, so maybe my name would never come up. I rebutted that the possibility of my name never coming up was about the same as the possibility of a summer in Florida without a hurricane.

By the time I stepped out of the shower I was close to being water dissolved but no closer to seeing anything positive about the situation. Pete Fountain was still playing on the CD, but as I reached for a towel I heard a ring on my cellphone that made me shoot out of the bathroom trailing water droplets. Only a handful of people have my cellphone number, and only three people—Michael, Paco, and Guidry—rate a special alert ring. Michael and Paco know they're on the elite list. Guidry doesn't have a clue.

I hoped Michael was calling to tell me he'd heard from Paco, but it was Guidry.

He said, "Are you at home?"

I admitted that I was.

"I'm just turning into your lane. I'll be there in two minutes."

Damp and gasping, I wriggled into a thigh-length spaghetti-strapped tank and pulled my wet hair into a knot. With Pete Fountain playing in the background, I met Guidry at the door with bare feet and a bare face. His gray eyes tried for objective and neuter, but his irises gave him away. Stand in front of a man with your nipples hard under knit, and his irises will expand like spreading inkblots. The other side of that, of course, was that my nipples had given me away first.

He said, "I wanted to talk to you about the girl."

My mind had been so stuck on Maureen that it took a moment to realize he meant Jaz. I gestured toward the love seat and dropped into the matching chair. I folded my legs under me, realized I was exposing a lot of thigh, and tugged the tank toward my knees. Ella hopped into the chair with me and settled into the corner. I was glad to have her there. She made a little warm mound behind my hip.

Guidry's eyes flicked toward the sound of Pete Fountain's clarinet.

I said, "I saw Jaz this morning at Hetty's house. She said she and her stepfather live nearby. She doesn't know the house number but I described Reba Chandler's house—you know, built on stilts with a tall stairway—and she said it looked like that."

His eyes said *I'm listening,* but his head leaned a fraction of an inch toward the music, so I wasn't sure if he was paying attention to me.

I said, "While we were talking, Jaz noticed the time and got scared. She said if her stepfather came home and found her gone, he'd kill her. I don't think she meant it literally, just, you know, the way kids talk. Anyway, she rushed out and I followed her. Drove behind her and watched where she went. She ran into the nature preserve behind the Key Royale, so I knew the only place she could be going was there, to the hotel."

Guidry's eyes had grown sharper on me, so I was pretty sure he was listening.

I said, "I talked myself into the Royale and one of the employees showed me around the place. They have honeymoon cottages that back up to the nature preserve, and he said rabbits come from there all the time. The cottages are built on tall stilts exactly like Reba's house, so I think Jaz must have described one of them to somebody, and that's why those boys came in Reba's house looking for her. She didn't have a house number to give them because those cottages are all named instead of numbered."

Guidry looked skeptical. "You think she lives in a honeymoon cottage at the Key Royale?"

"I know it doesn't make any sense, but I do. The guy who showed me around said those cottages rent for twenty thousand a weekend. Jaz's stepfather doesn't look like he could afford that, but I don't think there's any other explanation. I'm thinking he must work there as a security guard, but Don—that's the guy at the Royale who showed me around—said the hotel doesn't give living quarters to anybody except the managers. The employees I saw were all well dressed and sophisticated. Not like Jaz's stepfather."

He said, "Did you or Ms. Soames ever get a last name from the girl?"

"No, but I found out Jaz is short for Jasmine, pronounced Jas-*meen,* and she said that's what her mother named her. She resents her stepfather calling her Rosemary. When she mentioned her mother, she got teary and stopped talking. Hetty doesn't believe there's a mother in the picture, and she may be right. Hetty took her shopping last night and bought her some new clothes. She's also feeding her."

Pete Fountain began playing "Tin Roof Blues" and Guidry's eyes changed in a way that made me positive he was as aware of the music as he was of me.

I suddenly felt like a complete dolt. Maybe it hadn't been my nipples that had caused Guidry's pupils to dilate, maybe it had been Pete Fountain. Guidry was from New Orleans. His name was Jean Pierre. He spoke French. He came from a wealthy family, and he was smart as all get-out. New Orleans French Quarter jazz might turn him on more than I did.

I said, "Guidry, are you French Creole or French Cajun? What is Cajun, anyway?"

I swear to God I hadn't meant to say that. It wasn't an appropriate time or an appropriate question. Besides, I truly didn't *care* what kind of French he was. It was just that my mouth didn't know I didn't care.

Ella raised her head above my hip to look hard at me. She said, "Thrippp!" and curled up behind my back again. The music had apparently brought out her scatting tendencies. Either that, or she was embarrassed at my nosiness and didn't want to be seen with me.

Guidry's gray eyes examined my face for a moment, pretty much the way Ella had. When he answered he sounded a bit like a teacher whose patience is stretched.

"You've heard of the French and Indian War? When Canada fought France and Great Britain?"

I shook my head. I was sorry I'd asked. I didn't want a history lesson, I just wanted to know if he was Creole or Cajun.

"France and Great Britain both claimed an area in Canada that had been settled by Frenchmen. Part of the area was Acadia. Great Britain won the war and ordered all the French settlers to leave. A lot of them went to Louisiana. That's what the poem *Evangeline* is about. Since they'd come from Acadia, they called themselves *Acadian,* but the Americans in Louisiana pronounced it *Cajun.* French Creoles were already there when they came, and the Cajuns spoke a different French dialect. Still do. It's about as hard to find a pure Cajun today as it is to find a pure Creole. Lots of intermarrying, lots of different bloodlines."

"So you're Cajun?"

He grinned. "When did you get into genealogy?"

"I'm just curious."

"Okay, here's my family story. Too bad my sister isn't here, she could tell you all the details."

I assumed this time he meant a real sister, like in a family, not a nun who'd taught him to fear girls in school.

He said, "First-generation French colonists in Louisiana were just called *French.* Their children were called French *Creole* to identify them as American-born rather than immigrants. My French Creole several-times-great-grandfather met my several-times-great-grandmother at a Quadroon Ball."

I was only half listening. My mind was back on the fact that he had a sister. I wondered if he had more than one, and if he had any brothers.

He said, "You know what a quadroon is?"

"Old French money?"

He rubbed his forehead with his fingertips. "A quadroon was somebody less than a quarter black. A Quadroon Ball was where French Creole men were introduced to beautiful, well-educated young quadroon women."

I said, "Uh-huh."

I had a fuzzy mental image of a lovely young bride with skin the color of creamed coffee walking down the aisle to meet a proud French Creole groom.

As if he guessed what I was seeing in my mind, Guidry said, "The women were not introduced as potential wives, but as potential mistresses."

My neck drew back in distaste.

Guidry said, "Seems hard to believe now, but interracial marriage was illegal until the 1960s. People thought it would be the end of civilization if couples of different races married."

"But your grandfather—"

"My *great-great-great*-grandfather. According to family legend, he loved the woman he met at a Quadroon Ball at first sight, and loved her to the end of his life. They had four children, all sons. They were given his name, and he sent them to the best schools in the country."

Disillusioned, I said, "Did he also have a legal wife?"

"No, Guidry men are one-woman men."

My cheeks heated. Guidry had told me once that he'd no longer loved his wife when they divorced. I wondered if he had used up all his woman-love on her and would never love another.

He said, "Before you ask, we don't have a family legend about my mother's ancestors, but they were mostly French and Spanish."

As if he'd been deliberately providing background

music for Guidry's family story, Pete Fountain went silent on the CD player.

Guidry looked toward the silence. He sat up a little straighter and looked faintly embarrassed.

He said, "Before I climbed my family tree, we were talking about the girl named Jaz."

I said, "Guidry, there's something creepy about her and her stepfather. In the first place, why would a guy who wears polyester suits and drip-dry shirts rent something so expensive? And in the second place, those are one-bedroom honeymoon cottages, which brings up all kinds of awful possibilities if they're living there together. But Jaz is too young to live by herself, and there doesn't seem to be a mother in the picture. The whole thing is just weird."

Guidry said, "The bigger question is where the money is coming from."

"Do you still think Jaz is mixed up in a gang?"

"How old do you think she is?"

"Twelve or thirteen."

"When you were that age, were you smart enough to stay away from the guys with the coolest jackets and the hottest cars?"

I said, "When I was that age, I don't think I even knew a guy with a car."

That was true. I had been in high school before I knew a boy with his own car. He had been Maureen's boyfriend, Harry Henry, who had driven an old dented hearse with a rusty tailpipe that made sparks on the street.

Guidry said, "I'll see what I can find out about the stepfather's connection to the Key Royale. In the meantime, if you see Jaz again, tell her to stay away from those boys. Particularly right now."

"Is she in danger?"

"If you see her, try to get her to stay at Ms. Soames's."

As if he'd said what he'd come to say, he stood up. His face told me not to ask for an explanation, but I'd got the message. In the law enforcement world, something big was getting ready to happen regarding organized gangs. If Jaz was involved with a gang, she would be hurt. If Hetty and I could keep her away from gang members, she would be safe. Or as safe as a girl could be when she doesn't have caring parents.

But why tell *me* to try to make Jaz stay at Hetty's? I didn't have any influence over the girl. I didn't have any influence over Jaz or Maureen or Guidry or anybody else in the whole friggin' world. I didn't even have any influence over myself.

I stood up too. "If the stepfather's involved with a gang . . ."

I didn't finish the sentence. We both knew the futility of trying to save a child from a destructive family.

Guidry's eyes held mine for a moment. "I like that dress."

My nipples jerked up like soldiers saluting. His irises spread again. Okay, it had been my nipples all along, and not Pete Fountain.

Ella chose that moment to jump to the floor and twist around my ankles while she made scatting sounds.

Guidry looked down and grinned. "I see you've got your watchcat trained."

For two cents I would have told him I wasn't wearing underwear. Heck, I would have done it for free, but he didn't give me a chance. His hand hovered above my bare shoulder for an instant, and his head tilted to the side a little bit the way a man's does when he's ready to kiss you, but then he straightened his head and lifted his hand and went out the french doors like he'd suddenly remembered a pressing engagement on the other side of the world.

He didn't say goodbye until he was safely on the porch. Then he raised his hand and grunted, "Thanks, Dixie."

I didn't answer him because I suddenly felt like a hollow reed without wind to give me music. I lowered the shutters, shambled into the bedroom, and crawled into bed with the sheet pulled over my cold shoulders. When Ella slipped under the covers and settled behind me, I scooted backward a fraction to get closer. The next thing I knew, I was weeping hard, and I wasn't sure why.

I would like to think it was because my old friend's husband had been kidnapped, or because kids were growing up with nobody home to give them milk and cookies after school, but I don't believe that was the reason. There are times when tears just demand to be shed, and there's nothing you can do about it.

Sometimes I feel as if my heart has been held hostage for a long time by some unknown assailants—alien beings who have abducted me and transferred me to a world very similar to but not the same as the world I knew before Todd and Christy died. In that alternate universe, I go about my business, I talk and walk and eat and sleep and to all outward appearances lead a real life. But my true self is locked inside somewhere looking out, and I'm not entirely sure that other people are their true selves or empty vessels like me.

At times like those I think I should start a club for other empties. I could call it Empties Anonymous and we could have meetings and eat cookies and drink tea and not pretend to *be*. That would be a relief. To not have to pretend for the sake of others who love me that I am a person of substance. I'll bet other Empties feel the same way. We could all get together and support one another's not being.

When I was all cried out and not feeling so hollow anymore, I fell asleep and slept until almost time to leave for my afternoon rounds. With Ella on my desk, I made quick work of transferring notes to client cards, then got dressed in my usual cargo shorts and sleeveless T.

My thoughts kept going to Maureen, wondering what was happening now that she'd gone public about Victor's kidnapping. I wondered if she was cooperating with the sheriff's department. I wondered if they could be of any help to her now, or if it was too late.

I left Ella snoozing on my bed and headed for Tom Hale's condo. He and Billy Elliot were watching *Oprah,* where two couples were describing how they kept romance in their marriages by having open affairs. Oprah didn't seem to like the idea, but she was trying to be respectful. I'll bet sometimes after she talks to certain guests, Oprah goes backstage and hollers into a wadded-up towel.

Tom clicked the show off and turned his chair to watch me clip Billy Elliot's leash to his collar.

He said, "A marriage counselor on that show said romantic love lasts exactly eighteen months, no more and no less. I guess that means if people wait eighteen months to get married, they won't."

I said, "Oh, phooey, I know lots of people who've been married forever and they still have the hots for each other."

He grinned. "You oughta go on *Oprah*."

"Tom, did you see Maureen Salazar on the news?"

He was still grinning when he looked up at me, and the grin died as he registered my question.

"The oil broker's wife? Good God, Dixie, was Salazar the guy you asked me about yesterday?"

"You saw her?"

"She said her husband was kidnapped and that she'd given the kidnappers a million dollars to get him back. She got that money out of her home safe, didn't she?"

Billy Elliot whuffed to let us know he'd endured our chatter as long as possible, and I let him lead me out the door. Billy was right. My job was to run with him, not to prod Tom into speculating about why a man like Victor Salazar would keep buckets of cash in his home safe.

# 18

On the way to Big Bubba's house, I made a quick stop at the market for more fresh bananas. At the cashier's stand, a young girl at her mother's elbow was doing that maniacal thumb-dancing that kids do when they text-message. Her attention was so rapt on the minuscule screen that her mother had to poke her arm after she'd paid for her groceries and was ready to leave. The mother rolled her eyes at the rest of us so we could share in her long-suffering patience with her text-messaging kid, and several people muttered amused understanding.

As my underripe bananas moved forward on the conveyer belt, the checker said, "Kids are going to give themselves carpal thumb syndrome with those things."

A woman behind me said, "I caught my grandchildren text messaging their friends during our seder."

The checker read my total aloud and I handed her money. As I grabbed my bag of bananas, it hit me that I had never seen Jaz with one of the phones that every other kid in the world has. No BlackBerry, no iPhone, no anything, not even the old kind without a keyboard for texting.

Girls talk to one another. My generation did it by phone, now they do it via typed messages on teeny little computer screens. They tell secrets, what boys they like, what they had for lunch, what music they like, what TV shows they watch, and what they're doing right that minute. Why wasn't Jaz doing that?

I thought about that all the way to Big Bubba's house. I was convinced that Jaz had described one of the honeymoon cottages to somebody she knew, and that person had passed along the description to the thugs who'd come in Reba's house. How had she done that? It was entirely possible, of course, that Jaz had a cell phone at home and that she text-messaged like nobody's business when she was alone. I didn't think so, though. In fact, I could not imagine Jaz alone without seeing her huddled in fear.

Big Bubba was in a loud and aggressive mood. The floor around his cage glittered with seed residue, and he had painstakingly dropped every Cheerio into his water dish. His millet branch looked as if he'd held it in his beak and beat the bejesus out of it against the bars of his cage.

He hollered, "Did you miss me? Did you miss me? Did you miss me?"

He sounded as if he was fed up with being taken for granted, that he'd reached the limit of his patience, and that if he didn't get a lot more respect, the world could kiss his red tail feathers.

I turned off his TV and opened his cage door. I peeled one of his bananas while he clambered out. When he was atop the cage, I held the banana up to him so he could peck at it. He went at it like a woman hitting a newly stocked sales bin at Victoria's Secret.

I said, "You're getting bored, aren't you? Your mom will be home soon."

In actual fact, Big Bubba had spent a lot of his life waiting for Reba to come home from the college, but I knew the house felt more silent to him than usual.

I spent extra time playing with him on the lanai, and I gave him a shower. While he ran around squawking and flapping his wings to dry them, I put fresh seed in his cups. I vacuumed up all the flung-out seed hulls and hung a fresh millet branch in his cage. I threw away the soggy Cheerios and gave him fresh water. I made his world as clean and organized as possible, but I knew he wouldn't be completely happy until Reba came home. We all rely on that special someone to make us feel secure.

After I'd coaxed him back into his cage and chatted with him awhile longer, I covered his cage for the night and left him.

It had become habit now to stop at Hetty's house after I left Big Bubba, but when I got there I saw her and Ben on the sidewalk walking toward home. I parked in the driveway, got out of the Bronco, and leaned on the door and waited. Ben trotted along with the happy look of a youngster discovering the world. Hetty held his leash with enough slack to let him explore interesting rocks and plants alongside the sidewalk, but short enough to keep him focused.

When they reached me, I knelt to scratch the spot between Ben's shoulders while his tail did a delighted helicopter whirl.

Hetty said, "Come in for a cup of tea."

She went toward the front door, snapping her fingers at Ben as she went. At least I thought she was snapping her fingers at Ben, but I guess she could have been signaling me to follow.

Ben and I obediently trotted after her, and as I went in the door I noticed a dark sedan parked half a block away at the curb. It gave me a moment of paranoia because cars don't park on the street in that kind of neighborhood. I told myself I was being silly and went inside the house.

In the kitchen, Winston was asleep, stretched on his back on the windowsill with his front paws bent like a Japanese dancer. If humans slept as much as cats do, we might be as lovable as they are. Well, some of us might be.

I sat down at the table, and Ben lay at my feet. Hetty effortlessly filled a teakettle and got out cups. She had taken off the elastic bandage.

I said, "Did Jaz come back?"

She shook her head. "She seemed so scared when she left, I'm afraid she won't be back."

I said, "I followed her this morning, but she ran into the nature preserve behind the Key Royale. I think she and her stepfather are living there. If they are, I'm sure it's temporary. The only explanation I can think of is that he's a security guard."

"That would explain some things."

"It doesn't explain why those gang members know her or why they're looking for her."

Hetty shook cookies from a square plastic container onto a plate. "She said she didn't know those boys."

"Do you believe her?"

Hetty sighed and poured boiling water over tea bags in a pot. "No, I think she was lying."

"Well, then."

"Dixie, I've had kids, I've taught kids, I know kids. Jaz is a good kid."

"And her stepfather may not be working at the Key Royale. He may actually be a paying guest, and his money may come from gang involvement."

Hetty sighed again. "He did look like a gangster, didn't he?"

She poured two cups of tea and shoved one across the table to me.

She said, "It seems like such a straightforward thing to ask. With anybody else, you can just ask, 'Honey, what's your stepfather's name?' and they tell you. They don't jump up and run away because it's a secret."

I took a cookie from the plate and bit into it. It was tasty, not too sweet, a little crisp. Had a peanut butter flavor and a hint of blueberry. I looked more closely at it. It was a doggy biscuit.

I said, "Are you giving me doggy treats because I deserve them, or are you just trying to get on my good side?"

She looked at the cookies, then did a double take. "Oops, wrong container!"

"Never mind, I like it."

"It's healthy too. Organic peanut butter and blueberry."

Ben raised his head as if he might offer a biscuit review, then thought better of it.

As I walked toward my Bronco in Hetty's driveway, the dark sedan that had been parked at the curb pulled into the street and sped past. A trick of the late sun's angle cast a fierce spotlight on the driver's face. It was Jaz's stepfather. Hunched over the wheel, he gripped it with both hands like a man who'd been driven beyond his limit. The man had obviously been watching Hetty's house. The question was whether he had been hoping to catch Jaz there against his orders, or if he had been watching to learn more about Hetty. As in gathering information to pass along to burglars.

I pulled out my cell to dial Guidry. I got his voice mail, which was good, because my message was more anxious than informative.

I said, "Jaz hasn't come back to Hetty's, but I just saw her stepfather. He drives a dark sedan, but I didn't get a tag number. He was parked on Hetty's street watching her house, and then he drove away."

I went back and rang Hetty's doorbell. She opened the door looking worried. When I told her about Jaz's stepfather, she looked even more worried.

I said, "I called Lieutenant Guidry and told him, but just be extra careful. If you see or hear anything unusual, call nine-one-one."

I left Hetty's house feeling glum and depressed. It wasn't going to get any better, either. Paco was still God knew where and Michael wouldn't be home from the firehouse until the next morning. My own cupboards were as bare as Mother Hubbard's and my refrigerator was pitiful. If I ate out, I'd first have to go home and get cleaned up.

Any other woman would have been able to call a friend who didn't know a thing about Jaz or Maureen, and enjoy an evening of female talk. Any other woman would have been able to forget all about Paco being off on a dangerous undercover job while she laughed at another woman's tales of the perils of dating. Without much hope, I ran down my mental list of friends who might have dinner with me. There weren't any. Everybody I knew either had a family or a job or a lover that took up their evenings.

I was the only woman in the entire world who didn't have a list of friends she could call for an impromptu dinner. The only woman in the entire world who couldn't drop in on a good friend and eat with chopsticks from cute little take-out boxes like people on TV do. The only woman in the entire world who couldn't pick up spur-of-the-moment deli stuff to share with a close friend. Clever finger foods. Stuffed grape leaves. Delicate spring rolls. At least cheese fries.

It was flat depressing.

Thinking about the available friends I didn't have made me think about the friends I'd once had. Which was probably why I made a sudden turn south toward Turtle Beach. I wanted to talk to my old friend Harry Henry.

Okay, maybe I really wanted to find out what Harry knew about Maureen. What are old friends for if not to talk about another friend's kidnapped husband?

# 19

Turtle Beach doesn't have the floury white sand of Siesta Beach and Crescent Beach. Instead, its sand is dark and dense, the kind that turtles love to burrow into. Turtle Beach once led to a boat channel called Midnight Pass through which boats moved from the bay to the Gulf. But in a particularly boneheaded decision, the county tried to change nature's intention by moving the pass, with the result that now there's no pass at all, which pisses boaters off like you wouldn't believe.

It was near sunset when I parked the Bronco and walked out on the beach. A gray cloud cover had moved in to turn the light sepia, giving the beach and the people on it the look of an old photograph. A potbellied tourist threw bread at gulls while his companions, two women in lawn chairs they'd unfolded on the sand, looked in vain for the fabled sunset colors. The gulls squawked disdainfully at the man's bread and circled away. Disgusted, the man flapped his arms against his square hips and glared at the women as if it were their fault his crumbs had been rejected.

No doubt accustomed to taking the blame for life, they heaved themselves out of their chairs and refolded them. Slump-shouldered with disillusionment, all three trudged through the sand to their parking place, where they made a big to-do of brushing away the beach before getting in their sedan. The minute they drove away, the cloud cover parted and gulls swooped down and pecked at the bread. Clouds that had obscured the sun minutes ago now rode above the water like sky elephants with gilded backs. The sun slipped beneath the sea, leaving the sky shot with shafts of indigo and orange. Too bad those pessimists hadn't been willing to watch a cloudy sunset.

Harry wasn't among the people watching the day's spectacular end, so I walked down to the Sea Shack, an open-air seafood joint where beach bums and sunbrowned fishermen drink beer and play poker.

As far back as junior high, just hearing Harry Henry's name had been enough to send me and my girlfriends into giggling fits, and not just because he had two first names and was movie star handsome. From the time his voice changed, Harry had been a babe magnet, and some of the babes were twice his age. By the time he was sixteen, already six foot three and eminently swoonable, he was rumored to have screwed half the girls in high school. He was also said to have been the reason for a hair-pulling fight between the English teacher and the math teacher.

When he and Maureen got together, it had seemed almost inevitable to the rest of us. Maureen's reputation for being promiscuous hadn't been as well earned as Harry's, but once she realized that her body caused men to grow mush-minded when they looked at her, she'd used it. Somehow she and Harry didn't discover each other until our senior year, and after that they'd been inseparable. They were beautiful together too, with some extra quality that sets stars apart from ordinary people. All us less good-looking and less sexy classmates had expected them to stay that way, together forever, always set apart by their beauty. Somehow, the fact that they were both dumb as a box of rocks made them even more endearing to us. They were our high school's golden couple.

Then, before the ink was completely dry on our diplomas and our mortarboard tassels were still hanging from our rearview mirrors, Maureen had stunned us all by marrying a man none of us had ever heard of. Harry had taken it like a prize fighter who'd been dealt a major blow to the head. For a long time he'd wandered around in a bewildered daze, unable to comprehend that the girl he loved had actually married somebody else.

If Harry had possessed acting talent or ambition, he might have headed to Hollywood or a career as a male model. Instead, he'd stayed on Siesta Key and worked on chartered deep-sea fishing boats. He'd never married, but lived alone on an old houseboat at the Midnight Pass marina.

I found Harry at the Sea Shack. It was that peculiar quiet time when the light takes on a translucent quality and the sea seems to hold its breath waiting for the evening tide. Harry was at a back table on one of the Shack's benches. He was leaning against the sun-bleached wall, and he had a friend with him I'd never seen before—a long-haired dog with wide whiskers and a coat patterned like a tortoiseshell cat. The dog was sitting on the bench too, and it looked as if Harry was sharing from his plastic basket of fish and fries.

I stopped a waitress and asked her to bring me the house special and a beer, and went over and sat down on the bench across from Harry, swinging my legs over and under to face him. He and the dog looked at me with identical expressions of mild curiosity.

I said, "Harry, if that dog's hanging out with you, he must have pretty poor taste."

He grinned. The dog grinned. The dog wagged its tail. Harry grinned some more, and I had a feeling he was mentally wagging *his* tail.

He said, "I won him in a poker game. He's not much to look at, but he's one smart dog. I think he counts cards."

I said, "What is he, a Scottie and a Lab?"

Harry ruffled the dog's mottled fur affectionately. "Hell, Dixie, I don't know who his ancestors were. I figure he's an American dog, a little bit of every bloodline all mixed together. You don't want to get too prissy about pedigrees. That's the beginning of becoming a fossilized human being."

Harry was right. I had got so used to expensive dogs with pure bloodlines that I'd forgotten how much energy and intelligence nature invests in mongrels.

I said, "I'm sorry, dog. I hope I didn't hurt your feelings."

Harry said, "His name is Hugh Hefner. On account of he's old, but he's still chasing young bitches. I just call him Hef."

"Does he live in pajamas?"

"Naw, Hef goes nude. And don't get me wrong, Hef don't actually get personal with the females he chases, he just likes hanging out with them."

The waitress brought my beer and a plastic knife and fork wrapped in a paper napkin. The Sea Shack doesn't go in for frills. As she left, she patted Hef's head.

I took a sip of beer. "I guess you've heard about Mo's husband."

He looked out at the sunset-glinted water. "Kind of hard not to. She's on the TV every hour."

"Harry, did you ever meet him?"

"Who?"

"Mo's husband, Victor."

He grinned, and for a moment he looked young and handsome again, even with skin dried and crosshatched as an old leather boot.

"Sure, him and me hung out together all the time. We was real jet-skiers together."

I was pretty sure he meant jet-setters, but I let it pass.

"No kidding, Harry, did you?"

A flicker of pain flashed across his face. "Why do you ask me that, Dixie? I'm not good enough for Mo, remember?"

The waitress brought a red plastic basket filled with still-sizzling batter-fried strips of grouper and wide-cut french fries. Hef's ears cocked forward while I lifted out the little paper cups of tartar sauce and coleslaw and arranged them next to my beer bottle. I reached for a bottle of Tabasco at the end of the table and sprinkled hot pepper sauce on the fish. I turned the basket so the fries were on the right and the fish on the left. It's important to have your food at the right latitude before you eat it. I unwrapped my plastic fork and knife and smoothed my napkin on my lap. I forked up a bite of crisp grouper and put it in my mouth. I fanned my mouth and grabbed for the beer.

Harry grinned. "You still like stuff hot, huh?"

I gasped and drank some more beer. "Not *that* hot! Boy, that fish is right out of the fryer!"

He nodded proudly. "They do it good here."

Hef looked proud too.

I picked up a french fry with my fingers and waved it in the air to cool it.

I said, "Harry, I'm wondering if Mo is really that broken up about Victor being kidnapped. I mean, the kidnappers told her they'd kill him if she told anybody, and she's gone on TV and told it. Doesn't that seem odd to you?"

"It was my understanding," he said—and he began to squint at me with red-rimmed eyes—"that she was going to leave him."

I tossed the cooled fry to Hef, and he caught it like a pro.

"Leave him as in get a divorce?"

He nodded with the exaggerated care of somebody not wanting to give away too much. "That's what she said."

"When?"

His squint got squintier. "When did she tell me, or when was she leaving?"

"Both."

A pelican flapped to the railing by Harry's side, and he turned and studied the bird as if it might have a message for him.

"She told me that right from the beginning. She was always gonna leave him. She never said exactly when, though. One year it would be after Christmas because they were going skiing for Christmas, and for several years it was going to be after August because they always went someplace special in August. And a bunch of years it was going to be after her birthday because she always got a new diamond on her birthday."

The pelican tucked its head back on its curved neck and went to sleep. Hef looked at the bird and cocked his ears. He probably wished he could fold his neck like that. I know I do.

For a while I concentrated on the grouper and fries, with an occasional bite to Hef. Harry leaned his head against the wall and closed his eyes. Below us, the sea made slushing sounds as it began to rock itself to sleep.

I gave my last fry to Hef, drained the last of the beer, and tossed my crumpled napkin into the basket.

"Harry, did you ever feel like Mo was just stringing you along?"

His eyes opened and met mine, and for an instant the soft waning light made him look like the golden hunk he'd been in high school.

"Hell, Dixie, she's been stringing me along since the first day I met her. She holds up a razor, and I lick syrup off the edge."

I said, "And you've been seeing her ever since she married, haven't you?"

He glowered at me under sun-bleached eyebrows. "Like I said, Dixie, I'm not good enough for Mo. I haven't seen her in two or three years."

I sat for a moment looking into his eyes, knowing that he was lying, but also knowing that I had all I was going to get from him. I decided not to call him on it.

"Okay, Harry."

"Your brother okay?"

"Yeah, Michael's good."

"He's a good fisherman, that boy."

I swung my legs over the edge of the bench and stood up. "Thanks, Harry. You take care."

I leaned over the table and ruffled the top of Hef's head while Harry touched two fingers to the bill of his cap in a sardonic salute. "See you around, Dixie."

On the way out, I gave the waitress enough for Harry's dinner too. I figured I owed him that much.

The problem with sticking your nose into things that really aren't your business is that you're liable to find yourself face-to-face with a monster, and it's not somebody else's monster, it's *your* monster and you have to deal with it. I'd known Harry Henry practically my whole life, and I knew all his mannerisms. I knew how his eyes danced to the side and his lips got a little almost curve at one corner when he told a whopper. And I knew damn well that Harry had lied when he said it had been two or three years since he'd seen Maureen. I was sorry I'd gone to see him. I was sorry I'd talked to him. I was sorry I hadn't minded my own business and stayed out of it.

Nevertheless, I *had* talked to him, and he had lied to me. All the way home, I thought about what that lie meant. From everything else he'd said, I figured it was a pretty good bet that he and Maureen had been up to their beautiful necks in an affair all during Maureen's marriage. That didn't surprise me. And while my personal philosophy is that married people who don't love each other enough to be loyal should end the marriage instead of being liars and sneaks, Maureen's adultery wasn't any of my business. So why did I feel as if there was something worse than adultery going on between Maureen and Harry?

Even worse, why, if I was honest with myself, did I have a terrible hunch that a sweet, goofy guy like Harry was somehow involved in Victor's kidnapping?

# 20

I woke the next morning with Ella cuddled warm against my back. I left her in bed while I splashed my face with water and brushed my teeth. As I streaked down the hall to my closet-office for shorts and T and Keds, I saw that Ella was sitting up and yawning. Four A.M. is way too early for a cat.

She followed me to the front door, and I stopped a moment to kiss her head and tell her goodbye. I said, "Michael will be home at eight and get you."

It was probably my imagination, but her eyes seemed to light up at the sound of Michael's name. Lots of females have that reaction.

Outside, the sky was dark and dense as dryer lint. Along the shoreline, coquinas and mole crabs fed on the surf's salty broth of nutrients as gulls gobbled down the feeding mollusks. Nature is efficient. Going down the stairs, I trailed dew-moistened fingertips along the rail. In the carport, a snowy egret who was balanced on one knobby-kneed leg atop the roof of Paco's truck twisted his head full circle to watch me pass. A brown pelican on my Bronco unfolded himself, spread his wings to their full six-and-a-half-foot span, and flapped away.

I made it to Midnight Pass Road without waking the parakeets in the trees, and turned north. Tom Hale's condo is only a short hop away, so I was at his door in five minutes. Tom was still asleep, but Billy Elliot was waiting for me with a big happy grin. We had the parking lot entirely to ourselves for our run, and when I took him upstairs Billy's tail was wagging in pure happiness. I read somewhere that you can tell how satisfied a dog is by the direction its tail goes when it wags. If it circles to the right, the dog is happy. To the left, not so much. Billy's tail was definitely doing clockwise circles.

There was still no sound in Tom's apartment, but as I unsnapped Billy's leash I noticed a filmy pink scarf tossed on the sofa. It had been a long time since Tom had allowed a female guest to sleep over, and I was glad to see that he'd quit sulking over the loss of the last girlfriend. Especially since she hadn't been nearly good enough for him and Billy Elliot.

I made a circle of my thumb and forefinger and whispered, "Awright!" to Billy. He waved his tail to the right.

I had two new clients that morning, a husky male Shorthair named T-Quartz and his housemate, a snow-white Persian named Princess. T-Quartz was stolid and watchful, not ready yet to commit himself, but Princess threw caution to the winds and immediately made me her new best friend. I wondered if their names had affected their personalities. I wasn't familiar with their house yet, so I spent a bit longer with them and got to Max and Ruthie's house later than usual.

Ruthie and I were now so slick at our pill-pushing routine that it had become performance art. We could probably have sold tickets and drawn a crowd. Max beamed while we showed how smooth we were, and then he took Ruthie in his arms and told her she was absolutely the smartest cat in the entire world.

I left them basking in mutual adoration and zipped to Big Bubba's house. As I turned into his driveway, a dark sedan passed in the street behind me. The car slowed almost to a stop, and in the rearview mirror I saw the driver's head turn toward me. It was just a glimpse, but he looked like Jaz's stepfather. I put the Bronco in reverse to get a better look at him, but the car sped away.

I didn't like the idea of Jaz's stepfather seeing me in Reba's driveway. If he had something to do with gangs sent out to burglarize houses, I didn't want him to catch on that Reba was away.

Inside, Big Bubba squawked with excitement when I removed the cover from his cage. "Did you miss me? Did you miss me? Did you miss me?"

I laughed and opened his cage door. "Yes! Yes! Yes!"

He laughed too, as if he'd heard the funniest joke in the world. I left him climbing to the top of his cage and went to the kitchen for his banana and apple slices. For an extra treat, I got a couple of crackers as well. When I went back in the sunroom, he had sailed to the floor and was at the slider waiting for me to open it so he could go out on the lanai. Big Bubba was one smart bird.

As I opened the door, I said, "Your mama will be home in a few days."

He said, "Did you miss me?" He was smart, but repetitive.

While Big Bubba and his wild cousins yelled the latest avian news to one another, I put down clean carpet and fresh food and water. Then I got out the hand vac and sucked up all his seed hulls. When everything was clean and organized, I turned on Big Bubba's TV to his favorite cop show.

Except his cop show had been interrupted by a news flash. A hyperventilating newswoman was standing on a dock pointing to a boat belonging to the Sarasota Sheriff's Department. The boat was empty, but the woman wanted the world to know that it had recently been occupied by a dead body.

"The dead man is believed to be Victor Salazar," she said. She smiled while she said it, but she pulled her eyebrows close together to show that she could be as empathetic as the next person about a dead body. "Mr. Salazar was kidnapped several days ago, and his body was found early this morning by some fishermen. His widow, Maureen Salazar, is in seclusion and has not issued a statement since her husband's body was found."

Saddened and vaguely alarmed, I stood motionless as the scene shifted to a newsman back at the studio, who gave the particulars about Victor Salazar and his business. Salazar was sixty years old and a native of Venezuela, he said, and had extensive holdings in Venezuelan oil production. He didn't mention anything about oil trading, just oil ownership.

I was surprised at Victor's age. I'd thought he was a lot older because he'd seemed ancient to me when Maureen married him. But if he was only sixty, that meant he'd been forty-five when he married Maureen, and that didn't seem so old now. On the other hand, compared to Harry's thirty-three, sixty was old.

As I got Big Bubba back into his cage, my mind raced through all the ways I might get in touch with Maureen and tell her how sorry I was. Either by design or negligence, she had never given me a phone number, and I was sure it would be unlisted.

I changed the station to the Nature channel, told Big Bubba I would be back in the afternoon, and left him. He seemed subdued, as if he sensed my mood.

Back in my Bronco, I called Information and asked for Victor Salazar's phone number. As I had expected, it was unlisted. I asked for Maureen Salazar's number. It was unlisted too. Of course the numbers were unlisted, they were rich people. Harry Henry probably had a phone number for Maureen, but I felt squeamish about talking to Harry again. I might find out more than I wanted to know.

I needed breakfast, but before I went to the diner I drove half a block to Hetty Soames's house. At least she might have good news about Jaz.

She didn't.

Looking strained, Hetty said, "Dixie, something has happened to that child. She liked me and Ben. She wouldn't just disappear without saying goodbye."

I said, "I'm sorry, Hetty."

She said, "I have a really bad feeling about this. A *really* bad feeling."

I did too, but I didn't say so.

As I left Hetty's house to go pounce on breakfast, another dark sedan pulled close behind me. At first I suspected it was the same one I'd thought was driven by Jaz's stepfather, but some other cars got between us after I turned onto Midnight Pass Road and I decided I was being paranoid. Half the cars on the street are dark sedans, and one looks pretty much like all the rest.

As I entered the Village Diner, I glanced at the big-screen TV over the counter. It was turned low enough not to bother people who didn't want the latest bad news with their breakfast, but high enough so people at the counter could hear every word. I caught the name "Victor Salazar" and the word "kidnapped" but I didn't slow down.

Judy was prompt with my coffee. She said, "Did you hear about that kidnapped man? His wife paid them a million dollars and they drowned him anyway."

"I heard."

"Damn, if she'd known they were going to drown him anyway, she could have saved herself a million bucks."

Without waiting for a response, she swished away to dispense coffee to other caffeine-deprived people. I felt miserable. If Judy knew I was the person who had delivered the million dollars to Victor's kidnappers, she wouldn't see me as a friend anymore. She'd think of me as a person she didn't know very well, somebody who had weird secrets about weird things done in the middle of the night. If my role in the ransom payment ever came out, everybody I knew would look at me in a different way.

They might even look at me the same way I was looking at Harry Henry, as somebody involved in Victor's kidnapping. Just thinking that made me feel as if I were wandering in a maze. The Harry I'd always known wouldn't have had anything to do with kidnapping.

Judy brought my breakfast, seemed about to say something, decided not to, and left me alone with my dark thoughts.

One idea lay like a lion stretched on a rock in the sun, lazily swishing its tail while it waited for me to draw close enough to leap on me. I had to face the possibility that if Harry had anything to do with Victor's kidnapping, it would have been with Maureen's knowledge and consent. Harry not only had a history of letting Maureen use him, but I was positive he was currently involved with her. As in being her lover, which can make a man do all kinds of things he might not otherwise do. Harry had always been a fool when it came to Maureen. If she'd asked him for help, he would have helped her.

But if they were involved in the kidnapping, that meant they also had something to do with Victor's murder, and I couldn't believe that of either of them.

Which made me drop to the less onerous but more likely possibility that neither of them had been involved in the kidnapping, but that Maureen had leaped at the chance to get rid of Victor and keep his money. If she had wanted to leave him anyway, she might have seen his kidnapping as the best thing that ever happened to her. If he were returned, she'd be in the same spot she'd been before, a wife with a rich husband and a poor lover.

Maybe when she'd got the call from his kidnappers she had decided to do the thing that would make them kill Victor. They had told her not to report that Victor was gone, and the first thing she'd done was run to me. Then after I'd delivered the ransom money for her, she'd put on a distraught wife act and called a press conference to tell the world he'd been kidnapped. Even as she begged for Victor's release, she'd known her act might get him killed. And all the time, Harry may have known about her plan.

If all that were true, anything I did now would only help her cause. If I confessed to the investigators that I had been the person who carried the duffel bag full of money to the gazebo, it would simply corroborate that Maureen had paid the kidnappers. It would also make me look like sixteen kinds of an idiot. Which I probably was. The two people I had always believed were dumber than a sack of dirt may have played a clever trick on smart me. They both knew me as well as I knew them, and they had known how to push my loyalty buttons.

On the other hand, I didn't have a shred of proof that any of my dark suspicions were true. Once again, I was thrown back to the bottom line: Maureen had done nothing illegal when she chose to pay off Victor's kidnappers. I had done nothing illegal when I carried the money for her to the gazebo. Even Maureen's press conference to reveal that Victor had been kidnapped hadn't been illegal. Stupid, maybe, if she wanted Victor returned alive. Disloyal and unconscionable if she didn't, but not illegal.

The only truly unlawful things had been done by Victor's kidnappers—not Maureen, not Harry Henry, and not me.

Even so, the whole thing was ugly, and I wished I didn't even know about it. The fact that I not only knew about it, but was involved in it, made me so disgusted with myself that I didn't linger for another cup of coffee. I left money for Judy and went out without saying goodbye.

Like a homing pigeon, I sped south on Midnight Pass Road and made a right turn onto my lane where a discreet sign warns DEAD END, PRIVATE ROAD. I felt better just to be so close to home. I wanted to talk to Michael and try to get my life back on an even keel. Slowing so as not to freak out the parakeets in the oak trees, I began to relax as I looked out at the sun-spangled Gulf. Distant sailboats made white triangles against the blue horizon, and I could make out the white track of a water skier behind a speedboat.

Motion in the rearview mirror caught my eye, and my heart began to leap like a trapped beast when I saw still another dark sedan in the lane behind me.

Half the people in the world drive dark sedans, but they don't drive down private lanes unless they have reason to go to the house at the end of the lane. Cops drive unmarked sedans. If the car behind me was an unmarked cop's car, that could only mean that somebody from SIB was coming to notify Michael that something had happened to Paco.

# 21

It's funny how the world goes gray when you're faced with something you've always feared, as if a layer of cheesecloth settles over all the color and dulls it. I pulled into the carport next to Paco's truck and forced myself to open my door and slide out. If what I feared was true, I did not think I could bear it. Michael's car was gone, which was either good or bad. Good that he wouldn't be there to hear the news that would break his heart, bad that I would have to be the one who ultimately told him.

The sedan crawled to a stop on the shelled parking area, and the driver turned his head and looked squarely at me.

The hairs on the back of my neck rose, and I half turned to run away. It wasn't a deputy from SIB, it was Jaz's stepfather.

Throwing his door open, he lunged from the car. The gray screen that had lowered over my vision dissolved, so I saw him silhouetted against a sky blazed by a feral sun.

With bald accusation, he said, "Where's the girl?"

I took a half step backward toward the stairs to my apartment and played ignorant.

"What girl?"

He moved forward, but not just a half step. He was coming at me, and fast. "My stepdaughter! Is she here?"

There are times when I feel strong as a jungle tiger. This wasn't one of them. Pure and simple, I was afraid of the man. Afraid of his size. Afraid of the gun I knew he wore under his left arm.

Grabbing the remote from my shorts pocket to open my hurricane shutters, I turned and ran up my stairs.

As the shutters began their upward glide, he thundered to a huffing stop at the bottom step. Red faced, he yelled, "You don't know what you're involved in, lady."

I hate it when a sleazeball calls me lady. Makes me want to kick him where it would do the most good.

I looked over the railing and said, "I'm giving you two seconds to get in your car and leave."

I tried to make that sound like "otherwise I'll call down a rain of fire on your head," but I didn't really have an otherwise.

He must have known it, because he started up the stairs, moving with surprising speed for a man his size. My shutters made it to the top and clicked home, but I was trapped. He was halfway up the steps, and even if I pushed through my french doors and ran inside my apartment, he could come after me before I could lower the shutters again.

As he climbed higher, I did the only thing I could do. I ran to the top of the stairs, planted my foot in the middle of his chest, and pushed. Surprised and knocked off balance, he flailed the air while I ran to my door. He grabbed for the banister, missed it, and stumbled awkwardly to the bottom step just as Michael's car jerked to a stop downstairs.

Michael slammed out of his car, and I could tell from the expression on his face that he had seen me kick the man. That's all he needed to go into white-hot fury.

I yelled, "He's got a gun, Michael!"

Michael didn't even slow down.

The man looked up at me and then at Michael, and began making erasing motions with both hands. "Lady, you've got it all wrong."

I was afraid he'd go for his gun, but Michael reached him before he had time.

The only other time I'd ever seen Michael that mad was when I was twelve and he was fourteen, and a nasty boy at school had jerked up my T-shirt and pinched one of my newly budding nipples. Michael had come at him so hard and fast that the kid's nose was flattened and a front tooth was hanging by a bloody thread before I'd even got my shirt pulled back down.

The guy at the bottom of the stairs didn't fare any better. Michael smashed his fist into the man's gut, then hooked him with a thudding uppercut to the chin.

As much as I would have liked watching Michael beat the living snot out of him, I yelled, "Michael, stop!"

He grabbed the man's arm and twisted it behind his back so viciously that I cringed at the pain I imagined in the man's shoulder.

Michael gave me a grim smile. "Why?"

"Because Guidry is here."

It was true. Guidry's Blazer was rolling across the shell by the carport.

Without releasing the man, Michael waited for Guidry to park and get out of his car. Guidry wore the look of a man who cannot be surprised but is willing to be tested.

I skipped down some of the steps and jumped down the others, sort of a semivictorious hustle. I had somehow managed to magnetize a man who was probably the head of a gang of thieves and killers. My brother had the man in a death grip, and now Guidry could arrest him and thank me.

I said, "Guidry, this is the man I've been telling you about, the one who's Jaz's stepfather."

Guidry gave the man a curt nod. "I'm Lieutenant Guidry, Sarasota County Sheriff's Department."

To me, he said, "What's going on here?"

I said, "This man followed me home and threatened me. I kicked him down the stairs and Michael stopped him from escaping."

The man said, "That's not true. I didn't threaten her. My stepdaughter is missing and I think this woman knows where she is. I'm just trying to find my stepdaughter."

Guidry said, "Your stepdaughter would be the girl named Jaz?"

The man grimaced. "She calls herself that. It's really Rosemary."

Guidry said, "Whatever her name is, we have reason to believe she knows members of a gang wanted for murder."

The man heaved a huge sigh and wiped his face with

the hand Michael didn't have a grip on, rubbing it as if he wanted to erase his own skin.

He said, "Christ, I hate this job."

We all waited. I wondered if he was actually going to confess that he was the head of a gang that he sent out to sell drugs and rob people.

He said, "I'm a United States marshal, Lieutenant."

My mouth fell open, but Guidry merely regarded him with dispassionate eyes. He said, "Show me some ID."

Wincing a bit, the man reached into his breast pocket, drew out a slim wallet, and flipped it open to show his creds.

Guidry said, "Michael, let him go."

Michael narrowed his eyes and looked at the man for a long moment before he loosened his hold. Rotating his sore shoulder under his navy polyester, the man arched his back as if his entire spine hurt.

Michael said, "You need me here?"

Guidry shook his head and Michael walked toward his kitchen door. He was flinging his punching hand from his wrist to get the blood circulating, but otherwise he looked as if he had more important things on his mind.

Guidry said, "What's your connection to the girl?"

The marshal looked up at me as if he'd prefer not to speak in front of me, then made a what-the-hell shrug. "She was a witness to a drive-by killing in L.A. Right now she's the *only* witness."

Guidry said, "You've got her in the Witness Protection Program?"

"That's correct."

Guidry said, "I guess that explains why you're paying an exorbitant rate to keep her at the Key Royale."

"It's the safest place we could find. Guards at the gate, lots of security on the premises. Room service, maid service, unlimited movies on big-screen TV. It wasn't going to be forever, just until the trial next month."

With a surly glance at me, he said, "She stayed there until this woman and her friend interfered. After that, I believe she has been sneaking away. With all the security there, I don't know how she managed it, but I suspect she's left more than once."

Guidry said, "The manager at the Key Royale says they gave you a special off-season rate."

The man and I both stared at Guidry. I was surprised he'd got the Key Royale people to give up a detail like that, and I suppose the marshal was surprised they'd talked at all.

The man rubbed his face again. "One kid is more trouble than an entire Mafia family. Kids don't understand the danger they're in, they don't have any self-discipline, you have to watch them every minute or they'll call their old friends and give away their location."

I said, "Did Jaz call those boys who're looking for her?"

His face sagged. "I didn't know any boys were looking for her."

I said, "Three boys came in a house where I was working. One of them was named Paulie. They asked for Jaz by name."

Guidry said, "We got latents from that boy and identified him. Name was Paul Vanderson, one of the three charged with the drive-by killing in L.A."

The marshal said, "She wouldn't have called them. She's scared to death of them."

I said, "I think she gave somebody a description of the honeymoon cottage she was staying in at the Key Royale. The boys just went looking for a house that fit the description."

The man scowled. "I gave her a phone so she could call me if she needed anything, but I took it away from her because she was making calls to L.A. She claimed she only called a girl from her school, but if she told where she was, the girl could have spread it around."

I thought about going over and kicking him. I said, "What is it with you government people? Are you all dead from the neck up? You leave a girl that young alone, of course she'll call a friend! And of course the friend will talk about it! What were you thinking?"

For the first time, he looked faintly ashamed. "Look, terrorism is the focus now, and we're spread all over the place. We don't have the personnel to babysit teenagers. In the beginning, we assigned a female marshal to her, and the two of them holed up in a hotel room in Kansas. But the trial date got changed, that marshal got reassigned, and we brought her here where she'd have more freedom. I know it's not an ideal situation, but I checked on her twice a day. I brought her comic books and candy bars. I even took her to Target a couple of times for shampoo and stuff. It wasn't like she was in jail."

"Couldn't you have put her with a family someplace?"

He met my angry glare with dull eyes. "Until the murder trial is over, putting her with a family would expose them to grave danger."

I said, "What about Jaz's parents? Why aren't they with her?"

"Her mother split when she was a baby, father took off a few years later. She lived with a grandmother, but the old lady died a few months ago. She was in a foster home when she saw the shooting. Everybody on the street scattered, nobody will talk. She's the only one we've got."

His voice was gruff, but tension around his lips said he felt sadness along with his frustration and anger.

Guidry said, "How long has she been missing?"

"She wasn't at the hotel when I went to check on her last night. I checked again this morning and nothing had changed."

His eyes shifted to me, as if he still hoped I knew where Jaz was.

Guidry said, "Could she have run away?"

"Her things were all there. If she'd run away, she would have taken her personal things."

Guilt was pouring over me like hot oil. I hadn't encouraged Hetty to give Jaz sanctuary, but I hadn't discouraged it, either. With the best of intentions, Hetty and I had given Jaz an escape from boredom and loneliness, but the escape may have caused her to be killed.

I said, "I followed Jaz yesterday morning when she was on her way back to the hotel. She ran into the nature preserve behind the hotel, right at a spot where a Hummer was waiting at the curb. I think the guys from L.A. were in that Hummer. If I hadn't been on the street, they would have grabbed Jaz then. They probably went back yesterday afternoon and caught her when she was on the way back to Hetty's house."

We all fell silent, each of us knowing the worst might already have happened.

The marshal took out a card and handed it to Guidry. "We'll cooperate with any local investigation involving one of our charges, Lieutenant, but I doubt you'll find the girl alive." Bitterly, he added, "Without her, those guys will walk."

With a barely civil nod to me, he walked to his car and drove away.

I still didn't know his name and I still didn't like him. On the other hand, he had tried to keep Jaz safe. At least he got credit for that.

I said, "How did you know he was here?"

"I didn't. I came to talk to you about something else."

Even with my heart heavy because of Jaz, a little bubble like a champagne blip rose through the sorrow.

He said, "I'd like to talk to you about the murder of Victor Salazar."

I should have known. Now that Victor was dead, the investigation was no longer just a kidnapping but also a homicide. Guidry wasn't here for any personal reason. He was here strictly as a homicide detective.

The little bubble took on feet, and one of its feet was mired in quicksand. I could almost hear the sucking sound it made as it pulled its foot up and got ready to stand its ground.

I said, "You'd better come upstairs."

# 22

I went up the stairs ahead of Guidry. I felt like a bear with a thorn in its paw. Guidry could just ask me his detective questions and leave. If the only thing he was interested in was what I knew about homicides, that's all he would get.

I opened the french doors and pushed into my hot apartment. Ella was gone, which meant that Michael had come home earlier, moved her to his house, and then left again.

I said, "Sit down, I'll turn on the air conditioner."

He dropped to the love seat while I scooted into the bedroom and switched on the AC unit installed in the wall. I tossed my bag on the bed and went into the living room to face the music.

I said, "Let me save you some time. I knew all along about Victor Salazar being kidnapped. His wife is an old friend of mine, and she came right after she got the call from the kidnappers and told me. She said they'd demanded a million dollars in cash. They wanted it left in the gazebo at Maureen's boat dock. Maureen refused to let me call any law enforcement agency, and she asked me to go with her to deliver the money. I agreed to do it, and she came here and got me. After we drove to her house, she asked me to carry the money to the gazebo alone. I did what she asked, and she brought me home."

Flat voiced, Guidry said, "You carried a million dollars down to Mrs. Salazar's dock and left it for kidnappers."

I firmed my jaw and looked him in the eye. "It isn't illegal to pay off kidnappers, and that's what Maureen chose to do. She said it was what Victor had always told her to do if he got kidnapped."

Guidry said, "How well did you know Victor Salazar?"

"Barely. He and Maureen went off somewhere to get married, and I don't think I was in the same room with him more than once or twice. He wasn't what you'd call friendly."

"What do you know about his business?"

"Maureen said he was an oil broker."

"Tell me about the million dollars."

"It was in twenty-dollar bills. Maureen put it in a pink duffel bag."

"You saw the money?"

I crossed my legs, and a muscle twitched in Guidry's jaw.

I said, "The money was already in the duffel bag when Maureen came to get me."

"So you didn't actually see it."

Fine hairs on my arms stood up. "What are you getting at?"

Guidry studied me for a moment. "You trust Mrs. Salazar?"

My finger traced uneasy loops on my knee. "Maureen was a good friend in high school."

"Honest and aboveboard?"

I cleared my throat. "I wouldn't say Maureen was *dis*-honest. Not really. Not much."

He didn't answer, and when I finally looked at him, I knew he was waiting for an explanation. A personal explanation.

I said, "It was complicated. We both had alcoholic parents who'd abandoned us. Nobody else understood what that was like, so we sort of supported each other."

He let a beat go by, then said, "Mrs. Salazar told me she'd talked to you and that you'd delivered the money. I just wanted to corroborate what she said."

I took a deep breath. "On the news, they're saying that Victor drowned. Is that true?"

He shook his head. "He was already dead when somebody dumped him out of a boat."

"How?"

"Contact shot to the forehead."

"Like gangland execution style?"

"What makes you think that?"

I shrugged. "On TV crime shows, when somebody's shot in the forehead, it always means organized crime."

"You have any reason to think Victor Salazar was part of organized crime?"

"I told you, all I know about Victor Salazar is what Maureen has told me, and she says he's an oil broker. You know what an oil broker does?"

He said, "Salazar's ankles were tied to an anchor. Some snook fishermen snagged him in the Venice inlet by the riprap."

In warm water, it doesn't take long for a dead body to accumulate enough gas to float to the surface—but not a dead body bound to a heavy weight.

I said, "If he was attached to an anchor—"

Guidry compressed his lips as if he was afraid he might smile. "The rope they used was too long."

My mouth tried to find something to say, but all I could do was stare at him and imagine a dead body bobbing upright just under the water's surface, with a rope running from its ankles to an anchor on the silty bottom.

For Guidry, the fact that Victor had been anchored with a rope so long that it allowed him to float to the surface was an amusing fact in an otherwise gruesome homicide. He probably wasn't even terribly surprised, since most criminals are caught because they do stupid things that make it easy to catch them.

For me, the too-long rope was a red flag that signaled more strongly than ever that Harry Henry had been involved in Victor's kidnapping. Harry was the only person in the world dumb enough to anchor a dead body with a too-long rope.

Guidry and I didn't have much to say to each other after that. We said our goodbyes and he left, each of us mumbling something about talking later. I didn't know how Guidry felt, but I felt oddly ashamed, as if I'd blundered into an X-rated movie and hoped nobody saw me.

I would never have imagined Harry Henry capable of kidnapping or murdering anybody, but every intuitive bone in my body thrummed that he was up to his handsome cheekbones in Victor's death. Harry had been in love with Maureen since we were in high school, he was loyal as a dog, and if she had asked him to kidnap Victor, he would have done it. But would he commit murder for her?

My mind felt like a pinball machine, ricocheting between awful images of Jaz taken by young men who wanted to keep her from testifying against them in a murder trial, and the possibility that two people I'd known and liked practically all my life might have colluded to kill a man.

And then there was Michael, who was downstairs with a hand swollen from hitting a U.S. marshal. I had caused him to turn into an avenging angel, and all his vengeance had proven unnecessary. He probably felt foolish, and I needed to go down and explain everything to him.

But as I started down the stairs, Michael slammed out of his kitchen door and strode across the deck to the carport like a man on a mission. He didn't even notice me on the stairs, just got in his car and peeled out.

Everybody but me seemed to have a definite purpose.

Wearily, I went back inside, took a long shower, and crawled into bed. When I woke, I was a lot less tired but no less depressed about the state of my world. A peek over the porch railing at the cars in the carport told me that Michael had come home, so I got dressed in a hurry and went down to talk to him. It was time to tell my big brother everything that was going on.

I found him and Ella in the kitchen, Ella at her preferred

spot on a barstool, and Michael at the cooktop stirring something simmering in a huge pot.

I sniffed the air. "Is that chili?"

Even to me, my voice sounded pathetically hopeful. Michael waved his wooden spoon toward the butcher-block island.

"Get a bowl, I'll give you some." Then he did a double take at my face. "Other than kicking U.S. marshals down your stairs, what else have you been up to?"

I got one of our grandmother's red-fired chili bowls out of the cupboard and handed it to him. I poured myself a mug of coffee from the pot heating on the counter.

Michael ladled dark brown chili into the bowl, put Godzilla-sized pinches of grated cheddar cheese and chopped onions on top.

"Hold on," he said. "I've got corn sticks ready to come out of the oven."

Ella and I watched raptly while he opened the door on the wall oven and hauled out two special pans filled with steaming golden brown cornbread sticks. With synchronized flips of his wrists, he turned both pans over a dish towel spread on the countertop, and with a smart rap sent hot cornbread sticks tumbling out. He put two on a plate for me and set it on the butcher block next to my chili.

I sat down at the island bar. "I guess you've heard about Maureen's husband being kidnapped."

He did a get-on-with-it motion with his hand. It wasn't swollen, just a little red.

He said, "I know some snook fishermen found his body."

Careful not to let the inside of my lips touch it, I

crunched the tip of one of the hot cornbread sticks between my teeth. I chewed. I moaned softly. I took a bite of chili and moaned again. Venal sinners surprised to wake up in heaven would not have been more grateful.

Michael poured himself a mug of coffee and sat down across from me. Ella lowered her eyelids and gazed worshipfully at him.

"So what does Maureen's husband have to do with you?"

"You know that night she came here? That's what she came for, to tell me he'd been kidnapped. She'd got a call from the kidnappers asking for a million dollars."

"Okay."

"She wanted me to go with her to deliver it."

He raised an eyebrow. I ate several more bites of chili in case he snatched it away after I'd told him the rest of it.

I said, "She came and got me the next night and I carried a duffel bag full of money down to a gazebo at their boat dock. Then she brought me home."

He waited.

I said, "That's all. At least that's all I had to do with it. But Guidry told me that Victor had already been dead when he was thrown out of the boat. Somebody shot him. His body had been tied to an anchor, and the rope that tied him was too long. That's how he floated up high enough for fishermen to snag him."

Michael's eyes got a look that said he might laugh. "They tied him to an anchor with a long rope?"

I said, "It's not funny."

"It's a little bit funny."

I ate some more chili.

Michael said, "So what was the deal with the marshal? Who was he looking for?"

I was almost to the bottom of the chili bowl, so I ate the last of it and polished off the second breadstick before I answered him. I figured I'd need all the strength I could get.

"A couple of days ago, three teenage boys came in Reba Chandler's house while I was there with Big Bubba. The parrot, you know. I turned around and there they were. They seemed to think a girl named Jaz lived there."

"You know her?"

"She's a teenager I had seen at the vet's office, the same girl that marshal you slugged was looking for. He was with her at the vet's. He'd run over a rabbit and killed it, and she was upset about it. Cute girl. He claimed he was her stepfather, but he was lying. She's in witness protection and he's her guardian or whatever."

Michael erased the air with a flat palm. "I don't want to hear about the girl. I want to hear about the guys that came in on you."

"But they're all connected. They're all from L.A., and the boys are part of a gang there. One of them left latent prints on a jar of birdseed at Reba's house, so the fingerprint people were able to identify him. He's one of three guys who killed a boy in a drive-by shooting in L.A., and Jaz is the only witness willing to testify. That's why she's in witness protection. They hid her here to wait until the trial. Now Jaz has disappeared, and the marshal thinks the gang got her."

He went still. "Why did he think you'd know where she was?"

"He probably saw my car at Hetty's house and followed me."

Michael raised an eyebrow asking for more information. I hate it when he does that.

I said, "Hetty Soames has a new service-dog pup she's raising, and she took a shine to Jaz and offered her a job. She wrote her address for Jaz, so the marshal knew it. Jaz was secretive about where she lived—well, she was secretive about everything—so Guidry asked me to try to learn more about her. I've been stopping at Hetty's every day."

"Guidry has known about this?" Michael's voice was defensive and a trifle hurt.

"He's investigating a homicide that happened here a few days ago. A man was killed during a gang-related burglary. Some neighbors saw teenagers loitering outside the man's house earlier, and they matched the description of the boys who came into Reba's house. The sheriff's office got a positive match on prints at the murdered man's house and the prints left at Reba's house, so they knew they were the same guys."

"The gang members who killed a boy in L.A. also robbed and killed a man here?"

I could tell he was having a hard time finding slots in his brain to hold so many dismal bits of information. "Their trial in L.A. is the one Jaz is a witness in."

Michael stood up and got a cornbread stick and ate it in two bites. He does that when he's agitated. Probably a holdover from the time that feeding himself and me was the only escape he could find from our mother's self-consumed immaturity.

"Okay. And what else?"

"I'm afraid Harry Henry had something to do with Maureen's husband being kidnapped. I can't believe he'd kill him, but I think he's involved somehow."

"Harry Henry? Nah, Harry wouldn't do something like that."

"He told me Maureen had planned to get a divorce from the first day she married Victor. Then he said he hadn't seen her for two or three years, but I know he was lying about that. Besides, who else do you know who'd sink a dead body with an anchor but use a rope so long the body could float to the surface?"

Michael's eyes had gone slitty.

"What do you mean, he *told* you? Did you ask him about it?"

"Not exactly. We just talked a little bit at the Sea Shack."

Michael sat down and put his elbows on the table. He lowered his head between his hands and squeezed it for a long time while Ella widened her eyes and looked alarmed. When he raised his head, his eyes were considerably less cheery than they'd been when I first came in.

"Anything else?"

"No, that's it. Harry asked about you, by the way. Said you were a good fisherman."

"Hell, Dixie."

"I'm not involved in anything, Michael. It's just that I know all these people."

Michael sighed. "Let me get this straight. You've delivered ransom money to kidnappers. You've talked to a man who might have killed Maureen's husband. And you've spent time with a girl who's on the run from a murdering gang from L.A."

"It's not as bad as you make it sound."

"Stay away from Harry Henry."

"Aw, Harry's all right, he's just weird. He has a new dog, named him Hugh Hefner."

"Figures. Hugh Hefner's probably Harry's hero."

I got up and rinsed my bowl and cup and put them in the dishwasher. I went around the bar and kissed Ella's nose. Then I kissed Michael's cheek.

"Thanks for the chili. Don't worry about me. I'm cool."

When I closed the kitchen door, I could see them through the window. Michael was letting Ella lick crumbs from his fingertips. Ella looked blissful. Michael looked worried. On top of his concern about Paco, I had just given him another load to carry.

As for me, I didn't feel half as cool as I'd pretended. Laying it all out for Michael had made me feel like I was in the middle of a hurricane's eye. It was calm there for the time being, but hurricanes move on. When they do, you get slammed by winds from an entirely different direction than the one you've been facing.

I still had some time before I had to make afternoon rounds so I ran upstairs and got my car keys. I needed to talk to Cora Mathers.

# 23

Cora Mathers is an eighty-something-year-old friend whose granddaughter was once a client of mine. The granddaughter was murdered in a most brutal way, and I had been immensely impressed by Cora's strength when it happened. Afterward, she and I had sort of adopted each other.

Cora lives on the mainland in a lovely condo in Bayfront Village, a posh retirement tower on Tamiami Trail overlooking the bay. Her granddaughter bought the condo for her with money made in ways Cora has never suspected. As far as Cora knows, her granddaughter was a smart woman who made wise investments, and because she had a good heart she provided well for her cat and for her grandmother. The good heart part is true.

Driving north on the way to Bayfront Village, I swung off the Trail for a few blocks to Whole Foods. Leaving the Bronco in the parking garage, I hotfooted it inside and bought a dozen pink roses and a carton of frozen soup. As I loped back to the garage, a motorcycle arced around me and pulled into a parking spot. The driver's head was covered by a black helmet and he wore so much denim that I couldn't see his body, but I kept a hawk eye on his hands in case he flashed Paco's signal. He pulled off his helmet and turned his head to look at me. He had a broad freckled face, little piggy eyes, and a scowl that looked as if it had been there forever. He definitely wasn't Paco.

I pretended I hadn't been staring at him and got in the Bronco and raced off. When I pulled under Bayfront's portico, the parking attendant sprinted smartly to open the Bronco's door before I had time to get out. Rich people get service like that.

When he saw it was me, he lost the servile look but kept the grin.

He said, "You here to see Miz Mathers? Nice roses."

I slid out of the Bronco and looped the bag with the soup over my arm.

I said, "They're organic."

"You gonna eat them?"

"No, but I guess if somebody gets stuck by a thorn, it won't be a poisonous thorn."

"Ha! Next thing you know, they'll be selling organic fertilizer."

I sort of thought they already were, but I just smiled and left him to disappear my car into the bowels of the Bayfront's parking garage. I like that about ritzy places. They make you feel like royalty.

The front doors sighed open as I approached, and the concierge waved to me from her French Provincial desk. The lobby was busy with enthusiastic seniors making plans for music lessons and bridge parties and opera trips and gourmet dinners. For sure their lives were a lot more socially active than mine. Maybe you have to be old to have the time for quality fun. Gives me something else to look forward to.

As I moved toward the bank of elevators, the concierge picked up her phone to warn Cora that I was coming. She used to make me wait until Cora had given permission for me to come up, but now she knows Cora always wants to see me. I like that. It's good to know somebody always welcomes your presence.

Cora lives on the sixth floor, and when I got off the elevator she was already out in the hall, excited as a child to have company. When she was young, Cora probably stretched herself to an inch or two over five feet, but now that age has condensed her, she'd have to stand on tiptoe to reach five feet. She has wispy white hair like a baby chick and a skinny frame that moves on slow freckled legs. To make up for her slow feet, her brain moves at warp speed. When she looks at me with her pale blue eyes, I feel like I'm being examined by an eagle.

She said, "Why didn't you tell me you were coming? I'd of made some fresh chocolate bread. All I've got is leftover."

I said, "It's still good left over."

She said, "Oh my, what beautiful flowers. What else have you got there?"

"Some of that shrimp and corn chowder you like. The roses are organic, so you can stick your nose in them and not get poisoned. I guess the soup is too."

She laughed and began ministepping into her apartment so slowly that I had to march in place to keep from barreling into her. Cora's apartment is pale pink and soft turquoise everywhere you look, from the marble floors to the skirt on the round table between the galley kitchen and the living room. Glass doors open to a sun porch overlooking the bay, so she has an ever-changing view of water and clouds and sailboats.

An odor of chocolate always hangs in the air from the decadent chocolate bread Cora makes in an old bread-making machine—another gift from her granddaughter. She won't divulge the recipe, but at some point in the process she throws in bittersweet chocolate chips that never completely melt but make soft oozy blobs in the bread. She serves it in torn chunks, and when it's hot and slathered with butter Cora's chocolate bread would make hardened criminals break down and confess just to get a taste.

Her kitchen wasn't big enough for both of us, so she sat at her table and watched me work behind the open kitchen bar. She said, "Leave the soup out to thaw. I'll have it for supper."

While water heated in her teakettle, I put the roses in a clear glass pitcher and set them on the bar. I got a tray for our tea things and found half a loaf of chocolate bread.

Cora said, "Don't put it in the microwave, it'll get tough. Just tear off some hunks."

"I know."

She watched me get butter from the refrigerator, tea-cups from the cupboard, and pour hot water over tea bags in a pot. I brought the tray to the table and sat down across from her. She waited until I'd poured our tea and distributed our hunks of chocolate bread.

She said, "What's wrong?"

Cora is like Michael. One look at me and they both know what I'm feeling.

I took a sip of tea and tried to think which thing to tell. Like which disaster had precedence.

I said, "I met a teenaged girl a few days ago. Her name is Jasmine, but she's called Jaz. She's a cute girl, smart, likes pets. She's from L.A., and she saw some gang members shoot a boy. A whole street full of people saw it, but she's the only one willing to testify because everybody else is scared of the gang. The government has put her in witness protection to keep her safe until the trial. They moved her here and stuck her in a little apartment at a resort hotel on Siesta Key. She had an officer assigned to her, and he checked on her a couple of times a day, but she was lonely and called some old friends in L.A. Word got out where she was, and the gang came here looking for her. She's disappeared now, and the marshal who's been keeping an eye on her thinks they've killed her."

Sadness clouded Cora's eyes. "Does her family know?"

"There isn't a family. Her parents abandoned her when she was little, and her grandmother raised her. The grandmother died a few months ago and Jaz was put in a foster home. Poor kid never had much of a chance."

"That's not true. She had a grandmother. She must have done a good job too, to raise a girl so brave and honest."

I blinked at Cora. Until that moment, I hadn't seen Jaz as anything except a girl in trouble. But Cora was right. Jaz was incredibly brave to be willing to testify against a gang. None of the other witnesses had her courage. None of them had her honesty.

I tore off a bite of chocolate bread from my chunk and popped it in my mouth. It was almost as good as when it was piping hot.

I said, "I wish she hadn't been so honest about telling people where she was."

Cora said, "I blame the hospitals."

I tore off another bite and wondered if Cora's mind was going soft.

She said, "Used to be when babies were born, the hospital put them all in one room with a glass wall so people could look at them. They'd be all lined up in their little plastic bins, pink blankets around the girls and blue around the boys. Sometimes they put little stocking caps on their heads to match. They had strict viewing times, you couldn't just go see them any old time, so it was a special thing to get to look at them. Sometimes when things were so hard for me and I didn't know if I was going to make it, I'd go to the hospital and look at those babies. They were so new they still had God's fingerprints on them, and looking at them would make me remember that we all come perfect."

I said, "Those guys who killed a boy just for fun may have been perfect when they were born, but they're bad now."

Cora said, "That's because people don't ever get to see a whole roomful of new babies anymore, so they don't understand that no baby is born bad. People turn their backs on babies, let them go hungry and sick, and then when the babies grow up to be killers and thieves, they say, 'See there? I told you they were bad.' "

She raised her teacup and fixed me with her piercing old eyes. "That girl you're talking about could have turned out bad just like those boys, but she had a grandmother who loved her. That's why she's honest and brave. That's why my granddaughter was honest and brave too, because that's how I raised her."

I knew for a fact that Cora's granddaughter had *not* been honest. But it was true she'd been brave, and that was probably because Cora had raised her.

I said, "My grandmother raised me too."

"See? Grandmothers do it best."

I opened my mouth to say that Jaz could get killed no matter how honest and brave she was, then remembered what had happened to Cora's granddaughter and closed it. Cora was right about Jaz. None of the other witnesses had been honest enough to speak up.

The other side of complete honesty, of course, is that it's a mark of immaturity. If you're hiding from bad people who want to kill you, and the bad people ask bystanders where you are, you hope the bystanders will be mature enough to lie. If they're small children or immature adults, they'll point to your hiding place.

Jaz had the courage to agree to give honest testimony in court about the murder she'd seen. But immaturity had made her tell the truth to somebody about where she was, and now she had been found and possibly killed.

As if she were testing my own level of maturity, Cora said, "What's going on with you and that nice detective you're in love with?"

I swallowed a sip of tea wrong and for a moment sounded like a drowning person. "I'm not in love with him!"

She gave me one of those serene smiles unique to wise old women, the kind that makes their eyes almost disappear into fine wrinkles but still allows the flare in their eyes to pin you down like a laser beam.

She said, "I don't know why you keep saying that. It's plain as day you're in love with him."

My heart had started thumping like I'd been caught at something illicit. I said, "I don't *want* to be in love with him. I don't want to be in love with any man."

"None of us do, hon, but it usually don't make any difference what we want. We fall in love anyway."

I always forget that Cora was once a young woman. But of course she was, and of course there had been men in her life.

She smoothed butter on a bit of chocolate bread, then used the bread like a lecturer holding a pointer. "Just make sure you're not thinking you're in love when it's really pity you feel. Women do that all the time. Loving is the easiest thing in the world for a woman. A woman could go out and flag down ten men on the highway and there'd be two or three in the bunch she could love. Soon as a woman gets to know a man, finds out how he had a bad time in school, or had an old man that was mean to him, she falls in love. Especially if he's good-looking and smiles at her and talks halfway smart. But half the time it's not love, it's pity. Women always want to make up to a man for all the bad things the world has done to him, and they think that's love. Next thing you know they're marrying him, and that's like bringing home a dog that foams at the mouth just because you feel sorry for it. I don't care how much you think you can fix him, the wrong man will turn on you quick as a mad dog."

I said, "I don't feel sorry for Guidry."

"Well, that's good. But you've got to be sure that other stuff is right too. You know, the part in bed. People don't like to talk about it, but women need a lot more lovemaking than men do. Men talk about it more, but women want to do it more. And if you're with a man that don't like to do it much, or isn't any good at doing it, you'll get fat and cranky. Don't get mixed up with a cold man."

Oddly, I felt myself blushing. Not that talk about sex embarrassed me, but it made me remember what sex had been like with Todd. He had showed me a survey one time in which people who'd been happily married twenty, thirty, sixty years had sheepishly admitted to fantastic sex. They felt a bit freakish about it because they knew the lust part of love was supposed to die and be replaced with warm companionship, but their mutual lusts had never died. Todd had said, "I guess that means we'll still be chasing each other around when we're a hundred."

I thought about Judy saying that if I ever went to bed with Guidry, I'd probably kill him. But what if I was a firecracker ready to explode and Guidry turned out to have no sizzle?

Cora was watching me with an expectant look, so I must have been lost in thought longer than I realized.

I said, "If I ever fall in love again, I want it to bloom slowly, not explode like Fourth of July fireworks." I liked the sound of that. I thought it sounded wise and mature.

Cora didn't look impressed. "If love wants to bloom slowly, that's what it'll do. If it wants to bust out like firecrackers, it'll do that too. Why don't you just let it take care of itself?"

Why did everybody persist in telling me to quit trying to control everything? Good grief, you'd think I was some kind of control freak. I wished I could control them so they'd quit saying I controlled.

I couldn't think of any honest response, so I told her it was time to make my afternoon rounds. Before I left, I gathered up our tea things and tidied up the kitchen. I left the carton of soup sweating in the middle of the countertop so Cora wouldn't forget it, then kissed the top of her feathery head.

She said, "You're a good girl, Dixie, and I'm going to pray that missing girl's all right."

# 24

Before I left the Bayfront campus, my cellphone rang with the special ring reserved for Michael, Paco, or Guidry. With my heart rate up, I pulled to a stop and answered. It was Guidry.

He said, "Where are you?"

I pulled the phone away from my ear and glared at it. "Why do you want to know?"

"Sorry. What I meant to say was that I would appreciate knowing where you are . . . because I would like a moment of your time . . . if you would be so kind as to give it to me."

"I'm just leaving Bayfront Village, and I'm headed to the Sea Breeze condos on Midnight Pass to run with Billy Elliot."

"With who?"

"Whom. Billy Elliot. He's a Greyhound. We run in the parking lot."

"I'd like you to listen to something. It'll just take a minute. I'll meet you in the Sea Breeze lot."

At least he was being polite.

Even with lighter out-of-season traffic, it took me fifteen minutes to thread my way from Bayfront to Siesta Drive and the north bridge to the key, then to Midnight Pass Road and Tom's condo building. Guidry's Blazer was parked by the front door in a guest spot. When I parked beside him, he got out of his car and got into mine.

Guidry had developed new lines around his mouth in the last few days. Even in his fine linen jacket and perfectly cut slacks, he looked tired and drawn. I had to clench my hand into a fist because it wanted to reach over and trace the lines around his lips.

Reaching in a jacket pocket, he pulled out a small tape player and set it on the dash.

He said, "Mrs. Salazar kept the message she got from the kidnappers. I'd appreciate it if you'd listen to the call."

It was a reasonable request. I had known Maureen a long time, and Maureen had asked me to deliver her ransom money. It made sense that Guidry would think I might recognize the kidnapper's voice. I didn't think it was likely, but it was worth a shot.

Guidry hit the Play button, and a muffled man's voice said a word I didn't understand, followed by, "Salazar, we have your husband."

The voice went on to say all the things Maureen had told me the kidnapper said, but I wasn't listening.

Guidry said, "Anything about that voice you recognize?"

I felt icy cold. I said, "Play the beginning again."

He rewound the tape and started it again. Again the muffled voice, again the odd first word that sounded like "momissus." Was he saying, "*No,* Mrs. Salazar . . ." or perhaps trying for rapster chic with "*Yo,* Mrs. Salazar . . ."?

I raised my hand to stop the sound. "Play it again. Just the beginning."

It only took a few minutes to rewind and replay that opening, but it seemed like a lifetime. When I'd heard it again, I motioned Guidry to turn it off.

Guidry's gray eyes were steady on me.

For a moment I couldn't speak, but I had been raised by a grandmother who taught me to tell the truth.

I said, "There at the beginning, where it sounds like he's stuttering before he says 'Mrs. Salazar'?"

"Yeah?"

"He's not stuttering. He first says, 'Mo,' and then he corrects himself and says, 'Mrs. Salazar.' Only Maureen's close friends call her Mo."

"You know who it is." It wasn't a question.

I said, "He would not have killed Victor."

"Then he doesn't have anything to worry about."

I took a deep breath. "His name is Harry Henry. He's been in love with Maureen since we were in high school. Harry's sort of a beach bum, gets by working on fishing boats, but he's a good man. I don't believe he'd kidnap anybody, and I'm sure he wouldn't kill anybody. But I'm pretty sure that's Harry's voice on the recorder."

I didn't add that Harry was the only person I knew dumb enough to anchor a dead man with a rope so long the body could float to the surface.

Guidry slipped the player back in his pocket. "Once again, you've corroborated what Mrs. Salazar said."

"Maureen told you that was Harry's voice?"

"Why does that surprise you?"

About a million answers occurred to me, like, "because they've been lovers for over fifteen years and you'd think she'd be more loyal," or "because she didn't mention to me that it was Harry who'd called," or "because something is very fishy about this whole thing."

I said, "I guess you just never really know other people. Not even when you practically grew up with them."

"Mrs. Salazar said Mr. Henry lives on a houseboat docked at the Midnight Pass marina."

That was apparently another thing he wanted me to corroborate.

"I've never been on his boat, and I've never seen it, but I've heard that's where he lives."

"Okay. Thanks, Dixie."

He reached for the door handle, but I stopped him. "Guidry?"

"What?"

"Do you ever wish you hadn't come here? Do you miss New Orleans?"

For a second I thought he was going to open the door without answering, but then his face softened.

"I never wish I hadn't come here. But I do miss the New Orleans I grew up in, the way it was before the levees broke."

"Katrina."

He shook his head. "That name has become a catchword for disaster, but it wasn't Katrina that ruined the city, it was human negligence. The hurricane had already passed when the levees broke."

As if he regretted the bitterness in his voice, he firmed his lips and took a deep breath.

He said, "For tourists, New Orleans was great food, Preservation Hall, Mardi Gras craziness. But for people who lived there, New Orleans was the nutty old priest always haranguing people in Jackson Square, the transvestites strutting down Bourbon Street in their mesh hose and feathers, up-and-coming young musicians in the park, ordinary people starting their day with beignets at Café du Monde, all of them giving one another room, looking one another in the eye because they all *belonged.* And if a funeral parade came down the street, anybody who wanted to could join in, dance a little bit, clown around some, because we all knew life can't be taken too seriously or it'll kill you."

It was the longest speech I'd ever heard Guidry make, and when he finished he blushed a little bit under his tan as if he were embarrassed to have let me see how passionate he was about his hometown.

And right then and there, I finished falling in love with him. Just leaned over the edge of love's chasm and tumbled straight down. It didn't have anything to do with the fact that he looked like an Italian count with a vineyard in his backyard. It didn't have anything to do with the fact that he was cultured and intelligent, or that I'd seen him in action enough to know that his integrity was impeccable. It didn't even have anything to do with the fact that he was one heck of a kisser—oh, yes, he was. It had to do with that hidden passion he'd just exposed.

Lots of men are good-looking and smart and cultured. Well, not lots, but some. And a few have unquestionable integrity. Okay, they're mostly in the movies or in books, but some of them are for real. Guidry had all those qualities, plus passion for a city where people respected one another.

How could I not love him?

It scared me to death.

I said, "Guidry, do you think those guys killed Jaz?"

A spasm moved across his face like a shadow. "I don't know, Dixie. I hope to hell not."

His hand moved across the gap between our seats and his fingertips tapped my thigh. It was just a momentary touch, but all my nerve endings sizzled.

He pushed the car door open and left me feeling desolate.

# 25

I went into the Sea Breeze condos like somebody walking underwater. Even riding up in the mirrored elevator seemed an effort. When I looked at my reflections, I saw an endless procession of sad-eyed blond women in wrinkled cargo shorts and loose white T-shirts. None of those women knew where Paco was or if he was safe. They didn't know where Jaz was or if she was alive. And none of them could believe that Harry Henry had kidnapped and murdered Maureen's husband. But all the evidence said he had.

At Tom's apartment, Billy Elliot was whuffing eagerly at the door when I unlocked it and went in. The filmy pink scarf was gone from the sofa, and Tom was at the kitchen table working on some papers. As I knelt to clip Billy Elliot's leash on his collar, Tom wheeled into the living room.

He said, "I saw the news about Victor Salazar drowning."

He wasn't exactly asking a question, just leaving the

door open for any inside information I might want to provide. I didn't provide any. If the sheriff's department hadn't yet stated that Victor had been dead when he was dumped from a boat, it was because they didn't want it noised about. Besides, I had too many secrets buzzing in my head. If I let one of them slip out, the rest might fly out too. People always think they want to know other people's secrets, but secrets are like bee stings—too many at one time can be fatal.

I said, "Yeah, I saw it too."

"Have you talked to your friend?"

I shook my head. "She has an unlisted number and I don't have it."

I hustled Billy Elliot out the door before Tom could ask me anything else.

When I brought Billy back after our run, Tom was still working at the kitchen table. I hung up Billy Elliot's leash and smooched the top of his head.

I yelled, "Bye, Tom," and beat it. I definitely did not want Tom to ask me any questions about Maureen.

As I went toward the elevator I was sorry I hadn't had a chance to ask Tom about his new girlfriend. That's the trouble with keeping secrets to yourself. You do that, and you can't ask other people about theirs.

For the rest of the afternoon, my mind played with the question of what the heck Maureen was up to. She had been very convincing the night she'd come to beg me for help. She'd seemed truly distraught about the phone call she'd got telling her Victor had been kidnapped. I had believed every word, but now I was suspicious of everything she'd said.

She had told me she'd replayed the kidnapper's message so many times she knew it by heart, and yet she hadn't told me it was Harry Henry's voice. While it was possible she hadn't recognized the voice until later, that seemed a slim possibility. And when I'd asked her if she ever saw Harry, she'd immediately gone on the defensive and denied she did. Protested too much that she was a faithful wife.

From what Harry had said, Maureen had talked for years about leaving her husband for Harry, then always changed her mind. Harry had denied seeing Maureen for the last few years, but I hadn't believed him. Now I was even more convinced that he'd lied.

While I cleaned litter boxes, I wondered if Maureen had told Harry one time too many that she was going to leave Victor and then changed her mind. Would that have made Harry kidnap Victor? Kill him?

While I played roll-the-ball with cats, I wondered if Maureen and Harry had actually parted for a few years. If they had, maybe yearning for Maureen had caused Harry to go bonkers and kidnap Victor so he could have her.

While I washed water and food bowls, I wondered if the ransom call Harry had made to Maureen had been for real. Knowing Harry, he might have felt obliged to make the call because he knew from movies that a ransom call was what kidnappers did.

Driving from one cat's house to the next, I wondered what had happened to that duffel bag full of money I'd left in the gazebo. Had Harry come and got it? If so, where was it now?

Victor hadn't just been kidnapped, he'd been shot in the forehead. I doubted that Harry Henry had ever handled a gun, much less shot anybody. Furthermore, no matter how Guidry might downplay the mob execution angle, ordinary law-abiding people don't get shot in the head and then dumped out of a boat with their feet tied to an anchor. I kept remembering Tom's suspicious face when I'd said that Maureen had a home safe with over a million dollars in cash in it. According to Maureen, Victor had been an oil broker. But why would an oil broker keep that much cash in his house?

By the time I got to Big Bubba's house, I was worn out with thinking. To spare my arm the effort of moving it up and down while Big Bubba rode it and flapped his wings, I put him on his exercise wheel. He immediately jumped off. I didn't blame him. To a bird, exercise wheels are probably like treadmills are to humans, and riding a human's arm is probably like riding a mechanical bucking bull at a cowboy bar. Anybody would choose the bull.

Thirty minutes later, having done bird calisthenics with Big Bubba, I gave him fresh fruit and hung a new spray of millet in his cage. I draped the nighttime cover on his cage and left him muttering jokes to himself.

I weighed about two tons when I trudged up Hetty's walk. When she opened her front door, she looked as dispirited as I was. Ben was at her feet, the only one of us full of energy.

I said, "Hetty, I have to tell you something about Jaz."

She stepped aside to let me through the door. "Come in the kitchen, we can have tea while we talk."

Winston was asleep in a puddle of late sunshine

through the kitchen window. He didn't even open an eye when I came in.

While she made a pot of tea and put out a plate of cookies, Hetty talked nonstop about the weather and Ben and the mint growing on her windowsill. I knew she was talking to avoid hearing what I'd come to tell her.

When she'd run out of irrelevant words, she sat down at the table with me. "Okay, tell me. I know something has happened to Jaz."

I said, "She's missing, Hetty. I mean *officially* missing. You know the man who said he was her stepfather? Well, he lied. He's a U.S. marshal assigned to watch over her. She's in the government's Witness Protection Program because she's their only witness to a gang killing in Los Angeles. She was brought here to keep her safe until the trial. Those young thugs who came in Reba's house were looking for Jaz to shut her up."

Hetty listened intently, as if she were getting directions to a place she had urgent reason to visit.

Hoarsely, she whispered, "Dixie, have those boys killed Jaz?"

"Nobody knows. The marshal said she'd left all her personal things behind, so he doesn't think she went willingly."

Tears welled in Hetty's eyes. "Those new clothes we got at Wal-Mart—they were just cheap little shorts and tops, but she was excited as a kid at Christmas. I don't think she's had many things given to her."

"The marshal said her parents had abandoned her when she was very young, and her grandmother raised her. The grandmother died a few months ago and she's been in foster care."

Hetty looked at Ben, also in foster care, who was lying on her feet.

"How did you get the marshal to tell you all this? Isn't the Witness Protection Program supposed to be a secret?"

My face grew warm. "My brother beat him up, and then Guidry came and was going to arrest him. So he showed Guidry his credentials and explained it all."

"Your brother beat him up?"

My face got hotter. "I thought the marshal was going to attack me, so I kicked him down the stairs that go up to my garage apartment. My brother drove in just as I kicked him, and he thought I needed protecting. My brother's a little bit, um, physical when he gets mad."

Hetty hid a smile behind her hand. "I think that's nice. Brothers should protect their sisters."

"I guess the marshal could have been nasty about it, pressed charges or something, but he let it go."

Hetty's face grew sad again. "So Jaz is missing, and nobody knows where she is."

"I'm afraid so."

There wasn't anything else to say, and I needed to go home and sleep for a few million years.

As she walked me to the front door, Hetty said, "She's a good girl, Dixie. She deserves a lot better."

I thought of what Cora had said. "I guess they all deserve a lot better, Hetty."

At the door, she said, "If you hear anything, will you let me know?"

"Of course."

I was on the walk when Hetty called after me. "Dixie, if they find Jaz, does that mean she'll have to go back to California?"

At first I thought she meant if they found Jaz's body. But when I turned to look at her I realized she was referring to a living Jaz.

"I don't know, Hetty."

"I was just thinking, if they'd let her stay here in Florida, and if she wanted to, you know, I'd be pleased to have her live with me."

My eyes burned, and I had to make several tries before I could speak. "I'll tell them that."

As I drove away, I muttered, "Tell *who*? The government? The gang? Nobody *cares* where she lives."

That wasn't true, of course. Hetty cared.

When I got home, Michael had a light supper waiting on the deck. I charged upstairs for a fast shower and clean clothes and joined him. Ella was on a chaise in her diva pose, content in her harness with a thin leash attached to a leg of the chaise. The two place settings on the table looked pitifully few. There should have been three.

On the horizon, a thin band of white clouds promised to hide the sun's setting, but we took seats facing west just in case. Supper began with creamy vichyssoise, then switched to roasted chicken and a green salad. We ate hot french bread with it. We drank chilled white wine. We didn't talk much, just mostly said, "Mmmmm."

The cloud bank on the horizon glowed gold and saffron as the sun dipped behind it, and rays of pink and yellow shot toward the heavens. But the sun slipped into the sea without showing itself, a striptease artist coy behind a gauzy fan.

When the colors above the clouds had dulled, Michael brought out a plate of fat strawberries whose tips had been dipped in chocolate.

Michael ate one or two strawberries, I ate about half a dozen. Chocolate brings out the hog in me.

When I'd finally stuffed myself as much as possible, I said, "Guidry met me in Tom Hale's parking lot this afternoon. He wanted me to listen to a tape of the message Maureen got from the kidnappers."

"Yeah?"

"I'm almost positive it was Harry Henry's voice. He even called her Mo at first, and then changed the Mo to Mrs."

Michael snorted, either to indicate how dumb he thought Harry was to have given himself away like that, or to indicate how dumb he thought Harry was in general.

I said, "Guidry said Maureen had already told him it was Harry."

Michael moved his wineglass in little circles on the tabletop.

I said, "When she came to see me that night, she was so upset about that call. She quoted it word for word, exactly the way Harry had said it. Doesn't that seem weird to you? That she would have played it so many times she knew it by heart, but she didn't recognize Harry's voice until after Victor's body was found? Doesn't that seem weird?"

"Everything about that woman is weird."

"Cora Mathers thinks nobody would grow up bad if they were loved enough. Do you believe that?"

"Hell, Dixie, I don't know."

"Hetty Soames wants to be Jaz's foster mother if they find her alive."

"Hunh."

"Michael, do you have any idea where Paco is?"

He stood up and began gathering dishes to take inside.

He said, "Paco and I have an understanding. He doesn't tell me how to put out fires, and I don't tell him how to catch criminals. Paco is wherever he is. When he's finished doing whatever he's doing, he'll be home. End of discussion."

I carried Ella inside and helped Michael tidy up the kitchen. Then I kissed them both good night and went up to my apartment and fell into bed.

In my dreams, I entered a restaurant looking for the perfect stranger. I didn't have any notions of what that might be, just let my inner guide direct me. In the bar area, none of the line of people perched on stools met whatever criteria my guide had set, so I crossed over to the other side and looked at the diners sitting at tables. Nothing moved me toward any of them.

Just as I was beginning to think I'd got my dream message all wrong, a man came through double doors from a glass-walled kitchen. He wore a chef's tall hat and an immaculate white apron, and he carried a live stone crab in one hand. He stopped when he saw me, and for a second the only motion was the crab's waving claws. Diners fell silent watching us watch each other, and the waiters drew to attention against the walls.

I moved toward him, slowly and deliberately. He waited, the crab held shoulder high and beady-eyed. The room was silent as white.

I reached him and took the crab from his grip, holding it out to the side to escape its grasping claws.

The man said, "Good. I've been waiting for you to figure that out."

I woke up with a start and lay staring into the darkness. I didn't have a clue what the dream meant, but it wasn't any more confusing than my waking life.

# 26

The breeze was brisk and smelled of rain when I went out the next morning, and the curdled sky was not so tall. A few agitated gulls flapped above the waves, and on the beach a clawing surf tried to escape the pulsing sea. I stood on my porch a moment to inhale the salty day, then thumped down the stairs to the carport. Seabirds slept on every car, no doubt thinking themselves smart to get a pregame seat before the clouds burst.

At Tom Hale's dark apartment, I slipped in quickly and hustled Billy Elliot out with a minimum of smooching. At least between Billy and me. A faint scent of perfume in the air made me think Tom had an overnight guest again, so there may have been other smooching.

In the parking lot, security lamps cast wide pools of light on the oval track where Billy and I ran, but the sky was too overcast to let any dawning light through. We both looked up frequently. Billy probably hoped he'd get to sprint through a warm shower, I hoped the rain would hold off until Billy and I had finished our run. Besides

Ruthie and Big Bubba, my other clients for the day were seven cats—including two pairs—and a ferret. I would inevitably end up trailing cat hair. I hoped it wouldn't be stuck to wet clothes.

After Billy and I had made it around the last loop, and he had raised his leg one more time to announce to all the subsequent dogs on the track that he was still the number one honcho, we skipped back into the lobby. A jelly-bottomed woman in skin-tight lycra leggings popped out of the elevator before we got to it. She had slept-on hair and a bright-eyed Yorkie on a leash. The Yorkie was the size of a Hostess Sno Ball and was dancing with excitement. The woman looked as if she hadn't been awake more than two minutes.

Billy Elliot looked down at the Yorkie with keen interest.

As the woman opened the lobby door to go out, she said, "I've gotta housebreak this puppy."

She sounded as if she thought she needed to explain why she was going out before sunup looking like an unmade bed and leading a dog. Obviously a first-time dog owner.

As we got in the elevator, Billy Elliot looked over his shoulder for one last glimpse of the Yorkie—as if he wished he had one for himself. Whether we have two legs or four, I suppose we all want a companion of our own kind.

Back in Tom's apartment, the kitchen light was on and I could smell coffee brewing. I looked toward the kitchen but didn't see Tom, so I hugged Billy Elliot goodbye and slipped out. This time I was almost sure Tom had company.

I'm not sure what it is, but people make impressions on the air so that even if you can't see them, you know they're there. I just hoped this woman was better than Tom's last girlfriend. Not that it was any of my business, but Tom deserves the best.

The sky remained overcast and rain threatening for the rest of the morning. At every stop, I expected raindrops. I made a record fast stop to give Ruthie her next-to-last pill, and goosed the Bronco toward Big Bubba's.

It still hadn't rained when I got to his house. I hurried up the stairs, removed his night cover, and opened his cage door. I gave him an anxious once-over to make sure he hadn't gone bird nuts from boredom, but all his feathers were intact and shiny. He cocked his head and regarded me with the same scrutiny I was giving him, except I used both eyes.

He said, "Did you miss me?" Not angrily, just conversationally.

I said, "For breakfast this morning, may I suggest our best imported banana? It's served with toasted Cheerios and prime sunflower seeds on a bed of organic millet."

He said, "Get that man!" Then he laughed like a demented Santa Claus.

In the kitchen, I got his banana and some sliced apple. When I went back to the sunroom, he was sitting atop his cage looking toward the lanai. With no sun, the lanai probably didn't look very appealing to him.

I said, "It's cloudy today, with a ninety percent chance of rain. Temperatures will be in the high eighties. There are no major traffic problems."

He said, "Hello! Hello! Hello!"

I considered trying to persuade him to play on his exercise wheel, but I knew he'd rather watch dew evaporate. I unlocked the lanai slider and opened it so he could go out in the humid air.

I said, "While you're at the gym, I'll clean your house and put out your breakfast. Would you care for a news update?"

He waddled across the slider track to the lanai while I switched on the TV to a drug commercial featuring several lovely women wearing bedsheets tastefully pulled above their bosoms. A soothing female voice-over listed the consequences of taking the drug being advertised—blood clots, strokes, heart attacks, death—while the women in the sheets smiled benignly, bizarrely separate from the doublespeak.

The ad was replaced by local news people who were still covering kidnapping and murder.

An earnest woman with close-set eyes said, "Mrs. Salazar has not returned calls, and there have been no reported breaks in the case. A spokesperson for the Sarasota Sheriff's Department said the homicide investigation is ongoing."

The newswoman didn't say anything about Harry Henry being the person who'd made the ransom call to Maureen. I didn't know what that meant, but I was oddly pleased, as if it might all have been a misunderstanding, a case of mistaken identity that had been cleared up.

I'm too smart to fall for drug company propaganda, but gullible as a goose when it comes to old friends.

I changed the station to PBS so Big Bubba wouldn't get brainwashed by commercials, and left to go to Hetty's house. The sky was the color of mold, and the air had stilled. Trees and flowers were motionless. Even songbirds seemed to be holding their breath waiting for the clouds to let go.

With rain looking more probable every minute, I pulled as far as I could into Hetty's driveway so I wouldn't have so far to sprint when I left. When I rang the bell, Hetty and Ben let me in so quickly I thought they might have been watching for me. Lamps were lit in the shadowy house. By tacit agreement, we didn't move away from the front door, but stood in the foyer.

Hetty said, "Any word?"

"No. You?"

"Not a thing. She knows my number, Dixie. And I know she trusted me. She would call if she could."

I could have called too. Or Hetty could have called me. I had stopped for the same reason she'd been waiting for me—we needed each other's personal assurance that everything that could be done was being done.

I said, "I guess all we can do is wait."

"Wait for what?"

I didn't want to answer her. I was very afraid we were waiting for somebody to stumble on Jaz's body.

Perhaps because she feared I might voice those thoughts, she said, "It's going to storm any minute now."

I opened the door and stepped outside. I said, "If I hear anything, I'll let you know."

I trotted to the Bronco, and Hetty and Ben stood in the doorway and watched me back out. With the soft light behind them, they looked like the answer to a hopeless person's prayers.

The Village Diner was almost deserted, and the people inside were craning their necks toward the windows while they ate at double time. Judy scooted to my booth with my coffee, and Tanisha waved at me from the kitchen pass-through to let me know she was on my breakfast.

Judy said, "It's gonna come a real gully washer."

"Looks like it."

She said, "Dixie, did you know that kidnapped guy?"

"I went to school with his wife, but I only met him once or twice. Why?"

"Oh, they keep talking about it on the news, and they said the wife went to high school here, so I thought you might know them, all of you being natives."

"He wasn't from here."

"They said Venezuela."

"I think that's right."

"Something's mighty fishy about that whole thing, Dixie. I hope that wife isn't a good friend of yours because I'll bet a million dollars she did it."

I said, "You got a million dollars to pay me?"

"I'd have to pay it in installments, but I know I'm right."

"I don't know how she could kidnap her own husband. I mean, who would she be kidnapping him from? And then she'd have to pay herself off? I don't think so."

"Well, but see, what if she killed him and then got somebody else to dump him out of a boat? What if he was already dead when he drowned? They're not saying exactly what killed him, have you noticed that? They say they won't tell until they've done an autopsy. Why haven't they done that yet?"

That's the thing about being an ex-deputy. People think

they can ask me questions about criminal investigations and that I'll know the answers.

Tanisha dinged a bell to signal that my breakfast was ready, and Judy scooted away to get it. Good thing, because what she'd said made me feel like somebody had slapped me upside the head. I didn't know why I hadn't thought of it myself. Could Maureen have killed Victor? I wondered if Guidry had already considered the possibility.

If she had, then the money I'd carried to the gazebo hadn't gone to kidnappers at all, but back into Maureen's safe, and Maureen had used me sixteen ways from Thursday.

The rains came just as Judy put my breakfast down. The air inside the diner seemed to drop a few degrees, and the muffled roar of falling rain shrank the space to a refuge.

I ate my breakfast without a single glance at the windows. My mind was too busy thinking about what Judy had said to pay attention to a storm. For sure she'd been right about Victor being already dead when he was thrown overboard, and as soon as the medical examiner did an autopsy, that would be public knowledge.

If it also became public knowledge that Harry Henry had made the ransom call, the world would assume that Harry had killed Victor Salazar and that he had a million dollars in ransom money stashed somewhere. If Maureen had killed Victor herself, would she let Harry take the rap? It was a dumb question. Of course she would. If Maureen had to name the one person in the entire world who deserved her greatest loyalty, she would name herself.

I didn't linger over coffee, but left while the rain was still slanting down in opaque sheets. I was drenched by the time I got to the Bronco, and shivered when I started the motor and a blast of cold air came from the AC vents. I let the defogger run long enough to get rid of the moisture on the glass, started the wipers front and back, and eased into sparse traffic. I headed south toward home, but when I got to the turnoff to my lane, I kept going south.

I wanted to talk to Harry Henry again, and this time I wasn't going to let him lie to me.

# 27

At the marina, rain and steam rising from the bay shrouded boats and birds, and made the few scurrying people indistinct. Wet as a drowned rat, I walked down the wooden dock looking for Harry's houseboat. According to local gossip, it was a forty-foot relic from a time when houseboats were mostly boxy cabins set on pontoon-floated decks. Even without that description, I would have known it by the figurehead lashed to the front—a department store mannequin in a painted-on bikini. Harry probably thought it added a sophisticated touch.

Off the dock, a quintet of white yellow-billed pelicans sailed through the downpour like majestic dowager swans. One of their plain brown cousins had compactly folded himself neck-to-back on Harry's deck, and an immature blue heron with mud-colored feathers stood atop the cabin perfecting his neck stretches.

A skiff from an anchored pink catamaran was tied up

on one side of the houseboat, and a runabout was on the other side. A man shiny-wet as a dolphin was aboard the runabout gathering up empty beer cans and dropping them into a black garbage bag.

Nodding to him, I stepped off the dock to Harry's deck and pounded on the cabin door. "Harry, it's Dixie! Are you in there?"

The only response was the sound of rain and waves slapping against pontoons.

I circled the main cabin, peering into the shadows for Harry or Hef. All I saw were clean boards and carefully stored equipment. Harry might be eccentric, but he was neat. Fishing equipment took up the port side—rods of every type for freshwater fishing, a line of gaffs arranged from a three-footer to a six-footer, along with buoys, sinkers, cast nets, bait nets, fishing line, snorkels, and spear guns. Harry took his fishing seriously. He even had a chest-high stack of wooden crab traps ready—five of them, the legal limit for one person. A length of fine cotton twine had been tossed over the stack for tying the traps' exit doors closed. I like those exit doors. If a trap is left underwater too long, the twine disintegrates and the exit door swings open so the crab can escape.

Back at the door, I knocked again, just in case.

Behind me, the man from the runabout hollered, "Harry's not there."

I turned and yelled through the rain. "You have any idea where he is?"

"Key's above the door! Women use it all the time."

Before I could tell him that I wasn't one of Harry's

women, he gave me a knowing grin and walked away, swinging his plastic bag with a jaunty air as if he weren't soaking wet and walking through hard rain.

I waited until he was out of sight and then felt above the door for a key. Yep, it was there, but I pulled my hand down empty. It was one thing for a woman to use the key to open Harry's door if he'd *told* her to use it. But Harry didn't exactly expect me. And he hadn't exactly given me permission to enter his houseboat when he wasn't there. Which would make it a little bit like breaking and entering if I went in.

On the other hand, Harry's neighbor had told me to enter. You could even say he had given me *permission* to enter. He might not be authorized to give me permission, but how could I know that? I had shown up at Harry's door, and a man who could very well be his best friend in all the world had told me to use the key. So I asked myself what any responsible, law-abiding person would do. And the answer was that a reasonable person would use the key and go in and wait for Harry.

I reached up again and got the key. I looked around to make sure nobody was on any of the other slipped boats watching me—just in case I might be lying to myself. Then I slid the key into the lock and pushed the door open and hurried inside.

The cabin was as neat as the deck. Square room with pecky cypress walls hung with framed photographs of sea and shore life. Single bench bed covered by a quilt neatly tucked in. Immaculate galley kitchen with an eating bar. Shoved against the wall, a long wooden table with two drawers on its outer side. The top was loaded with careful stacks of *Sports Illustrated* and *Reader's Digest*. I didn't know what was in the drawers.

Three things were obvious: One, Harry wasn't home. Two, I was doing something that any court in the world would say was a violation of the law, not to mention just plain bad manners. Three, I wanted to know what was in those table drawers.

Their contents were as organized as everything else. The first one held checkbooks, boxes of printed checks, a hand calculator, a package of AA batteries, and a collection of pens and sharpened pencils. The second drawer had a phone book, some warranty papers for a boat motor, a digital camera, and a box of nice linen stationery. I opened the box. It didn't look as if Harry had ever used the stationery because the display envelope was still under a flat ribbon tied around the paper. The box also held a square pink envelope like greeting cards come in. My fingers trembled when I pulled out the paper folded inside it.

Even after fifteen years, I recognized the loopy handwriting, the humpbacked letters, the little open circles for dots on the *i*'s. I suppose people who don't grow up keep the same handwriting they had when they were teenagers. As I read it, I could hear Maureen's voice.

> Mrs. Salazar, we have your husband. If you want him returned alive, put a million dollars in small bills in a duffel bag and leave it in your gazebo at midnight tomorrow. Do not call the police or tell anybody. We will be watching you, and if you talk to anybody, we will kill your husband and feed him to the sharks.

Under my breath, I whispered, "Oh, Mo."

Now I knew why Maureen had been so sure what the kidnapper had said on the phone. She had written the script. Probably made several drafts before she'd decided on the final one, then gave it to Harry to read when he called her.

She had also sullied my memories of an innocent time that had been precious to me, a time before she chose money over love, and before I learned that choosing love doesn't mean you get to keep it.

The question was: What should I do about it?

Some old friendships are like cozy nests you can crawl into when you need comfort. Others are like giant squid, with tentacles lined with toothy suction cups that attach themselves to you and leave permanent scars.

I had let Maureen use me because her father had abandoned her and her mother had been a shrew. I had *understood* her, and I'd let compassion make me a martyr. So which one of us was the dumb one?

I pulled out my cellphone and punched in Guidry's number. His voice mail answered, which allowed me to be brisk and businesslike.

I said, "Maureen Salazar wrote the script that Harry Henry used when he called her to demand ransom money for Victor's kidnapping. If you should happen to get a search warrant to look for it on Harry's houseboat, you'll find it in a drawer in a long table."

I put the cellphone back in my pocket. But before I could replace the note in its stationery box in the drawer, the door to the cabin opened. I jammed the note in my pocket and turned around.

Maureen was dressed for rain. She wore a pink knee-length vinyl raincoat with matching shiny boots and a broad-brimmed hat. She looked cute and ridiculous and repellent.

With water still running off me onto Harry's immaculate floor, I said, "I know what you did."

She batted her eyes, all innocence. "I don't know what you're talking about."

"Oh, can it, Mo. I've had it with your lies."

She seemed to weigh her response options, and went with woman-to-woman confidential.

"Dixie, Victor wasn't a good husband like I always said. He used me like a toy—one of those ball-hitting things with the Ping-Pong paddle and the ball on a rubber band. You know? Well, he hit me one time too many, and my rubber band broke."

She paused and smiled, so pleased with her metaphor that I could see she was memorizing it so she could use it with the next person she met.

She said, "I tried to leave him, believe me, but I could never go through with it. He would cry and beg, and then he would hit me. And then when I promised not to leave, he'd give me a big piece of expensive jewelry. Harry thinks I stayed because of the jewelry, but that's not true. Victor was just a lot stronger than me."

Through cold lips, I said, "So you killed him?"

Her pink lips parted in surprise. "Is that what you think? That I killed my own husband? I can't believe you'd think that!"

The smart thing would have been to pretend to believe her. But I was beyond smart. I had gone into honest.

I said, "I don't know what to believe anymore. If you didn't kill him yourself, you know who did. So who was it, Mo? Who killed Victor?"

While I steeled myself to hear her name Harry, she studied her manicure. "I don't know his *name*. Victor never introduced us."

If that was going to be her story, Harry was doomed.

I said, "Victor didn't leave with some old buddies from South America, did he? You made all that up."

"We can't all be strong like you, Dixie."

"Being honest isn't a muscle test, Mo. It's a choice, like whether to wear underwear."

She tried for an arch smile. "I don't like underwear."

"Listen to me, Mo. Unless you can explain how Victor was killed, there's a very good chance that you, or Harry, or maybe both of you are going to be charged with murder. So start explaining and maybe I can help you avoid a lot of trouble."

She looked hopeful. "It was because of his business. Like I told you, he had a lot of enemies because of his business."

"His oil broker business."

"It wasn't exactly oil."

"Victor sold drugs, didn't he?"

"No, silly, he *imported* drugs. You make it sound like he was some street pusher. He dealt directly with the supplier—Colombia, Afghanistan, places like that. He had it delivered to men called captains, like in the army, and they passed the stuff out to people under them. He was a businessman. He didn't hurt anybody."

"You're talking about heroin and cocaine?"

She avoided my eyes. Even Maureen wasn't dumb enough to believe those drugs were harmless.

I thought of Jaz and all the other kids whose lives have been distorted by drugs. I thought of young men like Paulie and his friends, boys who sell drugs that people like Victor bring into the country. The guys at the bottom get money for fast cars and cool shoes before they end up dead or in prison. Men like Victor get megayachts and trophy women like Maureen and millions in cash in their home safes. It was cold comfort that Victor had ended up dead too, because for every "businessman" like Victor who disappears, a line of others are ready to take his place.

I said, "Tell me what happened when he was killed. The truth, please."

She said, "He was meeting somebody down at the gazebo, somebody who came in a boat. He did that a lot, so I didn't think anything about it. I heard a gunshot and then I heard a boat going away real fast. I knew something bad had happened so I went down to the gazebo and Victor was lying there dead."

She looked up at me with puzzled eyes. "There wasn't much blood. That surprised me. And it wasn't like his head was blown open or anything. It was just a neat little hole in his forehead."

I didn't offer any explanations, so after a pause she went on.

"I knew he was dead, and I knew the men trying to get Victor's business had done it. There wasn't anything I could do about him being dead, and if I called the cops and reported it, they would come investigating Victor's business. I thought they might take the money or the house, the cars and boats, maybe all of it. So I went to see Harry, and we came up with the idea of a kidnapping. See, if Victor was kidnapped, it wouldn't look odd that he'd disappeared, and nobody would know how he'd made his money. So Harry brought his boat around to the gazebo and we tied Victor's ankles to an anchor and then Harry took him out to deep water and dropped him overboard. Then he went home and waited until late that night and called me and left that message."

"And you came to see me."

"Yeah. You were cool to help me, Dixie."

"After I took the money to the gazebo and you drove me home, you went back to the gazebo and got the money, didn't you?"

She looked proud of herself. "It wasn't really money. It was phone books."

I felt like banging my head on Harry's walls. There hadn't been anybody watching me from a boat when I walked down that dark path to the gazebo. There hadn't been any money in the duffel bag. I had been a total dope.

I said, "Why the press conference?"

She looked surprised at the question. "That's what people *do*, Dixie. Rich people, I mean. When a rich person's been kidnapped, the family calls a press conference."

I said, "They've identified Harry's voice on the ransom call."

"I know. I feel bad about that."

"Do you understand? It means they think he kidnapped Victor."

"Well, they can't *prove* he did it. He doesn't have a record or anything. I don't think he'll have to serve time."

My hands itched to smack her. I took a deep breath and decided to come at her from another angle.

"You said Victor's killer was one of his rivals. You must have some idea who he was."

She shook her head. "It could have been a lot of people. See, some big shot from Colombia contacted them all and said he was coming here this week. He's going to put the entire North American operation in one broker's hands, so people are coming from all over the place to find out who the main guy will be. Victor expected it to be him. I think some other broker killed him to keep him from going to that meeting."

It made my head swim to hear Maureen speak of drug kingpins as brokers, but what she'd said made sense.

I said, "Did you hear a name for the guy coming from Colombia?"

"No, but Victor said he was one of Escobar's people. I don't know who Escobar is, but Victor said you don't screw around with one of his men. He sounded pretty scared."

I would have been scared too. Pablo Escobar was once the bad-ass head of the Medellín drug cartel in Colombia. He's been dead over a decade, but his former associates still use his name to instill fear. One of Escobar's men coming to Sarasota would send an earthquake through the drug world.

"You have to tell them the truth."

She shook her head like a four-year-old offered a bite of spinach. "I can't do that, Dixie. That would get me in a lot of trouble. You know, they might think I was Victor's business partner or something."

"If you don't tell, I will."

She looked at me as if she were seeing me for the first time. Baby gophers probably look like that the first time they poke their noses out of the ground and see daylight.

I said, "Mo, I know about the script you wrote for Harry. You directed him to make that ransom call."

Outraged, she said, "He told you about that?"

I pulled the note from my pocket. "I found it. I'm giving it to the police."

It was stupid of me to wave it at her. Maureen was tall and long armed and quick. With a look of feral cunning, she snatched the note from my hand and ran out the cabin door with me hot behind her.

# 28

Instead of leaping to the dock and running away, Maureen rounded the corner of the cabin toward the aft deck and disappeared into the shadows. Like a kid, she probably thought she could escape by making herself invisible. That if she hid from me, I wouldn't know where she was.

The rain had slackened to a fine mist, with steamy fog ghosting dark silhouettes of sleeping gulls and pelicans. Trembling with suppressed fury, I moved cautiously on the wet deck looking for her. Maureen had got away with using people all her life, and I was determined not to let her get away with framing Harry for kidnapping Victor. Maureen was taller than me by a good five inches, but I'd always been more athletic, and I had righteous outrage feeding me. When I found her, I knew I could overpower her.

I crept around a group of deck chairs, but she wasn't behind them. I peered behind a pile of coiled ropes and under a table lashed to the deck. She wasn't there. There was only one other place she could be. I stopped at the tower of Harry's crab traps. They made a perfect shield for a woman who thought she had the right to use old friends for her own selfish purposes.

I went still as a mongoose, waiting for her to give herself away.

After several silent minutes, the brim of her pink rain hat rose from behind the stack, then her big apprehensive eyes looked over its top at me.

By then I was a volcano ready to blow. All my anger and frustration and disappointment gathered into a bellow that would have traveled five miles in the jungle.

"DID YOU MISS ME?"

She recoiled as if I had put a bullet in her head, and pushed the stack of traps toward me. More furious with every moment, I caught the upper trap in both hands as it fell. I heaved it at her, and she made a noise like a squeaking mouse as she ducked away. She was afraid of me now. For the first time since she'd known me, she was seeing the side of me that had faced down evil and won, a side of me that had killed a man.

Made clumsy by fear and the mist-slick deck, she tried to run, but one of her pink vinyl boots crashed into the escape hole in one of the traps she'd knocked over. Flailing the air for balance, she grunted and kicked her leg as if she would shake it off, but it's not that easy to disengage your foot from a crab trap. Especially if you don't know the size and shape of the exit. Especially if you don't know you have to line your foot up exactly with the hole to extract it. Especially if you're being attacked by a she-devil from hell.

Lowering my voice to a normal level, I said, "Harry's been loyal to you for as long as he's known you. I won't let you hurt him any more than you already have."

Her mouth thinned, and I saw her mother's face. "Oh, you're so high and mighty! Always thinking you're smarter than everybody else, better than everybody else. In high school it was always, 'Don't sleep with boys, Mo, you'll get pregnant. Don't smoke dope, Mo, it'll make you a loser.' Well, look who's the loser now. I've got a big house and lots of money, and you're a pet sitter with a dead husband and a dead baby."

To this day I don't know why I moved toward her the way I did. To tell the truth, I don't remember *intending* anything, I simply surged forward. She shrieked and hobbled backward, eyes wide and scared. Awkwardly dragging the crab trap on one foot, she hit the low railing, lost her balance, and shrieked again. Her vinyl raincoat was slippery and the railing was wet. In a blink, she toppled over the railing and vanished into the rain-darkened water.

My anger evaporated. Now I was guilt stricken and horrified. Maureen had never been a strong swimmer. Neither was I. We were more at home on the beach than in the water. I ran to the forward deck and looked desperately for help. Not a soul. I ran back to the place where Maureen had gone over and looked into the water. The bay isn't deep, but Maureen was panicked and she had a heavy crab trap attached to one foot. She could easily become disoriented and not know which way was up.

People underwater for more than three minutes lose consciousness. After five minutes, their brains suffer permanent damage from lack of oxygen. I tried to estimate how long Maureen had been underwater. Half a minute, at least. Maybe more.

*Shit!*

Old deputy training made me put my cellphone in a protected spot out of the rain before I stepped over the railing. As I dropped into the dark water, I heard a man's shout and the barking of a dog.

My foot touched something, and I kicked away to come down beside it. My fingers felt Maureen's slick raincoat. After a jolt of fear when I thought I might be touching a shark, I moved forward to get a grip on her slippery arm. Maureen slewed toward me, clutching at my floating hair. Drowning people don't cooperate with their rescuers. They don't go limp and allow themselves to be lifted to the surface. Instead, they go wild with panic. They claw at their saviors, they try to climb them to reach air. Now we were both in danger of drowning. Maureen was weighted down by a crab trap, and I was weighted by Maureen.

As I struggled free of her, my body realized the danger I was in and made my throat close to keep water from going into my lungs. I had only been down a short time, but the smothering need to breathe sent me into the same blind terror Maureen felt.

A form suddenly moved against me, and two arms wrapped around me and tugged me upward. In seconds, my head was above water and I was coughing and gagging. I heard other men's voices shouting and the thunder of footsteps on the dock. Somebody boosted me toward the deck where strong hands hauled me onto the boards.

I crawled to the cabin wall and leaned against it while

Harry pulled Maureen out of the water. She was crying and gagging, and she'd lost her pink hat. Harry stretched her on the deck, gently eased the crab trap off her foot, and carried her into the cabin.

A man squatted beside me. He said, "Good thing Harry saw you jump in and ran for help. Your friend's going to be okay."

I said, "She's not my friend."

Hef came to my side and nuzzled my neck, which made me burst into tears and bury my face in his wet fur. After a while, Harry came back and there was some genial backslapping as he thanked the men who had helped save Maureen and me.

The men left, and Harry put his hands under my arms and lifted me upright. He didn't even breathe hard when he did it. Harry was strong.

He said, "Are you okay?"

Through my tears, I nodded. I was still wheezing and weak-kneed, but more upset than harmed.

He said, "Come on, let's get you inside so you can dry out."

I knelt to snag my phone from its protected spot and let Harry lead me inside the cabin. Hef followed me with his tail wagging. Mo had taken off her shiny raincoat and boots and was sitting on Harry's bed wrapped in a big towel. When I came in, she gave me a murderous look.

Harry brought me towels and led me to a chair.

I said, "You saved our lives. Thank you."

He grinned and shrugged. "I'm more at home in water than you two. What happened?"

Maureen said, "Dixie pushed me overboard. I nearly drowned."

I looked from her to Harry. I'd never thought either of them was perfect, but then who is? When you're young, you're more prone to overlook friends' faults and forgive their weaknesses because you know you're all still cooking and nobody's done. But we were adults now. All three of us had been in life's oven long enough to rise to our greatest heights.

I said, "I found the script Mo wrote for you to read when you made the fake ransom call. She took it from me and ran to the deck. I chased her and her foot got caught in a crab trap and she fell overboard."

Harry said, "I saw you jump in after her. Hef and I were coming home and I saw you. I yelled for help, and those other guys came running."

He didn't seem to get the implication of my knowing about the note and the fake ransom call.

I said, "Maureen told me that Victor was already dead when you tied the anchor to him and took him out to the inlet."

The corners of his lips tucked in, so I thought I might be connecting.

I said, "Unless Maureen comes clean and tells how Victor's drug-running rival killed him, you'll probably be charged with both kidnapping and murder."

He looked quizzically at me. Then he turned and looked at Maureen.

He said, "Mo, are you saying you *didn't* kill your old man? I mean, *for real* you didn't kill him?"

She glared at him. "I *told* you I didn't kill him!"

"I thought you just said that 'cause you didn't want me to know. That's the only reason I helped you."

Now it was my turn to finally get it. Harry had thought all along that Maureen had killed Victor. To protect her from a murder investigation, he'd agreed to make the fake ransom call. And on the theory that nobody could prove she'd killed him if his body was never found, Harry had taken Victor's corpse out in a boat and dumped him overboard. The poor guy had done it all to protect Maureen.

Maureen didn't share my sympathy for him.

She shrugged. "That's your problem, Harry. I *told* you. And that note Dixie found is in the water. Nobody will ever see it, and nobody can prove it ever existed. Anyway, you're the one who made the fake kidnapping call, not me."

Harry's face registered shocked pain. "You told me to!"

She said, "That's just your word against mine, Harry. Nobody will believe you."

I had forgotten that Harry could be quick when he needed to be. He was at her side in a nanosecond, leaning over her with one big hand gripping her arm.

He said, "You'd do that to me?"

Drawing her neck back, she swung her other arm up and slapped the air under his face. "Get your hands off me! Who the hell do you think you are? You're nobody!"

Harry flinched as if she had managed to hit him. Over her head, his eyes sought mine and sent me a look of sad acceptance. I had the feeling that Harry was more disappointed in Maureen for her hateful words than he was for her greed or dishonesty.

Hef didn't have Harry's old loyalty to Maureen. All Hef knew was that a person had tried to hurt his friend. Like a shot, the dog ran at Maureen with his teeth bared.

Still in Harry's grip, she kicked at Hef. "Get that damn dog away from me!"

Every man has his limits, and Maureen had just pushed dumb, good-natured Harry over his.

White faced, he said, "You don't kick my dog." To me, he said, "Dixie, get the cops out here."

She laughed. "Dummy, Dixie's my friend. She won't do that."

I pulled my cellphone from my pocket and punched in Guidry's number. This time he answered, and the sound of slapping windshield wipers told me he was in his car.

I said, "I'm with Harry Henry and Maureen Salazar on Harry's houseboat. They want to talk to you about how they faked Victor Salazar's kidnapping. Maureen would also like to tell you about the rival drug dealer she believes killed Victor."

"Are you speaking in code?"

I said, "Yes, his boat is in the Midnight Pass marina. Five minutes? That would be fine. We'll wait for you."

He said, "It's raining. Give me fifteen."

I slid the phone back in my pocket and smiled at Harry and Maureen. "The detective is on his way."

Guidry actually made it in ten minutes, and considering the rain he had to drive through, that was some kind of record. I opened the door when he knocked. With a quizzical glance at my dirty, bedraggled, waterlogged self, he strode inside.

Harry's grip on Maureen was still firm, and Maureen looked as if she would bolt in a second if she got a chance.

Maureen said, "I want my lawyer."

Guidry nodded. "Fine with me. He can meet us at the station."

Maureen said, "*She*. My lawyer is a woman."

She said it so defiantly that I felt sorry for her. Maureen was still stuck in an earlier time when it wasn't so common for women to become lawyers. I guess being the in-house bimbo of a drug dealer would keep you from noticing that a lot of old ideas had changed.

She was right about one thing, though. She definitely needed a lawyer.

# 29

With a promise from Guidry that Hef wouldn't have to spend the night in jail, I left the marina. Actually, I was pretty sure that Maureen's lawyer would have them home by midafternoon. Filing a false claim of kidnapping is only a misdemeanor, and so is illegally disposing of a corpse. More than likely, they'd each get off with a fine for those crimes. On the other hand, while I believed Maureen's story and expected the cops to eventually accept it, I expected them both to be suspects in Victor's murder.

On the way home, I thought how freaky it was that a group of big-time drug dealers were gathered somewhere in Sarasota right that minute. Every Floridian suspects that some of the tasteless megamansions that ruin our views have been built with money made from drug trafficking, but we like to believe they're *retired* drug traffickers. If what Maureen had said was true, a lot of them were still in business. I imagined their counterparts flying into Sarasota's private airport in their personal jets, each of them as rich and well armed as some countries, all of them in silk suits and dark glasses, all of them anxious about losing power to the man who would be named the new jefe of the North American drug-trafficking business. It made me feel like an extra in *The Sopranos.*

By the time I got to my lane, the rain had resolved into a gentle soaker. The oaks and sea grape along my drive were drooping with the weight of water, and all the parakeets were hidden under their leaves. I parked under the carport and squished up the stairs to my apartment. Inside, I was undressed by the time I got to the stacked washer and dryer in the hall alcove. Everything went in, wet shorts, soggy T-shirt, damp underwear, water-logged Keds. I had been in so much water, I wouldn't have been surprised if I'd sprouted fins.

I padded to the bathroom and hauled my tired self into the shower to let blessed warm water beat away the film of bay scum and disillusionment. I barely made it to bed before I fell into exhausted sleep.

I dreamed I went to a place with a lot of filmy white stuff that I guess was clouds. I was excited because I figured I was in heaven and that if I asked God nicely, he would send me to be with Todd and Christy. I came to a big golden gate with an arched top, the generic kind of gate you see in cartoons about heaven. I rang a doorbell and waited, a little annoyed that nobody was there to greet me. In a while, I heard a voice that wrapped around me with no source that I could see. It was a melodious voice that I associated with harps or cellos, the kinds of instruments you would expect in heaven.

The voice said, "Are you sure you want to enter here? You can't change your mind, you know."

I said I was sure, and the gate clicked open. I walked through and looked around. It was clear in there, with no rain or clouds, just pretty flowers and butterflies and songbirds and little gurgling streams—a standard heavenly environment.

The voice spoke again, and this time it was ahead of me. It said, "Come this way, honey."

That struck me as funny, to have an archangel or whatever he was call me *honey.* I followed the voice and came to a place where a lot of women were having a picnic. They had fried chicken and watermelon and potato salad and the little green olives I love so much. The women were all different ages and colors and shapes. The only thing they had in common were big satisfied smiles. These women were enjoying life, big time.

I said, "Excuse me, I'm looking for God."

They all turned their happy faces toward me and spoke with the sound of wind singing through silver flutes.

And the voice said, "Honey, I AM."

I woke up smiling, and lay for a minute feeling happier than I could remember feeling in a long time.

Then I remembered that Jaz was missing and perhaps killed, which made me get up and get busy so I wouldn't think about it. I'd done all I could do that day.

Naked, I padded to the kitchen to make a cup of tea. While I waited for the water to boil, I looked out the window over the sink. Rain was still falling and from the looks of the sky, it would continue to fall for a long time. As I carried my tea to the closet-office, I flipped on my CD player to let Patsy Cline's no-nonsense, no-equivocation, no-shit voice break the silence. With a fresh burst of energy, I returned phone calls to new and old clients, then whipped through all the clerical part of my business. Then, still naked, I hauled out the vacuum cleaner and sucked up all the dust in my apartment. I cleaned my bathroom too, and washed damp towels along with my wet clothes. Like Harry Henry, I like my environment to be clean and neat. It makes me feel as if I'm in control of my little corner of the world.

When I finished, I still had a little time before my afternoon rounds, so I got dressed in jeans and T-shirt and pulled on a reflective yellow rain slicker. I even put on the matching sou'wester hat with a dorky wide brim that drooped in the back like a dragging butterfly wing. Wearing all that rain stuff made me feel like a kindergarten kid, but at least I wouldn't get soaking wet again. Just sweaty and claustrophobic. I was careful going downstairs because the steps were slippery, and then I dashed across the deck to Michael's back door. He was sitting at the butcher-block island with a cup of coffee and a slice of pie in front of him. He looked miserable.

Ella sat beside him on her adoring stool, and when I came in she let her eyes open all the way for a moment. Cats do that in the dark, so maybe she thought my presence caused the lights to dim. Either that, or the sight of my big yellow self had made her think a lion had entered the kitchen.

Michael said, "Want some key lime pie?"

Like Guidry, he had new stress lines around his mouth. We were all too aware of dark fears lurking in the basement of our minds.

I shrugged off the coat and peeled off the hat and poured myself a cup of coffee. He sliced a wedge of pie for me, and I joined him at the island.

I said, "No word from Paco yet?"

He frowned. "I told you, Paco's fine. He'll call when he can."

"I just thought he might have called."

"I'll tell you when he does."

Ella watched us with a worried expression on her face.

I ate a few bites of pie. I drank some coffee. I said, "Guidry has taken Maureen and Harry to the sheriff's office for questioning."

Michael's eyebrows raised. Good, I had distracted him.

He said, "I'm almost afraid to ask you what those two numb-nuts managed to get arrested for."

"First you have to know that Maureen says her husband was a drug importer."

"A what?"

"A major drug trafficker in heroin and cocaine. Bought it direct from the big cartels in South America and Afghanistan. I'm talking *big* dealer. She calls it importing."

He made a face. "And she stayed with him?"

I said, "Remember, this is Maureen Rhinegold we're talking about. She's not any smarter now that she's Maureen Salazar. Anyway, she says there's a big shake-up going on in the drug world. Some Colombian top dog, one of Pablo Escobar's men, has come to Sarasota to meet with all the drug bosses in this country. He's going to name one American to head the whole North American drug operation. Maureen thinks somebody killed Victor so it wouldn't be him."

"She know who it was?"

"She claims she doesn't, but that may change if she looks at doing jail time for any part she had in Victor's business."

Michael looked slightly less miserable at the thought.

I said, "Harry thought Maureen had killed Victor. He helped her because he wanted to protect her from a murder rap. He made a fake ransom call so she could record it, and he took Victor's body out and dumped it in the Venice inlet."

"Poor stupid bastard."

"He had plenty of direction. Maureen wrote out the words for him to say when he made the fake ransom call. I imagine it was her idea to dump Victor overboard."

Michael grinned. "Too bad she didn't tell him to use a shorter rope on the anchor."

"It's not funny, Michael!"

He got up to rinse his plate at the sink. "Yeah, it is."

I didn't tell him about the near-drowning incident at the marina. It was too long a story to go into right then, but I would tell him later. I wanted him to know that Harry had saved my life.

He put the plate in the dishwasher and turned to lean against the counter. "What about that what's-her-name girl? Have they found her?"

I took a deep breath. "It's Jaz. Not yet."

He shook his head. "Doesn't sound good."

I said, "If those gang members were waiting for her when she left the resort to go back to Hetty's house, they could easily have grabbed her without anybody seeing. Even if she screamed, people are all shut up inside their houses with the air-conditioning on, so nobody would have heard her."

Michael crossed his arms, probably thinking what he'd like to do to the gang guys.

I said, "I keep thinking about those boys, especially the one they called Paulie. He seemed like a pretty good kid. Or at least not as cynical as the other two."

"Good kids don't kill other kids."

"Why didn't his mother pay closer attention to him? How could he be peddling drugs or robbing houses without her knowing? She'd have to be awfully busy or stupid not to notice. Or maybe she just didn't care."

Michael gave me a knowing look. "Why do you blame the mother? The kid had a father too."

I didn't answer because I knew it wasn't a real question. Michael knew why I blamed the mother.

I said, "If our grandparents hadn't taken us in, we might have ended up like Paulie."

He gave me a long, level look. "One of the guys at work has a wife who's close to nine months pregnant. He's nervous, so she got him some Chinese worry balls. He's supposed to rotate them in the palm of one hand to relax, but instead he's more tense than ever."

"Your point being?"

"You're rotating all that crap around just like they're worry balls, and it's not doing you a bit of good. Not doing those kids any good either. It doesn't matter why those guys turned bad. They killed another kid, and they'll have to pay for it. Period. End of story. Quit hooking everything to our mother leaving us. And for God's sake, stop wondering how we would have turned out if she hadn't, or if our grandparents hadn't taken us in. You can't ever find an answer, so quit worrying it to death."

That's one of the best things about having a family. They'll tell you when you're doing something dumb. Michael was right. It was senseless to dwell on questions I couldn't answer.

I said, "You're right."

"Damn straight I'm right. And I hope you've had your last conversation with Harry Henry and Maureen Rhinegold what's her name now."

"It's Salazar, and I have."

I thanked him for the pie, smooched the top of Ella's head, and got back into my slicker. When I yanked the yellow hat down around my ears, Ella looked alarmed.

I said, "I'm going to leave early for afternoon rounds."

Michael said, "We'll have meatloaf for dinner. Mashed potatoes. Rain food."

Too brightly, I said, "Great!"

Carnivore that I am, I love meatloaf, especially the kind Michael makes with tomato gravy. But Paco doesn't eat much meat, so the fact that Michael was planning meatloaf for supper meant he didn't expect Paco to be home.

I went upstairs to get my pet-sitting stuff and drove off through the soft rain. At least I didn't have to wear the dumb hat in the car. The parakeets were still hiding in the trees and the lane was soggy under the shell. When I looked across the Gulf to the horizon, it was hard to tell where the sea ended and the sky began. The entire world was gray and dreary.

I wondered if Guidry had finished questioning Maureen

and Harry. I wondered if they had posted bail and gone home. I wondered if Harry would ever forgive Maureen.

I caught myself thinking about them, and murmured, "Worry balls."

It was none of my business what happened with Maureen and Harry. My part in their drama was over. Furthermore, no way, no how, no time would I ever again allow myself to get involved in somebody else's problems. No matter how long I'd known them or how close we might once have been, people could just damn well take their problems to a nice therapist or a minister or a priest, because I was through.

That's what I swore, and I really meant it.

I should have remembered that any time you take a stand on something and say you'll never, no matter what, do that or go there or be involved in something, next thing you know you'll be up to your eyebrows in it.

At the Sea Breeze, I wore the hat while Billy Elliot and I ran. Either because he was embarrassed to be seen with me or because of the rain, he was willing to confine his run to only one lap around the parking lot's oval track. At the cats' houses, the order of the day was lethargic drowsiness. They'd put themselves into lull-land from looking out at the rain, and none of them wanted to play any vigorous games. I felt the same way, so I promised them we'd play twice as long the next time I came.

I took off the hat before I went into Big Bubba's house. The slicker was alarming enough, I didn't want him to think a yellow giant from the jungle was after him. He was so subdued by the relentless rain that he hardly acknowledged my presence.

I said, "Your mom will be home in a few days."

He said, "Get that man," but he didn't have his heart in it.

I left him with fresh fruit and a new millet strand and went out the front door. On the porch, I put the yellow rain hat back on and headed home. I didn't stop at Hetty's house. I couldn't bear to talk about Jaz right then. I didn't even pull the hat off inside the Bronco. All I could think of was going home and having comfort food with Michael.

At Old Stickney Point Road—so named after the city built a *new* Stickney Point approximately twenty-five feet from the old one—I hit the brakes to keep from broadsiding a khaki-colored Hummer that shot out in front of me and made a sharp turn onto Midnight Pass Road. The driver didn't even see me. His wipers weren't working, and he was bent over the steering wheel trying to locate the controls. The driver was Paulie, the kid who'd left fingerprints on Big Bubba's seed jar.

I dug under my slicker and winkled my cellphone from my tight jeans pocket to call Guidry. I got his voice mail.

I gave him a description and the tag number of the Hummer, even though I was sure it was a rental. I said, "I'm following him. I'll call you when I have an address."

Then I put my cellphone back in my pocket and held the steering wheel with both hands, peering through the insistent rain to keep watch on the young killer who might lead me to Jaz.

# 30

A pale sun sat low on the horizon and cast a sickly yellow light through the rain. Instead of making it easier to see, the light acted as a lens that blurred visibility. Since I was in familiar territory, I was able to navigate by known landmarks, but the Hummer in front of me slowed to a crawl at every eastbound lane. Each time, Paulie's head turned to look down the lane before he gunned the motor and sped off to the next intersection. All those lanes look alike and some of them don't have street signs, so it wasn't surprising that he had trouble finding the right one.

Paulie finally turned left toward the bay, and I swung in behind him. The street was typical of the key, winding and heavily wooded on both sides, with wide stretches of space between the houses. It was dark and gloomy under the trees, and my tires hit several low places that sent up sprays of dirty water. Paulie switched on his lights, but I drove without mine. I didn't want to call attention to myself.

The closer we got to the bay, the more often Paulie

slowed the Hummer and hesitated at driveways. I supposed he was searching for an address or for something familiar about a house.

He slowed even more when he came to a stretch where heavy rain had caused power and sewer damage. Several large panel trucks were parked along the curb, and a big orange backhoe was maneuvering into position in the middle of the street. Barriers had been erected in the street to mark a spot for digging, and a group of men in black rain slickers and rain hats stood by to watch the operation. Beyond the backhoe, an FPL truck with a raised cherry picker crane and two men inside the bucket stood beside a streetlight.

As if all the activity surprised him, Paulie came to a complete stop in the street and looked at the workers for a moment before he turned into the driveway of a one-story stucco house. The garage door began rising, and a curtain twitched aside at one of the lighted windows. A girl illuminated by inside lamplight peered out at the workmen in the street. She looked frantic, and her mouth opened as if she was trying to get their attention.

It was Jaz.

Somebody jerked her away, and the curtain closed.

While Paulie waited for the garage door to rise high enough to drive under, I came to a lurching stop at the curb behind a Verizon truck.

The garage door reached its tallest height and Paulie drove inside.

A voice somewhere in the dark recesses of my mind spoke in a flat, unemotional voice: *You know what you have to do.*

The thing about internal voices is that they call you to action *right then*. No time to think about it, no time for debates, no time to weigh consequences. Normal people would say what I did next was insane, but normal people have never met themselves face-to-face.

As the garage door began a rattling descent, I opened my car door and ran like hell. The garage door was about four feet from the ground when I got to it, and I swooped under it and duck-walked to the rear of the Hummer.

Paulie was hauling Siesta Grill take-out bags from the Hummer and trying to figure out how to carry all of them in one trip. Stacking them and balancing them taxed his brain, but he finally managed to gather them all in both arms. Without a free arm to keep his low-hanging pants from falling, he had to walk spraddle legged to the back door. He kicked the door to get somebody's attention, and when the door opened he dropped some of the bags.

The young guy who'd opened the door said, "Fuck, Paulie, you're spilling stuff!"

Paulie said, "So pick it up! I'm the one doing all the work here!"

He went inside and kicked the door shut, and I crept forward. Half the people I know never lock the inside doors to their garages. With luck, gang members wouldn't lock theirs either. I pressed an ear against the door and heard muffled male conversation, a couple of shouts, and then silence. I hoped the silence meant they had carried the food into another room.

Gingerly, I tried the doorknob. It turned, and I pushed the door open far enough to look inside. The kitchen was so messy and dirty it would have turned the stomach of an orangutan, but nobody was in it. From what I judged to be the living room, male voices argued over who had ordered what. The voices surprised me. I had expected young voices, but these were deep grown-up voices.

High on adrenaline, I crept forward. I didn't have a plan. I didn't have a weapon. I didn't have an idea of what I was going to do. All I knew was that young men who were members of a street gang had taken Jaz captive, and that she was still alive.

In the living room, a gruff voice said, "Goddam good thing you didn't bring us more pizza. Or those damn chicken buckets. I didn't come all this way to eat drive-through crap."

Several other men made vigorous agreeing noises, all of them apparently fed up with what they'd been eating. But who were they?

I moved faster. With all the noise they were making, plus the dull sound of the rain and the clatter of the backhoe digging up the street, I figured the sound of my Keds moving across the kitchen tile wouldn't be noticed.

Another man said, "At least one of those punks is good for something. I still don't know why you brought them."

A sharp voice said, "How many times do I have to explain it? I brought them to get that girl. If we let her testify, it'll bring a shitload of trouble on all of us."

Chilled, I listened to other men point out that the job hadn't been done yet. As if Jaz were a rabid animal they'd caught in a trap and needed to dispose of, their only point of agreement was that the longer she lived, the more all of them were in jeopardy.

Hugging the wall, I slipped out of the kitchen and into a dining area where a table was heaped with briefcases and laptops. The space formed the foot of an L between the kitchen and living room. Cautiously, I edged to the corner and tilted my head so one eye could peek into the living area.

About a dozen men were in the room, and it was immediately apparent what the pecking order was. Two of them sat on a long sofa with a two-man space between them. They wore expensive slacks and dress shirts. Their shoes were polished and they wore dark socks that didn't expose any leg. Each had a grandmotherly TV tray set up to hold food and a wineglass. Their food had been transferred from clamshell boxes to real plates, and they had real flatware. Three other similarly dressed and TV-trayed men sat in club chairs.

Other men were younger and dressed as if they were junior executives or midlevel employees. They sat on the floor with their legs stretched out and Styrofoam containers open on their laps. They had cans of beer rather than wine. The youngest, in sloppy jeans and droopy T-shirts, were Paulie and his two bottom-of-the-barrel friends. They were awkwardly serving the men on the sofa and chairs, fearfully making sure they had the dinner they'd ordered, pouring wine in their glasses, offering them extra napkins and salt and pepper from the carry-out bags.

At the far side of the room, a dark, broad-chested man with a curly black beard leaned in a doorway and watched the action. From the respectful way everybody looked at him, even the important guys on the sofa and chairs, I knew he was the most dangerous man in the room. He wore an exquisitely tailored black suit, black silk shirt, and black tie. Jet-black hair curved around his ears, and heavy gold bracelets glinted at his wrists. Even with the house darkened by rain, his eyes were hidden behind slim dark glasses. Everything about the man said he had an obsidian heart as black as his suit.

Realization hit, and my heart struggled against its cage like a panicked bird. The man in the doorway was the big shot Maureen had talked about, the one from Colombia who was here to appoint a North American drug czar, and the men who looked like executives were crime bosses. In a sickeningly rational move, the mob head from L.A. had brought Paulie and his friends to find Jaz and kill her. Without her, there would be no murder trial of his young street dealers, therefore no fallout that could hurt him.

With a take-out bag dangling from one hand, Paulie turned to the man leaning in the doorway. As if he were speaking to a coiled snake, he said, "Uh, sir, where do you want yours?"

Silently, the man crooked a finger at Paulie. Everybody in the room stopped eating to watch Paulie carry the bag to him. Without speaking, the man took the bag, and Paulie hurried away like a cowed dog to take a seat on the floor. At the door, the man extended the bag toward somebody inside the room.

Jaz stepped forward, took the bag from the man, and disappeared from view.

I must have made a movement, because the Colombian swiveled his head toward me. For a long moment we stared at each other, me like a yellow-crested bird, he with his eyes hidden behind those dark glasses.

Thinking that the best defense is a good offense, I stepped forward and let him see all of my reflective yellow glory. I must have been quite a surprise.

I said, “I’ve come for the girl.”

Cursing men leaped to their feet and grabbed for their guns. Dinners spilled, wineglasses fell to the floor, beer cans were kicked over. Behind the man in the doorway, Jaz came to look out at me with pinched terror in her face.

I squared my shoulders and tried to look tough. I wasn’t sure what I was going to say, but I thought if I talked fast enough I might be able to convince everybody that it would be a very good idea to let me take Jaz and leave.

I said, “I don’t have anything to do with this meeting, I don’t even know what it’s about. I’ve just come for Jaz. Let her go, and I won’t say anything to anybody.”

There was a long, cold pause, then the man in the doorway crooked a finger at me the same way he’d motioned Paulie to bring him the take-out bag. Jaz began to cry.

Oddly, everything seemed to become more distinct. Colors and scents and sounds were more vivid. I knew they were going to put me in that room with Jaz. I also knew they could not let me live to tell about it. If I ran, I would surely get a bullet in my back, and nobody would hear the shot over the noise in the street. The only good thing about this development was that Jaz would no longer be alone.

With a silent prayer that Michael would not be too devastated by my death, I moved forward. When I was close, the Colombian grabbed Jaz's wrist, pulled her from the room, and pushed her to me. Expecting him to order us to stand still while they executed us, I took her hand and squeezed it. Whatever happened, we were in this together.

Everything that happened next seemed to happen simultaneously, everything slapped on top of everything else.

First, the Colombian held his hand out straight in front of me in Paco's signal—his first two fingers making a V like open scissors.

Next, he turned toward the others and spoke in a loud voice. "Everybody freeze! You're all under arrest."

By some sleight of hand, a badge had materialized in the hand of the Colombian, except he was really Paco, and he was holding it out so all the men in the room could see it. A gun was in the other, and I knew he had taken it from a soft holster that had been hidden under his jacket. The jacket was now open, and the black holster displayed the word POLICE in big white letters.

In a low voice, he said, "My sister is coming out with the girl. Hold your fire."

I was so addled at the Colombian drug lord being Paco in disguise that for a second I thought he had cracked up and was talking to himself. Then I realized that in addition to a bulletproof vest under his silk shirt that added bulk to his chest, he was wired. He was speaking to somebody outside the house.

To me, he said, "*Go!*"

I gripped Jaz's hand and ran toward the kitchen. With a shrill yelp of fear, she let me pull her through the kitchen to the back door. We burst through the door into the garage and I blindly pawed the wall to hit the button that opened the garage door. When the door began to rise, I pulled Jaz toward it and we ducked under and ran across the boggy yard. At my Bronco, I stuffed her in, pulled myself inside, and gripped the steering wheel with both hands to keep from flying apart.

In the next instant, the backhoe that had been digging a hole in the street came to a stop, and the workmen around it yanked off their slickers and hats to reveal SWAT jackets and helmets. So did the backhoe driver. The cherry picker crane swung around to allow uniformed men inside the bucket to train their rifle sights on the front door. Patrol cars screeched from both directions to barricade the street, and the *whap-whap-whap* of a helicopter sounded overhead. A slew of men in dark flak jackets and helmets materialized out of nowhere. Every man had initials on his jacket—FBI, DEA, SCSD, SIB, SWAT—and every man carried an assault rifle.

A big voice spoke through a bullhorn. "Come out with your hands up!"

I gripped the steering wheel so hard my shoulders shook. Every man inside that house had a gun. Every man inside that house realized by now that Paco wasn't a big Colombian drug lord but an undercover cop who had tricked them. They had two choices: to add cop killing to the charges already against them, or to put down their weapons and come out.

Beside me, Jaz was frozen and confused, breathing in short laps like a stressed dog.

The front door opened and men began filing out with

their hands above their heads. I waited, stiff as stone, until Paco appeared in the door. He had put away his gun but still had the cloth holster open to show it was marked POLICE. Tensions run high in a situation like that, and I knew he didn't want any of the law enforcement people to mistake him for somebody else.

Within seconds, every man who'd come out of the house was handcuffed and led to the paneled trucks. The trucks were not plumbers' trucks or Verizon trucks or FPL trucks after all, but SWAT armored vehicles.

Paco separated himself from the others and slogged through the mist to the Bronco. He had taken off his dark glasses, but he still looked like a gangster. I rolled down my window and he leaned inside and kissed me, his beard prickly against my cheek.

"Go home," he said.

He gave Jaz a half smile and a thumbs-up, then turned and disappeared into the throng of uniformed lawmen.

I looked at Jaz and saw a new fear on her face. She was afraid of me.

She said, "Is he your *brother*?"

I said, "It's a long story, but he was just pretending to be a bad guy. He's really an undercover cop. You're safe now. Those guys who were after you are all going to jail. You don't have to hide anymore."

Her face crumpled and she dissolved into racking sobs. I gathered her into my arms and held her while she cried, patting her on the back like I once patted Christy.

She said, "He wouldn't . . . he wouldn't let them . . . hurt me. They wanted to, and he stopped them."

I squeezed her closer. "They can't ever hurt you again."

Jaz cried while the armored trucks drove off with their loads. She cried while men erected warning barriers around the hole they'd dug in the street. She cried while the truck with the cherry picker crane lumbered off. She cried as if she had barrels of tears that needed shedding.

After a final shudder, she went limp and pulled away.

Dully, she said, "Where do I have to go now?"

"My orders were to take you home."

In a tiny voice, she said, "I don't have a home."

I said, "Well, actually, you do. If you want it, that is. Hetty would like you to live with her."

The light breaking on her face was like a glorious sunrise.

# 31

The only sound on the way to Hetty's house was the *swish-swish* of the wipers.

When we got there, Jaz pushed out of the car and ran to the front door, her skinny legs churning. Hetty must have heard the car and looked through her peephole, because I heard her whoop of joy before she opened the door. While I stood behind her grinning, Jaz fell into Hetty's arms and the two swayed in the doorway for a long moment, squeezing each other as if they'd found a long-lost treasure.

Hetty finally pulled Jaz aside so I could pass through, and we all trooped to the kitchen, where Hetty busied herself making hot chocolate for Jaz. Ben ran to Jaz for a hug, and Winston graced her with a slow *I love you* eye blink.

I doubted Hetty would ever get all the story from Jaz, so I stayed long enough to fill her in on everything that had happened. Still dazed, Jaz didn't really understand it herself. She was a kid, and all she knew was that bad people had done bad things and had wanted to do more bad things to her, and now she was safe. It might be a decade or more before she understood the full implication of everything she'd been through.

When I left them, Hetty was already talking about the colors they might use for decorating Jaz's new room. A woman with less imagination might have been talking about transferring Jaz's school records from L.A. to Sarasota. Hetty knows how to set priorities.

I drove home on autopilot, too happy to do much more than steer the car. At home, I went straight to Michael's kitchen. He was at the stove enveloped in a cloud of steam, and he turned to me with a smile a mile wide.

He said, "Paco called. He's on his way home. I'm making bouillabaisse."

The butcher-block island was set for two, with wineglasses and cloth napkins. I didn't need to be told that, on this evening, three really would be a crowd.

Michael nodded toward the counter where an insulated hamper sat. "I packed the meatloaf and stuff for you. I put heated bricks in there, so it'll stay hot until you're ready for it."

I said, "Thanks. I love you."

"Love you too, kid."

The hamper was surprisingly heavy, but then Michael always gives a lot. I slopped out into the rain to cross the deck and go up my stairs. I left the hamper on my one-person breakfast bar and squished down the hall to my bathroom where I stood a long time under a hot shower. I was extremely alone.

When I was warm and scrubbed clean as new, I pulled

on a thick terry robe and went to the kitchen where the insulated hamper sat all by itself on the bar. I opened the lid and inhaled heavenly smells. I took inventory: a metal pan with Michael's meatloaf, a container of tomato gravy to pour over the meatloaf, a covered Pyrex dish filled with mashed potatoes, and another with skinny green beans and slivered almonds. There was even a square pan with warm blackberry cobbler. The cobbler called for vanilla ice cream which, wonder of wonders, I just happened to have in my refrigerator's little freezing compartment.

I closed the hamper's lid. I thought about Michael and Paco downstairs together. I thought about the ways people demonstrate love. I thought about how love lives in small acts as much as heroic ones—a smile, a word of support, a special dish, nice napkins for a dinner for two. I thought about how those small acts are reflections of courage and loyalty and commitment. Most of all, I thought about how love is unavailable to cowards.

I left the hamper on the bar and went to the living room and fished my cellphone from the bag I'd thrown on the sofa. I dialed Guidry's number.

He answered, which is a good thing because if he hadn't, I might have lost my nerve and not even left a message.

I said, "I have meatloaf and mashed potatoes. Would you like to have dinner with me?"

My heart beat once, twice, three times.

Guidry said, "I like meatloaf."

"Okay, then."

"Ten minutes?"

"Ten minutes is fine."

I clicked the phone shut and galloped to the hall closet. Breathing hard, I pawed through it until I found a five-pronged brass candelabra and five candles. The candles didn't match, and the candelabra needed polishing, but they would have to do. Charging to the living room, I set the candelabra on my coffee table, jammed the mismatched candles into it, and lit them. With the lamps turned off and only the kitchen light on, the candles looked just fine. Romantic, even. I found cloth napkins too, which were only slightly rumpled from lying in a drawer so long. I neatly refolded them and laid them next to silverware on the coffee table.

Last, I put on a CD of Regina Carter playing Paganini's violin, surely the most beautiful music ever made. Then, barefoot and breathless in my terry cloth robe, I opened my french doors to Guidry.

# 32

After we'd all had time to recover from the gigantic sting Paco and his cohorts had pulled off, Michael made a feast—leg of lamb butterflied and slowly roasted in his outdoor cooker, Bosc pears poached in peppermint schnapps, tabouli, leek and gorgonzola casserole, kibbe, prawn kebabs, burgers for the kids—and we invited half the people we knew. We gathered on the deck at sunset.

Guidry brought a case of assorted French wines. Tom Hale brought his new girlfriend, who passed my standards when she took off her sandals and ran with Billy Elliot along the shoreline. Jaz and Ben ran awhile too, but they were both so fascinated with the surf frothing on the shore that they sat down to watch it as if it were TV. Cora brought a fresh loaf of chocolate bread. Paco's SIB buddies and Michael's fellow firefighters brought their wives and kids. Max brought Jamaican ginger beer, and Reba Chandler brought a trove of Belgian chocolate. Ethan Crane came with a date, another attorney, and I was only a smidgen jealous. My old friend Pete Madeira brought his saxophone and played for us. Tanisha brought a basket of pies and in no time was exchanging recipes with Michael, while Judy couldn't resist going around to see if everybody had been served.

All the talk was how federal, state, and local agencies had cooperated in the raid on that house full of mob bosses. After months of planning and maneuvering, thousands of man-hours, lots of hard work, some lucky breaks, and Paco's undercover pose, they had gathered enough hard evidence of interstate racketeering to end the careers of several mob bosses and the underlings who served them. They were all being held without bail. If Victor Salazar hadn't been killed, he would have been with them.

Charges against gang members who had come to kill Jaz to keep her from testifying against them for a crime in California had expanded to counts in Florida of witness intimidation, murder, robbery, drug trafficking, wrongful imprisonment, and kidnapping. Paulie had agreed to testify against the others in exchange for leniency, but they would all spend the best years of their lives in prison. With the new charges, Jaz's testimony was no longer needed. She was free to become fully herself, with all the possibilities she'd had when she came with God's fingerprints still on her.

A sadder and wiser Harry Henry was in seclusion with Hef on his houseboat. Harry had been charged with illegally disposing of a body—not anything he'd go to jail for—and Maureen was charged with filing a false police report. She wouldn't go to jail for that either. She might have to reimburse the sheriff's department for the cost of investigating Victor's reported kidnapping, but that was roughly what she spent every week on her hair and nails. Federal agents were looking into whether her house or cars or boats had been used to promote interstate drug trafficking. If they had, she might lose some of them. But neither she nor Harry had killed anybody or kidnapped anybody, and Maureen had hired an expensive lawyer, so she probably wouldn't lose much. Except for Harry. Maureen had no idea how big a loss *that* was.

We ate in the afterglow of sunset, some of us at the long table my grandfather had built and some draped over chairs or chaises. The children trooped down to the water's edge and ate with the surf tickling their toes. Cora sat in an Adirondack chair with Ella sprawled across her lap. Guidry sat at the table beside me, so close I could feel his warmth against my hip.

Hetty and Jaz stayed long enough to eat, but left early because Hetty didn't want Jaz stressed by talk of her rescue. Hetty was now Jaz's official guardian, and Jaz wore the stunned look of a lottery winner not yet able to believe her good fortune. She didn't recognize a clean-shaven, short-haired Paco in faded jeans, and I don't think she yet realized what had actually happened in that house. But Hetty knew, and while Jaz carried a stack of plastic containers filled with leftovers to the car, Hetty went to Paco and gave him a tight hug.

"Thank you for protecting my girl," she said.

The white smile he flashed was embarrassed. "It was my pleasure. Truly."

After Hetty and Jaz left, the limo driver who'd brought

Cora from Bayfront Village looked at me with eyes round and admiring, as if he were in the presence of a rock star.

He said, "I saw you on the news, that helicopter shot of you and that girl running from the house, all those policemen swarming from behind cars and houses with those big guns."

Softly lit by a citronella candle, Cora said, "Dixie's like Wonder Woman."

One of the children ran to show her mother a cowrie shell, and people gathered around to look at it. Guidry's arm slid around me and pulled me close. I saw Michael's watchful eyes on us, hope and caution hanging in the balance.

With his lips moving against my ear, Guidry murmured, "Hey, Wonder Woman."

My head turned, and the sounds of the party drifted away.

I started to say, "Hey, yourself," but my lips got covered by his.

Have I mentioned that Guidry is a great kisser?

Oh, yes, he is.